VOICES IN THE WARDROBE

Recent Titles by Marlys Millhiser

VOICES IN THE WARDROBE

Marlys Millhiser

This first world edition published in Great Britain 2005 by
SEVERN HOUSE PUBLISHERS LTD of
9–15 High Street, Sutton, Surrey SM1 1DF.
This first world edition published in the USA 2005 by
SEVERN HOUSE PUBLISHERS INC of
595 Madison Avenue, New York, N.Y. 10022.

British Library Cataloguing in Publication Data

Millhiser, Marlys
    Voices in the wardrobe
    1.   Health resorts - California - San Diego - Fiction
    2.   Serial murder investigation - California - San Diego - Fiction
    3.   Detective and mystery stories
    I.   Title
    813.5'4 [F]

    ISBN-10 : 0-7278-6273-1

For Deborah Schneider and Cathy Gleason

Typeset by Palimpsest Book Production Ltd.,
Polmont, Stirlingshire, Scotland.
Printed and bound in Great Britain by
MPG Books Ltd., Bodmin, Cornwall.

One

Water trickled over rocks to tinkle into the little pools of a brook. Birds from exotic places (like outdoors somewhere) trilled and twee'd and chirruped.

"How does all this feel to you?" Maggie Stutzman asked in a dreamy tone, from the next eddy pool over.

"Makes me want to pee," Charlie Greene answered between clinched teeth. Faraway thunder rolled gently, the water splashed into the brook instead of trickling, and the eerie sound of a freaking flute "luuw-ooted" for no reason. "I want a cigarette."

"Charlie, you don't smoke."

"Well, I'm going to start. How did I let you talk me into this? I hate deprivation."

"What deprivation? Already today we've had a granite body scrub, a hydroptimale facial, a deep tissue massage and realignment, and our first intestinal cleansing—"

"Oh yeah, that one was a real hoot." Charlie, a Hollywood literary agent, had accompanied her ex-friend to this house of torture because she had some business to attend to close by in San Diego and because Maggie Stutzman was in serious trouble. And because before today they'd been best friends. They were also neighbors at home in Long Beach and had seen each other through any number of life's vicissitudes.

The eddy pools were, fittingly, kidney-shaped black bathtubs set into the floor of an enclosed deck and surrounded by potted plants so guests couldn't see each other, but the ocean view was left open at the foot. There were five such pools, the others vacant.

1

"The Sea Spa at the Marina del Sol is legendary, the Taj Mahal of natural health, beauty, and awareness clinics in the whole world." When she wasn't being weird, Maggie Stutzman was a lawyer for an estate-planning firm in Long Beach.

"I read the brochure too." They hadn't even had coffee. Just some kind of tea that smelled like mango but tasted like brine left over from a ship's bilge and stored in a museum for two hundred years. "You said there'd be twin beds."

"Well, it's a king—not like we have to breathe on each other."

"For damn skinny kings." The thunder grew louder, lightning cracked, wind lashed at groaning trees, and the rain drops pounded the poor brook—the flute replaced by another instrument Charlie didn't know nor care to. The way-weird about all this was that the Sea Spa at the Marina del Sol was sheathed in glaring sunshine and sat on the ocean front. All you had to do was sit up and look out the window to see the Pacific rolling in some impressive surf and hear gulls and stuff. Of course, in their condition sitting up would not be cool. But who needed brooks and flutes?

"Charlie—have you ever thought about Prozac?"

"I want a drink."

"If you were on Prozac you wouldn't need a drink."

"No, Maggie, if I weren't wrapped in seaweed with a cucumber stuffed up my ass I wouldn't need a drink."

Even Charlie had to admit that the dining room of the Sea Spa at the Marina del Sol was impressive. Pink marble floors, intimate tables for two with pink linen tablecloths and napkins, one gorgeous fat red blossom of some kind in a stem vase at each table. Crystal chandeliers that tinkled gently like wind chimes in the tiny bit of ocean breeze allowed into the room through spaced slats above the windows. They could be closed tight when the Pacific kicked up. The Spa sat on a point so the scene from the curved glass front of sea and sky and surf was one usually conscripted for private use by the inordinately rich.

After the lime and avocado "rinse" they had been allowed

2

to return to their room for a heavenly shower and shampoo and to don real clothes for dinner. Since they'd had nothing all day but tea and chalk bowel-cleansing yuck, dinner sounded exciting even at five in the afternoon.

"So, what wonderful events are on the docket for tomorrow?" Charlie asked.

"A colonic rinse, garden salad and tea, Pilates 101—"

"Stop right there, say no more, say no more."

"What, Pilates? It's a—"

"No, colonic rinse."

"Well, I don't know what that is, but I'm sure—"

"Maggie, can you say en-e-ma?"

And then came their dinner with a prune juice cocktail, soup broth (read hot water without salt) and a cup of hot ship bilge.

"I don't think I can take even another day of this. How you can handle five more is beyond me." Charlie had agreed to bring Maggie down and stay the weekend. "Spa" to her meant rest and soothing massage, coddling, skin and hair treatments—not enemas. Part of what Maggie was here for was to cure the depression brought on by drugs—in her case prescription.

"We have to cleanse our systems. I told you that. And tonight is the hormone, mind, and spirit presentation."

"The what?"

"Oh look, that's her, Dr. Judy." There was actually a little of the old fire sparking in Maggie Stutzman's eyes.

Charlie recognized the doctor because a much younger version of her hung on a wall in Luella Ridgeway's office at Congdon and Morse Representation, Inc. in Beverly Hills where Charlie Greene worked too. C & M represented Dr. Judy. "What's she doing here?"

"Charlie, they gave you a copy of the program when you registered."

"I got so excited at the thought of food, I left it in the room." Charlie pushed away the disgusting stuff in the fine china.

3

One of those lady motivational doctors so popular on local PBS begging weeks, Dr. Judy spoke before audiences of mostly women of various ages about woman stuff, used the latest in visual presentation gizmos like lighted wands and clickers that check off on state-of-the-art number charts, five reasons why hormone replacement therapy is too good for you and so on. Why estrogen won't give you breast cancer, if used correctly. More women die in automobile accidents than from breast cancer anyway. Well, duh.

Dr. Judy's hair, smile, and makeup were camera-ready, her dress long and flowing to avoid revealing her figure. She was very tall and had a hump forming where her neck met her back. She exuded a benign good humor gesturing, rocking back and forth in conversation with the Spa's proprietors, Warren and Caroline VanZant, who had greeted Charlie and Maggie last night.

A snappy little number in black clicked stiletto heels across the room toward them and marked something on her clipboard. "These two front and center, older ladies on either side," snappy number informed the young gofer following her. You could even hear her tongue clicking. "If they're done eating, they can report to makeup." She flashed her teeth, her eyes looking through Charlie and Maggie, and clicked her heels over to the next table.

"The doctor's taping tonight? Here? There's a studio?"

"Charlie, where are you going? I need you. I need you now."

"And I'm here for you. If not exactly in this building every minute, at least close by. I'm not going across country for godsake, just out for a real dinner."

The lobby was more crystal and marble. Why would people who could afford this place want to treat their bodies to torture? Her heels did a little clicking of their own and she wondered about driving the truck in them but her goal was to get out of this palace of woe NOW.

A large bald-headed person, in white slacks and knit shirt, stood at the ornate gate to the parking lot and put a hand out at her approach. "Sorry, patients can't leave without permission. Now just toddle back in there for your TV debut."

"Excuse me? I am not a patient." Charlie slipped out the gate with a nasty look at the creep just as a film crew member with a badge slipped in through it.

"Stop her," the gatekeeper yelled at another location type getting out of a van. "These are all addicts in here and they can't leave."

Charlie and the location type stared at the bald guy in white pants who watched them from well behind the gate, watched them exchange shrugs and go about their business. The would-be guard didn't offer to come after her himself.

Charlie almost split her skirt higher trying to climb up into the Dodge Ram. She waved at the bald guard still behind the gate as she turned the pickup around and roared off toward the winding road out of here.

"Mitch? Charlie. Have you eaten yet?" The only telephones allowed at the Spa were at the front desk, cell phones expressly forbidden. Charlie had left hers in the truck. She was barely out of the parking lot before she had it to her face.

"It's only five thirty. You want me to come up there?"

"No, I'm on my way. I'll pick you up. Where's the Catamaran from the Five?"

"Too far and it's rush hour. Stay on La Jolla to Mission Boulevard. It'll be on your left, on the bay side. I'll make reservations for somewhere. What are you in the mood for?"

"Lobster."

"Whoa. Things that bad, huh? How's Maggie?"

"Tell you when I see you. Have to watch the road."

"How are you dressed?"

"To kill."

"Gotcha, I know just the place," said the superstar in that voice.

Two

"**D**on't you think this is a bit of an over-reaction?" It wasn't dark yet, but Mitch Hilsten's eyes fairly glowed in it anyway. How'd he do that?

"You didn't get crushed by five SUVs trying to escape a runaway semi on the 405. What do you know?"

"Yeah, but a Dodge Ram with an extended cab? What are you going to haul, palm trees?"

"I liked the color and the hood ornament." The pickup was a metallic blue that made a statement and so did the head of a male bighorn sheep on its front. "And I can see over the traffic, be ready for trouble sooner." And it had eight cylinders, whatever they were, and an imposing grill that screamed— don't mess with me, dude—made out of fake chrome.

"Can't wait for the parking valet to get a load of it. Turn left at the next light. Libby wants you to call her."

"Libby talked to you?" Charlie's daughter hated the superstar with convincing ferocity.

"Left a message on my machine. Probably on your cell too. Spa wouldn't bring you to the phone. No phone calls allowed. Why does Libby hate me so?"

"You're a heartthrob for women over thirty-five, Hilsten. She thinks you're gross." Libby was eighteen.

"Even as a father figure?"

"Don't take it personally. She thinks I'm gross too. It's all the press we get."

"We hardly ever see each other."

"Yeah, but when we do at least one of us tends to get naked." And wherever you are there's a camera lurking. "Tell me you didn't make the reservations in your name?"

An oncoming stoplight picked up the glint of his teeth as well the glow of his powder blues. "Keith Anderson."

"Dammit, Mitch, that's one of your most famous roles. And the fact that you're in San Diego has been press for a week." There were few superstars over forty these days.

"Hum, thought the name sounded familiar. But it's a very ordinary name. Turn right here and follow the road to the end. Why won't the Sea Spa allow you to a phone? Is that even legal?"

"I don't know but it's weird. Had to leave my cell in the truck. This jerk at the gate tried to keep me from leaving. Said I was an addict."

"What kind of a spa is this?"

"It's lavish, elegant, and cruel. And incredibly expensive. Not at all what I thought it would be. But Maggie seems okay with it. We're all hoping for anything that will work." It had taken sizable donations from friends, neighbors, and co-workers. "Dr. Judy is taping a segment there tonight."

Charlie punched her cell pad for messages. Libby had left a voice message that Ed Esterhazie wanted to know if Maggie would be able to make it to the wedding. And that Kenny Cowper had called. And that she'd picked up Tuxedo at the vet's and he'd put the cat on Diazepam and Science Diet. Oh great, more medical bills. The only investments Charlie had that were going up instead of tanking were pharmaceut-icals. And what that damn cat would do to the house if he didn't like the food was not worth contemplating. Bad enough when Charlie bought the wrong kitty litter. The critter came in his cat door to do his do-do, even use his box if the litter was right, otherwise any of a number of corners, preferably carpeted. Then went back out to cat.

When she tried to call Libby all she got was Libby's voice mail on *her* cellular. It was scary and lamentable but Charlie and her daughter communicated more by messages left on telephone voice mail and written notes left by magnets on the fridge than any other way these days.

Kenny Cowper had left a message too, but Charlie would put that off until tomorrow. One stud was more than enough in her life at the moment. The parking valet made no horrified response to her Dodge Ram with the cool hubcaps and horned ram on the hood and massive fake grill. He helped her, her split skirt, and killer heels down from the cab, nodded at Mitch with a wink, and roared off in the metallic blue bomber.

"What do you get in that, four miles to the gallon?" Her escort watched the spectacle and exhaust fade into the scenery. "Tell me you just leased that sucker."

"Mitch, how can anyone who made *Bambo* and is now going to produce and direct *Jane of the Jungle*, possibly make fun of a pickup truck?"

He gave her that smile, took her elbow, and guided her to the also smiling maitre d' who awaited them on the steps of Crustacione de la Mer.

The tablecloths here were white linen, snooty waiters wore white and black. Most of the guests had dressed down in tourist attire. Maybe that's what made the waiters so snooty. The napkins, chairs, and floor tile were black. Charlie's lobster came on a black plate, Mitch's seared mahi on white. Charlie was sheathed in black. He wore white. If not for a chick in bright red at the next table and the superstar's powder blues, their corner of the room could have been in a pre-color film.

"You're going to get sick," Mitch Hilsten warned her a couple of hours later. "I have never seen you finish off a plate of food before. And that was no small lobster. Your face is even red."

Charlie nodded at the waiter offering more wine and her first cup of coffee in over twenty-four hours. She half-expected she'd be sick too, but her body at the moment was sending messages of ecstatic thank-yous, waves of them. And the coffee, strong and pungent, started right to work on a lingering headache. Okay, so she *was* an addict. At least she was off all the drugs prescribed after the accident on the 405.

"My face is red because I had a granite rub this afternoon."

"They rubbed granite on you? Or you on a hunk of granite?"

Charlie rolled her eyes in answer. She hadn't seen Mitch Hilsten for close to a year and, although they occasionally corresponded by phone or e-mail, there was much to catch up on. Unlike most Hollywood notables with whom she came in contact, it wasn't all about him. They talked about his daughters, both graduated from college and married now—no children. Libby's disinterest in applying for college.

"At least she's going to graduate from high school. She has this vague plan to live away from home for a year. Let's not talk about that, or I *will* get sick."

So they talked about his reason for being in San Diego. He was going to direct and co-produce a major studio film, a not-so-rare event these days—but *Jane of the Jungle*? They'd be shooting some preliminary scenes in the marina below the Sea Spa, doing some interiors in a special yacht, and more in local studios and on local beaches to save money. "We'll shoot as few as possible in Belize and Arizona. I'm psyched." That smile again.

Charlie had seen a treatment of that story somewhere. Thought it was awful—thought the published book, *Goddess of Glory*, even worse. *Jane of the Jungle* concerns a Bedouin princess captured by the Taliban who makes her escape by way of stuntmen and women, camels, and digital reality. By commandeering an Arabian prince's luxurious yacht, and with the help of a stud-city CIA agent, she sails to an undisclosed jungle where the story gets worse. Ought to offend three-fourths of the world, but that's Hollywood.

"Oh, Ed Esterhazie wants to know if you'd like to come to his wedding."

"Esterhazie Cement?"

"Concrete."

"You know Esterhazie Concrete?"

"Our kids attend Wilson High together in Long Beach."

"Esterhazie Concrete sends his kid to public school?"

"No accounting for the whims of the rich. He's invested some money in film productions. Good man to know."

"I know. When, where, which wife is this, and do I get to go with you?"

"Next Sunday, in his lovely garden, wife number three, and yes." This was all interspersed with more coffee and with discreet menus, napkins, whatever for him to sign. They gave up and wandered out into the night, waited for the roar of the metallic blue Ram, Charlie enjoying the night and the freedom away from the Sea Spa at the Marina del Sol. "Can't tell you how much I dread going back to that place."

"How do you know they'll let you in?" Mitch asked as she drove him to his hotel. "They didn't want to let you out."

"They have to. Maggie freaked when I left but I promised I'd be back. They have my money. They can't keep me out. Can they?"

He decided to follow in his rental to be sure she got in. "I want to see the marina below at night anyway."

Charlie drove faster than he did so she waited for him at the wye where the street to the Sea Spa turned off to climb the cliff through a canyon of crowded homes with only one stop sign along the way. She didn't know the make of his car but she wouldn't want to be followed by one at night if she were out walking— black, dark windows, low, sinister. The headlights, sort of oval, blinked as he came up behind her and she gunned the Ram over the crest where the houses ended, onto an empty curving road to Maggie and the house of torture, thinking of two things at once.

One was admitting she took some comfort in the fact he was behind her and that no matter how she tried to see as little of Mitch Hilsten as possible, he was becoming like family. The other was, there seemed to be a lot of night lighting at the Spa. Everybody should be in bed now resting up for their enemas.

Charlie lowered her window to be swamped by the indescribably rich scent of the Pacific saturating the night, the sparkle of boat lights approaching the marina below and of

aircraft in the heavens above. All eclipsed by the radiance
of the Sea Spa. Every window dazzled with light from within,
crystal glittering in most. Every patio and deck and garden
walk was lit as well, sea breeze moving exotic vegetation to
give a jiggling effect to the outdoor lighting. It would have
been lovely if it weren't for all the flashing lights of emergency and official vehicles. Uniforms directed Charlie and
Mitch where to park and walked them to the wrought gold-
colored gate where a sheriff's deputy checked names on a
clipboard.

"Ohgod, Mitch. Maggie pleaded with me not to leave her."

"You don't know this is about Maggie. Could be a drug
bust or something. Oh, sorry, I didn't—"

"Name?" the clipboard deputy asked Charlie but stared at
Mitch. "And reason for your visit?"

"Charlie Greene. I have a room here. Is Maggie all right?"

"Mitch Hilsten—"

"I know."

"I had dinner with Ms. Greene and escorted her back here."

Charlie could have pulled out a rapid fire whatever and
shot up half the parking lot before the deputy took her eyes
off Mitch. Until he said, "Please tell me there hasn't been
another murder."

Now Charlie got the deputy's full attention. She even
checked her clipboard, "Charlie Greene. Well, there goes that
theory. Last one unaccounted for. What do you mean by
'another murder?'"

"Well, wherever Charlie goes there always seem to be a
lot of—oh, sorry Charlie."

"Thanks a whole lot, Hilsten. I owe you one."

Three

Maggie Stutzman had thick black hair and lovely pale skin and eyes that had once snapped with intelligence, good humor, curiosity, verve. "Nobody didn't like" Margaret Mildred Stutzman. But gradually over maybe a year, maybe longer, Charlie's best friend began to withdraw, grow solemn, gain weight. Her gynecologist prescribed hormones to even out the early onset of menopause, her therapist Prozac to even out her moods, her dentist Vicodin for a root canal gone wrong. One night when Maggie didn't show for a potluck, Charlie crossed the courtyard to find her neighbor passed out next to a wine glass half full and the bottle half empty.

Betty Beesom, eighty-four, who lived on another corner of the courtyard, declared that Maggie should stop drinking alcohol. Charlie's mother, back in Boulder, who'd undergone a mastectomy, thought she should get off the hormones. Charlie, who'd felt so much better when off the painkillers after injuries in an automobile accident, thought Maggie should get off the Vicodin. Jacob Forney, who occupied the last corner of the courtyard, warned that Maggie had a classic case of depression and thought she should see a shrink. Poor Maggie, who was already seeing a shrink, didn't know what to do. So she started baking rich desserts and putting on weight which only made her more depressed. And then her massage therapist recommended a week at the Sea Spa at the Marina del Sol.

Right now, Maggie Stutzman wore that scary empty look which could be replaced by a nervous terror or, just as easily, sudden but still nervous rashes of surprising humor. She scared the hell out of Charlie and herself too.

She stood between Charlie and Mitch at the foot of one of the black kidney-shaped tubs on the enclosed deck where they did ghastly procedures and then wrapped people in gag-awful seaweed and left them nearly immobile to listen to birdies tweet and thunder roll over mountain streams while the biggest ocean in the world pounded a beach below.

At the head of the pool, surrounded in potted plants that towered above him, the bald jerk who'd tried to keep her from leaving tonight glared at Charlie Greene. Even though the phony "eddies" had been turned off, there was water splashed all around this particular pool and yellow crime-scene tape too.

On the other side of Mitch, a patient plainclothes asked, "You have witnesses to corroborate that Ms. Greene was with you all evening?"

"Andre Lyon, the Maitre d' at Crustacione de la Mer. You have to admit she is rather distinctive. And the waiter, soaked in disdain when she insisted her lobster be simply boiled and served with drawn butter. And the parking valet who was duly impressed someone in that outfit would drive up in a pickup truck."

"She drives a pickup?" Warren VanZant, the Spa's owner, said on the other side of Charlie and peered down at her lack of cleavage through some pretty racy eyeglasses. His hair a gray fringe, he was tall, lean, muscular, and his voice came up from somewhere down around his navel. If she'd had any cleavage worth staring at she'd have penetrated one of his tennis shoes with a killer heel.

Maggie giggled suddenly.

"Maggie," Charlie warned, but too late.

"Well, there goes your case, Detective. Guess you'll just have to settle for me." And she held out her wrists for hand-cuffs. "That's okay, Charlie, I want to die."

"What do you mean, you want to die? Jesus."

"Detective Solomon," Caroline VanZant leaned around her

13

husband to address the other side of the row, "Ms. Stutzman has been through a rigorous day of herbal cleansing and needs much rest before anything she says can be taken seriously."

"She's an addict," announced the jerk under the potted palms at the head of the eddy pool. "Just like Ms. Greene. Just like everybody here. Very probably including yourself, sir."

"That's enough, Dashiell." Mrs. VanZant was short, plump, with a sincere comforting smile, large rose-tinted eyeglasses, and a soft whispery voice that could take on a cleaver-sharp edge when she needed it to.

"Are you admitting to the murder, Ms. Stutzman?"

"Have you questioned the entire production crew?" Charlie asked the laid-back plainclothes. They seemed to be mysteriously absent.

"Don't fool yourselves, anybody who takes one drink a week is an alcoholic. Any alcoholic is drawn to drugs," Dashiell said.

"I want to die." Maggie giggled. Maggie had found Dr. Judy face down dead in the eddy pool.

"You just walked out and left me. Why should I listen to you about anything?"

They sat cross-legged, facing each other, in the center of the bed for skinny kings. This room was draped in Victoriana, layers of cloth and ruffles, the four-poster so high little stools sat on each side to help you mount. "Well, I came back didn't I? I'm here now and you do not want to die. In California they just put you in prison anyway, I think. Tell me again what happened."

The PA system announced lights out. They ignored it.

"I walked out on the deck because the night was beautiful and the stars and because I felt so good about her presentation. She said there is orgasm after menopause."

"Well of course there is." Charlie raised her arms toward the silly ruffled canopy above. "I could have told you that. My mom told me."

"Edwina has orgasms?"

They stared at each other like little girls at a slumber party for a whole minute. Charlie blinked first. "Well, okay, I have a little trouble with that one too, but that still doesn't explain why you say you want to die."

"Because now I feel terrible. It's not worth it."

"What's not worth what?"

"Life's not worth living."

"Just a minute ago you said you felt good about what Dr. Judy said at her presentation. Life's always been full of good news and bad news. Have you had your Prozac?"

The lights had gone out in Maggie's eyes again. There was just a weary waiting. "You went off and left me. You should have stayed away."

"This isn't about me. I won't be your excuse." Charlie assured herself she didn't feel a bit guilty, even though she enjoyed the evening so much and the best lobster, coffee, and wine she'd ever had, ever, ever, ever. She crawled off the bed to find Maggie's drug bag. The only pieces of furniture that didn't have either fringe or ruffles were the two wardrobes, no closets. One of the wardrobes concealed the television. "Okay, Dr. Judy was face down in the eddy pool. Was there any blood in the water? Was there a knife sticking out of her? What did you see, Maggie?"

"Don't start playing detective with me. I know you're lousy at it. What I need is my friend back."

"Well, I'm back." Charlie crawled to the middle of the bed with a glass of water and a sack of meds. The first one she pulled out was Diazepam. "Jeez, Maggie, this is what the vet just put Tuxedo on. Next thing you know the Spa will put you on Science Diet."

"Tuxedo's not sick, is he?"

"Libby just picked him up after his checkup and that was the prescription. You know, Science Diet might well taste better than the food at this place. What I'm really wondering I guess is, how did you know Dr. Judy was murdered and not just drowned in the pool by accident? The water's

15

fairly deep in those things if you're not weighted down with seaweed and cucumbers and buoyed by Jacuzzi bubbles."

"So what did you have for dessert?" Maggie asked out of the blue where she mostly lived nowadays.

"I didn't. I was too full of lobster."

"So what did Mitch have?"

"Crème brulée." And I don't feel guilty, dammit. I needed a break. "Now you answer my question."

"Caramel?"

"Caramel and raspberry. Maggie, about the dead doctor?"

"I'm addicted to food too."

Charlie climbed down off the bed again. Damn thing needed a gangplank. This time she came back with tissues, the box covered with pink gauzy ruffled stuff dotted with rhinestones. Where did people come up with this crap? "Everybody is."

"You're not. Look at you." Her poor friend sobbed. On a cushy, if over-dramatized bed, wrapped in a cushy house terrycloth robe. Out in the damn eddy pool, strangled with seaweed and rectally tortured, she'd been dreamy-happy. "You never even clean up your plate."

"Did tonight. Ask Mitch. Maggie, was there blood in the water? A wound on the back of her head? Where's the Prozac? Jesus, how many pills do you take? Why don't you answer my question?"

"Which one?"

They looked at the plastic bottles tumbled together on the lavish coverlet and Charlie hadn't emptied the bag yet. Maggie Stutzman reached for another tissue and the remote. "Leave me alone."

"I did and you got mad at me and found a dead body."

The television inside the wardrobe began to talk. It was creepier than the PA. How could Maggie turn it on without the door open? The ocean smell crept into the room through the gauze and ruffles and tassels at the window just as a man, unseen, inside the wardrobe asked, "Do you suffer from fatigue, irregularity, insomnia, arthritis? There is help.

16

Clinical studies have shown amazing results with Aviatrix."
The sound of a small propellor plane soaring and diving to
the tune of a woman's giggle. "Ask your doctor if Aviatrix
is right for you. Possible side effects may include nausea
headache jaundice intestinal bleeding heart murmurs and dry
mouth."

"Where's the Prozac?"

"I threw it away. It didn't help."

"That's the one pill they warned you not to stop taking,
Maggie. It's to keep you from being depressed. Or was that
the hormones?" But Charlie couldn't help but think how
depressed she'd feel too if she had to take all these pills. She
hadn't had to take this much medication to recover from a
near fatal car accident.

Four

The footboard, really a beautifully carved horizontal pole, came up to Caroline VanZant's chest as she peered across the drugstore on the bed. "You have prescriptions for all this?"

"I was so embarrassed because I couldn't even walk upstairs without pain in my knees," said a haunted woman in the wardrobe. But then a World War II dance band began to boogie and the woman, no longer haunted, said, "But now I can dance the night away." And a man said, "Ask your doctor if Celebrate is right for you. Side effects may include vision problems, diarrhea, fainting spells and dry mouth."

"How can the remote work without opening the door?" Charlie asked, but then noticed the strategically placed slit in the door's paneling.

"Dashiell's idea." Caroline's wan smile and puckered brow reminded Charlie of her own ambivalent take on Libby.

"Now, only five percent down and no interest payments for a whole year. This is Dealing Dirk and I guarantee the lowest prices on all makes of new and used cars in Southern California. Don't wait another day."

Charlie took the remote from Maggie's hand and turned off the voices in the wardrobe. Her friend didn't seem to notice. Charlie did have to aim the business end at just the right angle, but it was a clever idea for a jerk to come up with. She wasn't sure why anyone would want to listen to a TV like you would a radio. She and Caroline turned over the plastic bottles one by one in a line, with prescription stickers facing up.

"There's got to be lots of bucks here," Charlie said in awe.

"How many doctors does she have?" Mrs. VanZant pushed the big rose-colored glasses back up her nose to magnify her astonishment. "How old is she?"

"Well, there's a gynecologist, a dermatologist, a psychiatrist, a dentist, a heart specialist, a massage therapist." Charlie realized they were talking about Maggie like she wasn't there. "Who else, Maggie?"

Maggie didn't even look up, let alone bother to answer.

"And that doesn't include the alternative types. She's forty-one, two. This all started with early menopause and kind of snowballed. Biological clock running out, all that stuff. Wonder what would happen if we went cold turkey here?"

"That could get scary. Better talk to her psychiatrist first. Does she suffer from hot flashes?"

"No *she* doesn't because *she* takes estrogen," Maggie Stutzman spoke up for herself. "And I hate pills!" She swept the whole lot of them off the bed with one swipe of her arm.

Charlie Greene sat in her own cushy spa robe that came with matching slip-on slippers, hers a tad large but she could walk without losing them if she was careful. She sat in the administrative office with Detective Solomon, the laid-back plainclothes, Mitch Hilsten, and Warren VanZant whose wife was upstairs babysitting Maggie Stutzman. The snappy number in black with the clicking heels cooled them outside in a hallway lounge staring daggers at Dashiell, the hairless twit.

Charlie, after a far too long day and a far too magnificent dinner, was weary. And she had the feeling she dare not sleep tonight.

VanZant looked every bit as tired as she felt. "Judith was in good form and the audience eager—although I can't believe there's anyone over forty left in the world who hasn't heard her spiel at least once—if not that, read the book. She sold a great many of them here tonight."

"So what was she doing out on the deck? No one will answer that question. What's the deal here? Hey, I got all

19

night. Do you?" Detective Solomon screwed up one cheek in a faux grin, leaned back in the padded chair behind the desk, and scratched the bridge of his nose.

"I would hate to have the estate sue me. She had a secret she didn't want public. We all pretended not to know."

"This is a murder investigation, Mr. VanZant."

"And there are witnesses in the room," Warren countered.

Solomon allowed the grin to morph into a lazy smile, reached for a manila envelope on the desk, and pulled out a baggy. "Yes or no, Mr. VanZant."

Warren nodded and looked away. The plastic baggy contained the stained filter end of a used cigarette.

"Dr. Judy smoked?" Charlie came awake. "The press will have a holiday with that."

The detective turned his attention to Charlie and Mitch. "And neither of you had any prior knowledge of or contact with Dr. Judith Judd while she was living?"

"I know her agent. We both work at Congdon and Morse on Wilshire in Beverly Hills. I should call Luella, huh?"

"I have to admit I've never heard of her before tonight. I'm down here scouting a few locations and Charlie has a convention to attend."

"It's a screenwriters' conference, godsaveusall. What am I going to do, Mitch? I can't leave Maggie."

"I thought, Mr. Hilsten, that through your relationship with Miss Greene, you might have come in contact with Judith Judd, at a party or something."

"I've never met her, how would he meet her through me? Luella handles talent. I handle writers. And we do *not* have a relationship."

Detective Solomon glanced at Mitch, who shrugged, and turned his amusement back to Charlie with widened eyes exaggerated by a subtle lifting of the forehead. "Writers aren't talent?"

"Not in Hollywood. They're vendors. Not that there can't be a few very expensive vendors."

"Perhaps we could have someone watch out for your friend

while you're at the convention. You could come back at night to be with her," VanZant offered.

"Oh yeah, like old lovable Dashiell. I don't think so."

He stiffened and looked down at Charlie through those interesting glasses again. "Old lovable Dashiell is my wife's son by her first marriage. We both recognize that he has problems and are proud that he is dealing with them instead of denying them."

"And he's driving you both nuts."

"Right."

Mitch cleared his throat to clear the air. "Charlie, what's your schedule for the week? Maybe I can help find someone to cover for you part of the time."

"I have to go with Keegan tomorrow night to a dinner with the conference bigwigs, be on a panel Monday morning, and spend time evaluating pitches Tuesday afternoon. I was supposed to be back on Thursday night for the banquet but had already decided to be unable to make it because I have things scheduled at the office on Wednesday, am concerned about Libby's activities Wednesday and Thursday nights, and there's the wedding on Sunday. Not to mention I have a job."

"What if you drafted Libby to help you out with Maggie this week? Might keep them both out of trouble. They are pretty close as I remember."

"That is the dumbest idea you've come up with to date," Charlie told the superstar, "and that is saying a whole lot."

"You two sure *sound* like you have a relationship."

"We're just friends, Detective Solomon." Charlie was gritting her teeth again. The dentist had warned her about that.

All three men shrugged this time. Charlie figured old Dashiell was doing the same outside in the hall/lounge. "And ohmygod, Mitch, it just might work."

"I have good dumb ideas all the time. You never listen to me."

"You sound *married*."

"My daughter's eighteen and I've pretty much lost control," Charlie explained to the other two men in the room.

21

"Like what happened to Caroline with Dashiell," Warren VanZant said helpfully.

Maggie groaned and rolled over in her sleep when Charlie crawled into bed beside her. For a few seconds she reminded herself she must not sleep deeply, must awaken if Maggie got up. Two seconds later Maggie was coming out of the bathroom, roughing her damp hair with one hand. Even Victorian excess at the windows couldn't block out the California sun.

"Did you know you snore, Greene?" Fresh and dewy from the shower, you'd never guess Maggie Stutzman had found a dead doctor in the ebony eddy pool the night before.

"I do not snore. What time is it?"

"Ten something. You even slept through wake-up call." She pointed at the round thing in the ceiling over the door. "We missed the enema and the Rolfing."

"Oh damn." Charlie almost broke her neck falling off the bed and missing the stool. "I thought the Rolfing was the cucumber yesterday."

"It wasn't a cucumber—it just looked like one."

"Felt like two."

They actually both laughed at the same time—at the same thing. That hadn't happened in months. "The cucumber we get in the garden salad for lunch. Shower's all yours."

According to the abundant literature deposited about the place, the Sea Spa at the Marina del Sol had been built originally as a private home, bankrupted the owners before it was finished, became a rambling hotel which didn't make it either, and had been turned into a spa. With the change in direction, concepts, architects, owners, contractors and fortunes the end result was a warren of cottages, footpaths, and gardens outside—different uses than intended inside. The parts were generally lovely, the whole confusing.

An example was their bathroom. It would have been a triangle but for one corner which was elongated for no discernable purpose. Quality tile and ornate appointments, an overlarge shower, marble pedestal sink, tiered rack for towels and makeup kits, pedestal stool, and this oblong end that held an out-of-place full length wood-framed mirror on a platform and uprights and trunnions so it could tilt. So you could watch yourself do things you seriously did not want to see yourself doing, but couldn't get away far enough to see things you might like to check out—such as what your hair and outfit might look like to those behind you.

Basking under the hot pelt of the water and the aroma of lavender shower gel dispensed from a purple thing attached to the tile, Charlie considered the fact that one of the reasons her friendship with Maggie had been so successful was that they both seemed to sense how hard to push and when to back off. And they rarely had to say "I'm sorry," an inbred female habit. So, when she was toweled and dressed, she didn't ask all the questions trying to burst her brain, just followed Maggie down to the dining room for a cup of hot ship bilge which they carried out onto the deck and the crime scene. The tape was down, the eddies stilled, and out the window—the surf was up.

"Do you remember last night?"

"Some of it. Dr. Judy's skirt sort of ballooned like air had gotten trapped under it in back. Her hair floated higher than she did. Probably the Jacuzzi bubbles. I don't remember blood but that doesn't mean there wasn't any. I slept so good last night. Charlie, I'm not even hungry."

"You don't crave anything?"

"Only one. Chocolate."

"Have you had your pills?"

"Caroline VanZant took the whole sack of them with her. And I slept so good." Maggie's tears ran down her face anyway.

"What?"

"I don't know. I'm not even sad. I'm glad I'm here. I think I'll get help here, Charlie."

Charlie sure hoped so. How could life get so bad you wanted to be deprived? Dead maybe, but—"Maybe you can get your enema this afternoon."

Five

Caroline VanZant bustled out with her own cup of bilge and two pills for Maggie. "Now listen, I've talked to three doctors, one of them yours, listed the medications you've been taking and the problems you're having. The only thing all agreed on was the hormone therapy. Knock 'em down and we'll work with the rest. Glad you both slept in this morning. You needed it."

"Come on, Maggie," Charlie urged. "It's not for the rest of your life. Just to get you through a rough time." This medication had finally proved dangerous if taken far into post-menopause as had been prescribed for years and as many breast-cancer patients had suspected for years too. They were still considered helpful for women at the onset of this wonderful time in their lives if their hot flashes were unbearable and there was no family history of breast cancer. But the jury was still out and enthusiasts for hormone replacement therapy questioned the stats on this one. And no, natural or phyto estrogens didn't really cut it.

"We've lightened up on her regimen," Caroline said in that soft, sweet voice you wished your mother had. "I've got police and press downstairs to deal with. Could you stay with her through lunch, Ms. Greene? We'll try to work out something later."

Charlie rather thought she could leave Maggie with anyone but Dashiell until she met Sue who apparently had not received word of the lightening up of Maggie's regimen.

Sue, according to her name badge, had a ponytail and a clipboard like the female sheriff's deputy and the snappy number. "Are you Charlie and Maggie? What are you doing dressed like that? You should have reported to the pool half an hour ago."

They were wearing spa sweats and tank tops. Without much hope, Charlie tried, "We didn't bring our suits."

"Your suits are down at the pool. Come along, ladies."

"Don't leave me again, Charlie," Maggie pleaded with a look that tore at Charlie's gut far worse than any enema could have, not that she'd ever had one.

"If that damn flute from the eddy-pool deck starts up down here, I'm going to drown that dork," Charlie whispered and narrowly escaped a lung or two full of chlorinated lavender water. The pool, very large and very warm, was empty except for her, Maggie, and Raoul—their hydro-hypno-aroma-dream-therapy specialist. Not that anybody asked, but Charlie would have preferred a dolphin. The lavender was for aroma, the chlorine for burning your eyes. Raoul was for irritation.

"Butt up, Marg-a-r-r-retta. Breathe more deeply. Char-r-r-lemagne, head back, chin up, deeper breathing for you also. Arms out. Now flooooaat, gently. The water is your frienda, remember." Seemed like he rolled the wrong "r's" or something. One thing was certain, he thought he was a stud. Charlie, which *was* actually short for Charlemagne but only irritating people called her that, could not fathom why.

What gives here? On the way down, the elevator and halls were as empty of others as the pool. Were Charlie and Maggie simply so out of sync in the "regimen," having skipped earlier tortures, that they had the facilities to themselves? Were there different stages of spa treatments so that no one had the same schedule unless they arrived together? Had the murder of Dr. Judy Judd made everyone but them check out early? Or was everyone else up in the lobby waiting to be questioned in the office by Detective Solomon?

"Nowwww, allowww the dreams of wondrous, peaceful places to washa over you, seep inside your heads. Looooz yourselves in what you desire most at the momennnnto—if

you could have anything at this momennnnto—let it be so
in your minds—and then flooooat off deeper into the real
you, you have just begun to discover." Somebody Charlie's
mother's age might find his voice sexy.

It was like church, a leap of faith sort of thing, with an
ancient hippie-like cast to it. Was Charlie being baptized
without knowing it? She had a headache again. She dreamed
of floating in a pool of caffeinated espresso while sipping a
latte from a straw. She could almost feel the grit of residue
from fresh-ground coffee in that hard place to get to between
the fourth and little toe, the residue that leaves a stain in the
sink when you rinse out your cup.

And then she was trying to remember who Raoul reminded
her of—some old actor or a combination. That's the trouble
with working in Hollywood, even on the fringes, your frame
of reference sucks. Who . . . ?

"Ahhh, Char-r-r-lemagne, you allow your butta to sink you
will surely drown," Ricardo Montalban crooned in her ear
and ratcheted up her lower torso so suddenly she took in
more lavender and chlorine at the top end. "You must concentrate anda relax at the same time. Nobody saida perfection
of tranquility is easy." He held her up so she could cough to
the point of retching spit—even the bilge seeming to have
moved on down her digestive tract. He wore lots of interesting hair on his chest, his arms looked shaved, his mustache
quivered when he spoke. All of his hair was white.

If the pool water didn't wash out her contacts the tears
just might.

Ricardo Montalban and Mr. Rogers? Or Count Dracula—
who was that guy—Vincent Price. Raoul kind of switched
between the two—but Mr. Rogers was not entirely absent either.

The pool was on the lowest level, the number of levels
varying by the whim of changing designs and landscaping.
It was ground level here and looked out on hillocks of rock
formations instead of gardens. If Maggie got into one of her
moods at the Sea Spa at the Marina del Sol, she could get
real lost and right fast.

Charlie had a room at the convention hotel. Could she possibly get back here after the dinner and take Maggie to her room there, bring her back the next morning? She couldn't quite trust this place—maybe it was the murder, maybe it was Raoul.

Sue had them back in their spa sweats and tank tops and off to the garden salad lunch, their hair still dripping, almost before Raoul had finished intoning. Did embarrassing people by forcing them to look horrible make it easier to convince them to take enemas? The garden salad was actually not too bad. Cup of soup, crusty bread, and a glass of wine would have helped. They actually served the ship bilge over ice—without lemon and sugar of course. Did the VanZants dine on this stuff? And Sue was their server. She kept track of what they ate on her clipboard.

"So, what did Dr. Judy say last night besides there's orgasm after menopause?"

"Oh, things like, 'excuse me, I'm just going to run out and fall face down in the second eddy pool from the left.'"

"Maggie."

"Things like hormone therapy is the only thing that will save your sanity during menopause. I think Raoul's a plant, don't you?"

"You mean like a philodendron? With him, more like seaweed."

The blossoms in the stem vases today were blue. There were maybe half the people here now than last night. Unoccupied tables were not set up and had no blossoms. Perhaps the crowd that had been here for Dr. Judy left last night.

"You're afraid to talk to me because you think I'm crazy, huh?"

"No, I'm afraid to talk to you because *you* think you're crazy. Maggie, you are suffering from depression due to a screw-up in your chemicals. We just straighten out your chemicals and you'll be fine." And what the hell am I to do in the meantime? I've got a fancy dinner to go to tonight.

"You've got parsley stuck between your two front teeth, Greene. I think Raoul is a spy either for the psych squad or maybe the sheriff's department."

Charlie washed her mouth out with iced ship bilge, speared a cucumber slice and thought better of it. "What makes you think that?"

But their conversation was at an end. Apparently they were to be treated to a lecture rather than dessert. Well, this place was advertised as offering an intense program for busy people. And were there any other kind of people who could afford it these days?

Their server, Sue-of-the-clipboard, introduced herself to the tiny gathering in the large room as Sue Rippon. She was probably early forties, trying to pass for early twenties. Athletic and firm extremities, a little too wide at the waist and hips, Sue remembered how to swing her ponytail and smile big, but the bouncy sparkle was fading. Would that be Charlie in six, eight years? Was that Charlie now?

Sue proceeded to explain the importance of cleansing the colon and the wonderful benefits that would ensue. Charlie kind of zoned-out but thought the message was that colons are dirty. Noooo, really? They are the sewers of the body and it was important that they not become the landfill. Hence they needed flushing, scrubbing, and sanitizing. The result would be an enormous increase in energy because all the slime, waste, sludge, and garbage would be scraped away leaving the body renewed and ensuring that the liver and digestive track could be young again after years of refuse abuse. All the nutrients from digesting foods could be absorbed from intestines no longer coated with grease. Sue could say "grease" and conjure nasty images. It was the way she wrinkled a once-perky nose while pruning her lips and widening her eyes. It brought up visions of murk and bubbling, hissing, fuming poisons—stench beyond bearing.

And as a final treat all were presented with a plastic cup of dirt. There was dessert after all.

"Come on, Charlie, it's medicine."

"God, you'll take anything offered you. Without questioning it, or how it will mix with other stuff you're taking. Can you say Roto-Rooter?"

"I spit out the hormone therapy pill when you weren't looking. I've had nothing today. Or last night. I'm ready to cleanse my system." Maggie continued to spoon up the dirt and rinse it down with a big gulp of water to make it a clay in her body.

"Even Dr. Judy prescribed hormone replacement therapy, don't forget. Your face is red and your forehead's wet. You, girl, are having a hot flash already."

Okay Greene, what are we doing here? You are at the end of your rope with this depression business because you have other things you want to do. Remember how often Maggie has been patient with you and your life problems?

"Oh shut up. Maggie? I didn't mean you. I was talking to myself. Maggie?"

But Margaret Mildred Stutzman had already shut Charlie out with a chilling blankness in her eyes.

Six

Today the snappy number wore flats and low riders displaying the jewel in her navel. She sat in the office with Detective Solomon when Charlie went looking for Caroline VanZant.

"Come in, Ms. Greene. I take it you've met Ms. Singer?"

Ms. Singer looked blank until he named names. "Charlie Greene, Ruth Ann Singer."

Charlie Greene. The name she remembered. The face she forgot—trait of an over-organized species. "That's her, Detective, the woman who didn't come to the auditorium for Dr. Judd's presentation, waited outside to kill Judith instead." Ruth Ann tapped her foot in irritation like a grade-school teacher Charlie's daughter, Libby, once had. "Don't let her walk around like this. Put her in jail or something."

Charlie and the cop exchanged shrugs. Something about this room made people do that. He said, "I'm afraid her alibi is airtight."

"But I told you I have it on the video. She's the only one who wasn't in her seat. It couldn't have been anyone else."

"I'm looking for Caroline," Charlie said, happy to ignore her accuser.

Solomon thought Caroline had gone to the auditorium. "Out the hall and to your left. Just follow the signs."

The auditorium was really the studio and again photos of its transformations and printed explanations of its history were displayed on the walls on either side of the doors. Originally built as a lavish private screening room for an old-time producer, it had become, before it was finished, an even more

30

lavish recording and filming studio for the producer's heir to record his own music which was in the latest fad—which no one could any longer remember. But the place was lost to the family before the son of privilege could make his mark.

The seats were spacious and the rows tiered, all with a clear view of the stage or screen depending on the need and with no pillars or ceiling supports to interfere with the line of sight. The screen was normally hidden behind a curtain when not in use. A large flat monitor hung to one side of the podium to display succinct and numbered points or "steps" in logic, leaving a large area of stage for the speaker to perform and prance and gesture. It looked rather cold now without the special lighting that would enhance the colors for the TV screens at home.

At a quick glance Charlie figured the room could seat at least fifty people in a semicircle around the stage. Cameras could zoom in on particularly interesting expressions of the audience as well as different angles of the speaker. And the windowed control room from which the director could direct the shots by line of sight as well as from the video bank, was state of the art maybe twenty, thirty years ago.

Caroline discussed the dead doctor's choreography last night with the lady deputy who had met Charlie and Mitch after the amazing lobster dinner. She followed them around the stage and screen backdrop to discover a door that led to a hall which eventually led to the eddy-pool deck. Charlie stood there as they talked and watched the particular pool in question. It had been drained. She could see nothing important there now either, other than to imagine the Jacuzzi bubbles making Judith Judd's clothes billow when she was dead. The undrained pools lay dormant but still held water as was normal when no one was in them. Did the murderer turn on the bubbles for the dead doctor?

Charlie, don't. We let the sheriff's department handle this one. We do not become involved with murder ever again. "It's getting embarrassing."

"What's embarrassing?" The deputy, blonde and blue eyed, but with a determined jaw line, looked up from her clipboard. Hadn't everyone heard of PDAs?

"Nothing, just talking to myself." That's what's embarrassing.

"I'll be with you in a minute," Caroline VanZant told Charlie and disappeared back down the hall to the studio with the cop.

So Dr. Judy, after her performance and the questions from the audience, both on camera and off, slipped out this way to smoke and quiet her nerves. Charlie followed the trail back to the studio's rear door. It was not a straight line, few of those in this gerrymandered place.

There was no doorknob on this side of the studio's door, just a keyhole in a small round plate. Interesting. No surprises from the uninvited during taping?

Since the inner room of the studio was round, hallways made no sense to the linear mentality. Charlie could turn her back to the door without a knob and look down three hallways—one that branched into two just up or down a ways and one that went off toward the eddy-pool deck. But even more odd was the fact that in all this space and everywhere she'd been except the dining room there was hardly anyone around. Seemed to be more staff than paying customers. And this was a very expensive space.

"Are you one of the inmates?" a deep but young voice snuck up on Charlie from yet another hall that circled the round room behind her and which she'd failed to count. An eager, superior, inquisitive squint—"press" written all over him. "I'm Jerry Parks, *Union-Tribune.*" For some reason the word "ferret" came to mind. Charlie had no idea what a ferret looked like. The word probably suggested to her by the verb and the press's need to search out the facts? He dressed normally for Southern California—casual.

Charlie took off running down one of the wye corridors. With any luck she'd lose him before she got lost herself. What she needed to do now was arrange some surveillance for Maggie, get cleaned up, dressed, and check into her room at the convention hotel in time for the cocktail party and dinner in Keegan Monroe's honor.

Keegan, the celebrity speaker at this conference for aspiring screenwriters, was a major portion of Charlie's income. She represented many writers, both screen and book, some of them talented, but only a minuscule, lucky few made enough of a splash to hit "big time." Which was about the only time that mattered these days. And talent was in the eyes of the beholder.

And she must get a call into Luella about her client's murder.

Heads up. We're lost. Charlie's stupid common sense, or whatever it was, finally kicked in. But not before she found herself and her common sense outside, facing a labyrinth of pebbled pathways between statues, cactus, palms, ornate benches, pools, fountains, and discreet sheds for implements to care for all this.

Charlie slipped inside a shed that had a partially opened door to watch her ferret streak by only to turn back and pass her hiding place again, this time slowly looking around. He seemed to glance at the crack in the door that hid her, began to approach it, but then raced off yelling, "Hey, wait, I just want to ask a few questions."

He'd apparently seen someone he thought was Charlie or maybe someone who looked more knowledgeable. It gave her the chance she needed to escape but she did so with the growing dread of what would happen if fragile Maggie Stutzman found herself in this situation. If it panicked Charlie what would it do to her friend?

This place sat on a bluff or promontory. It had cliffs on the seaside.

Charlie was still worrying about that when she checked into the Hyatt Islandia. Her room overlooked long docks with the moored boats of a marina as did the spa she'd just left. Marinas were not unusual along most coastlines or inland lakes or rivers for that matter, but this area was particularly rife. Charlie had never understood the lure.

But then, she was not a person of leisure. All she wanted was time to do the work she loved. Ridiculed, but loved. She unpacked and called Luella Ridgeway who of course had heard of the fate of her client and was even now driving south on her way to the Sea Spa at the Marina del Sol.

"Charlie, I thought you were going to a conference in San Diego not a spa in the North County."

"I'm at the conference hotel right now. The Islandia. But I spent the last two nights at the Sea Spa with Maggie. Luella, she found Judy Judd's body."

"Oh, Jesus. I was about to ask you how poor Maggie's doing. But right now I think I know. What happened to Judith—what do you know?"

"Nothing, but Maggie's still there. And Luella, if you take my place looking after Maggie for a day or two and spend the night there, you're going to learn more than you will any other way. Just don't leave her alone—if you know what I mean."

"I know what you mean and I don't have the time, but for my client and your Maggie, I'll try to steal some from something else. I'm packed for a night at least. But will they let me in?"

"The VanZants, the proprietors or managers of the Spa, are worried too. I'll call Caroline and tell her you're coming. I'm tied up tonight and for a couple of days but keep your cell even if you're told it's forbidden and I'll check in with you when I can and don't hesitate to call me. And Luella? Be careful. There's something uncomfortable about that place."

"Oh Charlie, with you everything is a menace and a mystery."

"Yeah. Murder does that to me." But Charlie had no more than rung off than she felt a certain relief, lightening of the load. She straightened and drew in some serious oxygen and her back, neck, and shoulders sang with relief. Luella Ridgeway was small and no longer young, but she was one savvy lady. She didn't miss much and put up with less.

When Keegan Monroe, famous screenwriter—well okay, as famous as screenwriters ever get—called from the lobby, Charlie Greene was back in her dressed-to-kill outfit with all the lavender and chlorine washed from her hair and looking forward to the evening. And, after another day without the good life, prepared to party.

Seven

The pre-conference dinner for the speakers had two purposes as did most dinners of this sort, no matter the type of information or talents being shared. One was so that the speakers could hobnob with each other, not nearly so tantalizing for them as supposed. And the other was to give the organizers a chance to hobnob with those who actually worked in the industry, perhaps wrangle an inside tip, make an important contact, convince someone on the inside to look at a treatment, script, teleplay, sometimes even a published novel that would make a hit film.

That was all drearily predictable. What wasn't was that the dinner was held at Le Crustacione. Without Mitch Hilsten and the metallic Dodge Ram Charlie made not a ripple, but this time she behaved herself and had poached fillet of sole. It was still fabulous. What wasn't were the two other Hollywood literary agents at the long table in a private dining room she would not have guessed existed in so snooty a joint. It overlooked the parking lot and the bus that had brought them instead of the *mer*. But everyone was so busy impressing everyone, Charlie suspected few noticed.

The gentleman who'd sat beside her on that bus explained that this way they had a designated driver and could start the conference off with a bang—nudge, nudge.

Charlie sat next to Keegan now. The chief organizer Dr. Howard, administrator of one of the many "film institutes" that littered the area, sat on the other side of Charlie's main source of income. On *her* other side sat one of the other agents. In younger more jaded days she'd have told herself everybody had to make a living—that's the way the world is—get used to it. Now she very carefully avoided touching the jerk with her shoulder or arm, leaned closer into Keegan with her knees.

This guy, Jason North, was a predator. They existed in every profession where dreams most often pay better than reality. He was known for scrawling *Spielberg 2:30, Evan Black 5:00* across a chalkboard in his office to lure aspiring screenwriters to leave scripts and fees with him, wait for a phone call that would never come. Budding screenwriters were seduced by advertising in the trades, on the Internet, newspapers, magazines. These predators bought the mailing lists of conferences such as this. These sharks were bottom feeders.

The other shark she knew by sight, but had forgotten his name. He sat across the table and down far enough that she couldn't hear him but he kept gesturing toward her and Keegan to the woman next to him, and nodding at Charlie like they were buds. She ate more of her sole than she should have and nodded at the waiter, prepared to refill her wine glass, instead of the shark.

Okay, so this is not nirvana—but it's also not spa deprivation and murder. And you get to sleep in a bed without Maggie tonight and Luella is there to cover for you and you should be deliriously delighted.

"I am."

"You am what?" Her client turned to her and smiled fondly. Keegan had thinning hair and carried too much weight but she had been his agent when he hit, and that was a bond like no other.

"I am talking to myself."

"I don't understand how anyone so transparent can be such a good agent." Keegan Monroe had never been impressive looking, his hair and mustache grew thinner while his body thickened. But his bolo ties, turquoise jewelry, and cowboy boots were back in style, what with the current leadership in Washington. "Which reminds me, since this could be as close

to getting you all to myself as I'll have this week, I'm looking for an editor to edit a novel manuscript. The best there
is. Where do I go?"

Charlie nearly choked on her lemon sole. "You finished a
novel?"

"Well no, but I have a treatment—"

"Proposal."

"Right. And I want to publish with an e-publisher, print
on demand. But I've heard there's no critical, talented edit-
ing so they get little review space and if they do reviewers
feel free to trash them."

"Reviewers are free to trash any book, Keegan."

"With all the downsizing there must be some good editors
willing to freelance. I can pay. And this way I would have
complete control of the storyline."

"Bookstores don't order books they know they can't return.
Why not write a book about screenwriting? Your name could
get you a New York publisher, your credits could convince
the chains to buy the book."

"That's crass commercialism and you know it."

"Keegan, commercialism doesn't get any crasser than
Hollywood."

"I like to think there are loftier instincts in the old-line
prestigious houses in New York publishing."

"Once you had an editor in New York, the next book you
send her could be your novel. You'd have a foot in the door."
If you ever finished it. Charlie'd had several houses inter-
ested in him and one even offered an advance. He never
completed the book. Even in Folsom Prison he couldn't finish
a novel. But he did write a screenplay there that earned him
an invitation to Cannes and he did gain a lot of weight when
he got out, both events inspired by prison food. "And self-
publishing a book, which is what original I-books are, is
likely to get you slammed by snooty reviewers. Self-
published books have no promotion budget." Most other published books in this corporate world didn't either, truth be
known.

"I'll make it a mystery and go to those conventions around the country to promote it."

"And there you will meet thousands of I-published writers instead of book-buying fans—all trying to do what you are doing." But she made a mental note to hunt up a poor unemployed editor of merit to work with him.

Charlie opted out of the party continuation back at the hotel and went up to her room to face the music. She had messages on her cell and the phone light blinked on her room phone. She slipped into her night shirt (a man's V-neck undershirt) and the hotel terrycloth robe, not as luxurious as the one at the Sea Spa at the Marina del Sol, and washed her face. Munching a chocolate mint the maid left on her pillow, she took the cell out to the deck that overlooked a row of sailboats dipping and nodding at their moorings below and moonlight showering down from above. The sound of the bay lapping at the marina's docks reminded her of the eddy pool of cucumber, seaweed, and murder fame.

It felt so good being alone and on her own, having her life back. But she listened to Luella Ridgeway's message. "Charlie, Maggie's relatively stable but call me when you can. I snuck my cellular into the room. This is a weird place and I live with weird every day, but—"

Libby Abigail Greene—"Mom, do you know how to make a cat, who smeared the kitchen with poop and Science Diet, take a pill?"

Richard Morse of Congdon and Morse, Inc. who employed both Luella and Charlie. "What the fuck's going on down there? I just saw the score on Judy Judd's murder on TV. Luella's not answering my calls. I'm getting royally pissed, babe. Why hasn't anybody filled me in on all this? Heads are going to roll around here, I'm warning you."

Charlie rubbed the back of her neck. She was going to need a massage pretty soon. Luella was in the room with Maggie so not as free to speak as they both would have liked.

"I like the VanZants but the help is creepy and there's hardly anybody here but the aforementioned and a cop now and then."

Charlie could hear muted voices in the background. "Has she opened the wardrobe doors?"

"No, just listens. It is kind of interesting though. I don't pay any attention to the commercials when I'm watching TV unless one of the agency's clients are involved, but did you realize half the commercials are prescription drugs and the other half car dealers?"

"Yeah, it used to be ask your doctor, now it's tell your doctor. Kinda scary. Richard the Lionhearted is trying to get hold of you."

"I know. He's going to expect me to solve Judy's murder while I'm here. That's your department."

"No Luella, my department is writers. Judy was your client."

"And Maggie Stutzman is your friend."

Libby actually picked up her cell but she wasn't home with Tuxedo the terrible tomcat unless all of Wilson High was over for a party. "Where are you? This is your mother answering your distress signal, dammit."

"Hi Mom, I'm at the Smelly Socks concert. It rocks. Can you hear?"

What Charlie could hear was the slight slur in her daughter's consonants. "What about the cat barf and shit all over the kitchen? Did you clean it up?"

"Itch your kitchen."

"And it's your cat. Did you figure out what to do with the pill?"

"Yeah, Doug shtuck it in a piece of cheese. I left before I found out if the cheese stayed down."

"You clean that mess up before I get home, toots."

"Gotta go now, bye."

Charlie went back in the room and closed the balcony door on the peaceful night. Her stomach started the familiar burn. She looked at the light blinking on the room phone and considered ignoring it, turned on the television in the wardrobe, and muted the familiar Aviatrix commercial, then listened to the message on the hotel voice mail. It was Kenny

39

Cowper, a.k.a. Kenneth Cooper, and another of Charlie's clients. He was staying in the hotel. Kenny was a book author. What the hell was he doing at this conference? He was also stud city and the last complication she could handle now.

She jotted down his room number though. He was better than a massage—but no.

Charlie unmuted the TV for the eleven o'clock news. Might as well, she wasn't going to get any sleep tonight anyway. Dr. Judith Judd had not died of drowning in the eddy pool at the Sea Spa at the Marina del Sol. She'd been strangled first and then either fell in or was deposited there.

Eight

Charlie woke up groggy from having slept so hard, surprised she'd slept at all. She ordered room service, showered, shampooed, dried and tamed her hair as best she could. She'd had it cut shorter than usual which made the curls go ballistic, so she tied it back with a navy blue scarf to match a severe tuxedo suit she'd don when she finished eating and offset it with a naughty, blazing-white, frilled peek-a-boo blouse.

When her breakfast came she took it and the newspaper out onto the balcony, dressed again in the hotel robe. Fog rolled sluggishly off the bay as if it too needed coffee. She wasn't due to go on until ten.

Vegetarian eggs hollandaise, a pot of coffee, luscious thick toast. A yacht pulled out from the next pier over. An article about the Sea Spa at the Marina del Sol, with a picture of Dr. Judy alive, began on the front page of the *San Diego Union-Tribune*. Apparently she'd choked on a plastic water bottle. Police were not convinced that the plastic bottle was "self-administered."

Judy's ties to the Spa were curious. She owned a portion of it, had lent the VanZants money to pay expenses and taxes more than once and in return was allowed to tape many of her medical-showbiz stunts free in its odd studio/auditorium and had the Spa's paying customers as an on-set audience. She hired film crews piecemeal from the out-of-work, disenchanted, and nonunion scabs adrift in Sou Cal. Where do reporters come up with such odd bits of information? This by-line was none other than Jerry Parks', the guy who'd chased her around the spa.

41

Charlie and Luella better get a fragile Maggie away from the place. But what would they do with her? She couldn't be on her own. Funny, Charlie and Maggie used to worry about what they would do with Betty Beesom, their aging neighbor, when she could no longer be left alone.

Charlie, Dr. Judy is Luella's problem. Maggie is yours. You're in this all by yourself, sweetie.

"Maybe she's got relatives I don't know about," Charlie told the patronizing voice in her head. Maggie had a brother and a sister. The sister in Michigan got stuck with the care for their ailing mother for so many years she no longer spoke to her siblings. The brother ran dive boats for tourists in Hawaii. Maggie's last communication with either of them had been at their mother's funeral. It was not cordial. "Maybe her friends at work will help out some more."

A featured article on Mitch Hilsten graced the *Union-Tribune* as well, rife with "filmspeak" that some reporter had picked up on TV or at a conference like this one. Moira Moriarty, dusky, smooth, and perfect, oval face, oval eyes, looked so tiny standing between Mitch Hilsten and Samuel Houston who would play the gutsy CIA agent. He was in the process of growing one of those short beards that encircle the mouth. Mitch was not very tall—five ten, eleven at the most. Moira was very small and her leading man could appear very leading in contrast.

Moira would certainly look the part of a beautiful Bedouin princess—did Bedouins even have princesses? Didn't matter. The real problem was that Moira was, in real life, an Irish Jew from the Bronx and though coaches had trained most of the accent out of her speech, traces lingered. Charlie had visions of movie theaters blowing up all around the globe.

Jane of the Jungle was the CIA agent's fond term for her and already her real name was being linked romantically with both Sam Houston and Mitch Hilsten. Made good press. There was also a smaller picture of Charlie and Mitch squinting in the exhaust of the metallic blue Dodge Ram as the valet roared off outside Le Crustacione de la Mer night before last. *"But the famous actor-turned-director continues to dine with his previous girlfriend, Charlie Greene, a Hollywood agent, at C & M on Wilshire."*

On this morning's panel were Charlie, the two sharks, Sarah Newman—a story editor from Troll Productions—and Dr. Howard moderating. Attendees packed the sizable room and stood against the walls in back and some sat in the aisles. Keegan Monroe sat front row center. On one side of him sat Jerry Parks, the reporter who'd chased Charlie through the halls and pebbled paths of the Sea Spa at the Marina del Sol yesterday and written the article on Judith Judd in this morning's paper.

On the other side of Keegan, Kenny Cowper/Kenneth Cooper smirked up at her. All she needed now was for Mitch Hilsten to walk into the room and she'd wet her tuxedo.

The assembled consisted mostly of males, probably eighty percent or more. The moderator's questions centered almost exclusively on how to circumvent the security at agencies and studios to get material inside to be considered. The sharks proudly announced the lack of security at their offices. They worked solo with an office assistant for scheduling, did their own reading, and were not tied down by agency-like procedures. They agreed on most everything, but treated each other with loathing and disdain.

Sarah explained she had an assistant and accepted only agented material. Charlie explained hers was a small agency where she was the lone literary agent and others handled actors, speakers, minor athletes, commercial artists, even some ministers and circus performers. She had an assistant and two outside readers and they were all months behind. The readers culled most of the material, sent the rest to Charlie's assistant who culled most of the rest, and she saw maybe two percent of the original submissions. Out of that she might take none or perhaps find a home for one.

"You must understand the supply far outweighs the

demand, and that most of the writing in Hollywood is assigned. I spend much of my time handling the latter, like Keegan here. The chances against my selling your screenplay are astronomical. But every now and then I can sell *you* on the basis of what you send me. I can rarely, but sometimes help you become one of those assigned to write or help to write a screenplay. And sometimes I'll send the writer's work on to a small independent film maker who might not make anybody any money but who might gain the writer some credits upon which to build a career."

"That's why you want an independent agent. With me your dreams are safer," said one of the sharks.

"With me, your checkbook is safer. Remember the show-biz cliché, don't give up your day job. Writing is showbiz, not art. A very few manage to make showbiz art as Keegan did with *Open and Shut*. It took many years of hard work and a lot of luck, even for him."

"You sure know how to put a damper on enthusiasm," Kenny Cowper, a.k.a. Kenneth Cooper, said as he caught up with her in the hallway after she'd finally escaped the auditorium and handed out the business cards of the outside readers—only their PO boxes printed on them, hoping they didn't up and quit on her. "I mean, why did you come if you weren't looking for writers?"

"Only for Keegan. Most of my writers are freelance advertising types, if truth be known."

"They work for ad agencies."

"The good ones have their own agent to see they don't get screwed."

"You are such a negative person. How can you represent anybody?"

"It's called survival, Cowper." She may have been depressing but she'd turned down too many lunch invitations to count, requests for home and office phone numbers, or for her assistant's at second best. During the question and answer sessions she and Sarah had been barraged with the issue of why weren't they worried that they'd miss the script of a lifetime—worded in many different ways.

Sarah had summed it up nicely. "I'm more worried I'll be crushed under the weight of all the submissions I get from agents. Most of my successes come from acquiring film rights to books and letting others hire the screenwriters."

The moderator and the sharks snuffled, rolled their eyes. But it was Sarah and Charlie who took the longest to make it to the back of the room to the hallway and they met again in the ladies. "I had to come because of Keegan, but who talked you into this?"

"My sister married Grant Howard, the leader of this show," the story editor answered from the stall next door. "I've wormed my way out of it for five years, but got caught this time. Did you notice not a word was mentioned that my office is in NYC? Not on the West Coast? I thought you'd blow the whistle on me."

"What kind of doctor is Grant Howard?"

"Nobody ever says and if you ask you get that look and don't try again."

Out at the sink and paper towel dispensers, Charlie asked, "Did you get any feeling for *The Rites of Winter*?"

"You know, I just read it when I saw you were on the program. It's not for us, but you might try Uranus. They're planning a cable series for the older folks—forty, fifty somethings. It might be a fit."

Now Charlie walked along beside her towering author from Iowa, bemused at the fact that someone at one production company would suggest another for something the first rejected. Could Sarah be moving? Was she being fired/downsized?

Charlie walked. Kenny sort of minced to keep down with her. He had to be six four if he was an inch—and that boy had some inches.

Charlie!

Well? "So what are you doing at this conference? Are you going into screenwriting now?"

45

"Why should I tell you? You haven't sold the Myrtle book yet."

Actually, you know I think I might have. "There's some interest, Kenny. Have you continued with it? I mean past the proposal stage?"

"I've finished it, Charlie."

Their first mistake was to stop in the middle of the hall and turn toward each other. She, looking way up, trying to stop the satisfied smile breaking her face just as a professional stole a still shot that would complicate her life for a long time to come.

Oh, boy.

Nine

"Whoa girl, you drive a Dodge Ram? Who'd a thought?" Kenny drove his rental, a bright red something-to-ruther.

He'd been explaining to her why he was at the conference and trying to lay a guilt trip on her for not returning his calls. All the while Charlie was hurrying out to the parking lot, intent upon rushing to the Sea Spa, and postponing him, when she saw more cameras and the ferret from the *Union-Tribune* sniffing around her truck.

So, planning to tell her client to shove off, midway through the sentence Charlie changed to, "Kenny? Where's your car? I need to make a fast getaway." Studs are suckers for that kind of talk.

When they were nearly there she thought to mention they'd need to eat before they reached their destination. Charlie couldn't believe it when he pulled into a Carl's Junior for lunch. Kenny was a sometime health nut. "But this is junk food."

"I'm on vacation. So why that heart-stopping smile when I said I'd finished the Myrtle book? You know, I haven't felt that good since my mommy told me I'd passed potty training."

"I have a nibble on the proposal."

"Who?" he said around a loaded burger.

"Pitman's." She tore her burger into ragged halves and passed one over to his side of the table, sneaking a couple of his fries in return. "I just found out Friday. You must have had a boring winter in Iowa to finish it this soon."

"They turned down the last one after nibbles."

"New editor. This one could be different." Charlie met this creature last October when she and her mother traveled to Iowa on family matters. And she learned more about family than she'd ever wanted to know. Charlie had grown up thinking she'd been adopted from an agency in Boulder where she was raised and her daughter born. She and Libby had dark, almost black eyes in stark contrast to their light hair, Libby a platinum blonde and Charlie's hair with more of a bronze shade. But when Charlie visited Myrtle, Iowa for the first and she vowed last time, she found at least a fourth of the people there had the same color eyes— including Kenny Cowper who wrote under the name of Kenneth Cooper.

"Nice old Iowa" had been something of a surprise. And so had Kenny Cowper.

"So tell me again why you are at this conference?"

"I thought an exposé on charlatans in the entertainment industry might be a possible article. And I thought it would be fun to hand deliver a completed book manuscript to my new agent."

"You've already got an assignment for this article."

"Right. But you get to check out the contract. I have divorced Jethro Larue for good."

As Kenny had predicted, Jeth Larue, a fairly formidable New York literary agent, had not liked Kenny's proposal for a book dealing largely with the conundrum of nursing homes and those who dwell interminably and helplessly within. Jeth had a mother so incarcerated whom he couldn't bear to visit and found the whole subject distasteful. He was also of the age where he was the next generation up for this lovely existence.

Kenny's title for it was *The Curse of Myrtle, Iowa, the United States, and The Developed World*. Neither he nor Charlie thought that would be the final title but both were too involved in the problem it posed to think up the perfect one and Charlie figured this title would entice enough curiosity to get a close examination. If accepted, it would be his fifth published book, plus he had credits as an investigative reporter for the *Miami Herald* and at least ten article credits with major news magazines.

Plus which he was way more than presentable, too way more, and the guy could pitch, an indispensable asset in an industry in which major decision makers too often have little inclination to read. Agents and editors read what their assistants pass on and then must pitch to higher levels to wheedle contracts. That's one of the reasons why new material is often presented as similar to the latest bestseller or star in a genre or category. Plus, the stud had business savvy. His first agent didn't know the half there. Kenny'd been born and raised in Myrtle, moved to Florida, and returned to save its only pool hall. He'd renamed it Viagra's. It was a hit.

"Does that sudden photo op back at the Islandia mean I get my picture with you in the paper instead of Hilsten tomorrow?"

There was only one official San Diego sheriff's car in the parking lot at the Sea Spa at the Marina del Sol, but quite a few other cars. And when Charlie and Kenny entered, after ignoring Dashiell the gatekeeper, the place seemed to be humming. No one at the front desk or in the office, or in Maggie's room, but they followed sound to find her in a mirrored gym on the pool level sweating out an exercise-dance routine to the rhythms of Swank Swill with twenty-five, maybe thirty others. Unlike the screenwriters' conference, all but three of those participating here were female.

"Thought you said the place was almost closed down by the murder." Kenny inspected the weightlifting and torture machine room next door through the windows. "They got some cool stuff here."

Raoul had a few sacrifices in the pool and several others sat on the side watching. Maggie'd waved at them from the distressed line in the gym. Charlie said, "Let's go find either the VanZants, the law, or Luella Ridgeway. Maggie's smiling so I'm not rescuing her yet."

"You don't make a lot more sense than my last agent."

They found Detective Solomon in the auditorium with Caroline and Warren VanZant.

"Well, here's our famous Hollywood agent. In my minuscule experience of such things, I thought agents kept a lower profile. Our *Union-Tribune* is usually more immune to celebrity. And who is this gentleman?"

"I'm her bodyguard." Kenny Cowper bent to smile sardonically upon them all.

"He's one of my authors, Kenneth Cooper," Charlie said. "Caroline, I just saw Maggie and she seemed happy. Have you adjusted her drugs some more?"

"Drugs?" Solomon looked away from Kenny to study the Spa's proprietor.

"Medications," Charlie corrected and tried to smile with conviction.

But Caroline VanZant was still torturing her neck looking up at Kenny. "Kenneth Cooper? The author?"

"Never heard of him," Solomon said. "Now if we can get past the celebrity thing here, I want to know again exactly who was where when Judith Judd died. Not the clientele, I'm talking staff, you, your son."

"Sorry, talk to you later," and Charlie motioned the author out of the room and down the hall to the eddy-pool deck where every pool was filled with Jacuzzi bubbles, suffering cucumbers, bubbling brooks, and thunder in the distance. Charlie finally recognized what was so strange about Solomon's appearance: he had no eyebrows.

Dashiell squinted suspicion from the palms at the head of the pools. Charlie ignored him and walked to the windows, looking for Luella among the paths and plantings and cottages below. There was a long sweep of sea and she even got a glimpse of an edge of the famous marina. She didn't know "sea talk" but there was apparently an inlet or something at the north side of this promontory or point, whatever, that allowed the gentling of the swells that crashed against its end.

"You got a problem with that?" Kenny Cowper said behind her and she turned to see him leaning over Dashiell.

Charlie caught herself before she said, "Kenny, leave it."

She'd watched this dog food commercial one of her clients had snared, too many times. It was about training dogs to stop inappropriate behavior of all sorts apparently but when used to keep a dog from Pooch Svelte, it elicited a snarl from a Chihuahua, a Doberman, and something shaggy in between.

She led her author off by the arm, but the bald jerk brought them both up short. "He's a sex addict. Be careful, Miss Greene."

And good old Kenny had to turn around and retort, "Oh yeah? Well, she's a pervert."

And several sufferers made the mistake of trying to sit up and bend tight seaweed wraps and cucumbers to get a look at such an extraordinary couple and the eddy pools were much disturbed.

"I can't take you anywhere," Charlie groused when they walked outside among the sheds and paths and cottages. She'd seen some people wandering out here when she'd slipped upstairs to check Maggie's room. Luella's bag was still there and her Lexus in the parking lot.

"Wait a minute—is this the spa where that lady doctor was murdered?" Kenny asked now.

"Yeah, and my friend Maggie found her and when I got back she said she did it because she wanted to die. She's gone wacko on us."

"Did she kill the doctor?"

"She's suicidal, not homicidal. And on and off. Depression and prescription drugs. Screwed-up hormones."

"Rough."

"I was going to take her back to the Islandia with me, but now I don't know."

"I've heard women are pretty much ruled by their hormones. Must be really rough for women like you."

"What's that supposed to mean?"

Kenny started off down a path to a row of small, mostly one-room cottages with porches. He looked in windows, tried some doors—the investigative reporter in him perking up. Most of the cottages appeared empty of furnishings. Two had wicker chairs on the porch that the wind had blown over. The sea breeze smelled wet and salty, tried to tug her hair from its navy blue tie down. The sun was dry and hot and forced Charlie to unbutton her tuxedo jacket. That reminded her of the other Tuxedo in her life and in her house and the effects of Science Diet mixed with Diazepam.

"You know that blouse is illegal?"

"Be careful, it's easy to get lost out here."

"Tell me about it. There's not a straight path to anywhere, inside or out. Is there a point to that, I wonder? This sure isn't Iowa."

"Tell me about it."

"You know you send mixed signals?"

Charlie was happy to hear her cell go off in her purse. She could turn her back on him. It was Ronald Dorland, a fairly new client with a book out last year. He'd had some minor success with filmwriting assignments before that and was astonished when she answered instead of her voice-mail message. He couldn't understand the first royalty statement for his book.

"You don't want to know," Charlie told him.

"But I do. I took it to my accountant, Charlie. He didn't understand it either."

"Join the crowd. Let's see, that would be Bootstrap, a subsidiary of Wonderhouse who just merged with Dallywood, a subsidiary of Sherman/Sturtz just bought out by a German brewery whose name I can't pronounce whose parent company makes titanium nuts and bolts and body parts for repairs." Charlie should know, she had one of their plates implanted in her neck. "And itself part of a conglomerate specializing in diversification run by a management firm— SORRI."

"But my publisher is Zulu Press, not any of those other publishers."

"Merged with Bootstrap two years ago."

"Which all means what?"

"Get kneepads."

"I thought agents were supposed to keep authors from getting screwed."

"Look, most writers never get published at all. I was able to get you a contract for a two thousand advance—you are now on the bottom rung of a very tall ladder. It's either the beginning of a climb or you fall off and expire as an author or turn to self-publishing, which is pretty much the same thing. With that advance you're lucky the books got out of the warehouse. With that advance there is no clout for an agent to use." Charlie's commission on that advance didn't pay its share of the paperwork or overhead.

"So I'm never going to see any royalties? This is just like Hollywood."

"Look at it this way, Ronald, kneepads are cheap."

Ten

"K neepads," Kenny said, wide-eyed and for once not in total sarcastic control of a situation. "You talking praying or sodomy? Was that a client?"

"Well, it wasn't a gardener. Ronald published his first book last year and just received his first royalty statement."

"Oh. You were talking—"

"Right."

Luella Ridgeway, dressed in slacks and flats instead of business suit and heels, appeared from an angled walkway, talking on her cell. "Hang on a minute. Charlie, I need paper and pen. You have any in your purse?"

Before Charlie could make a move, a small notepad opened to a clean page descended from the porch above with a ballpoint and muscled forearm for a writing surface. Luella paused to stare up at the command center of this instant office, glance puzzlement at Charlie. "Okay, go ahead."

Luella was small, smart, swift, and savvy. She used the proffered desk as if she expected no less from the world as Kenny held the pad still for her so she could hold the cell and the pen. He had to bend almost double over the railing. Charlie wished she had a camera.

"You're sure? What's the source on that? Okay. Go on." Finally, she thanked her informant and punched off, tore out the pages she'd used and handed the notepad and pen back to the desk whom she thanked also and asked Charlie, "He for hire?"

"I only handle his writing talents. Luella Ridgeway,

Kenneth Cooper. Luella is Dr. Judy's agent, also Congdon and Morse. So what you got?"

"Well, I've talked to her doctor, her lawyer, and her daughter."

"She had a daughter?"

"And a granddaughter. And an ex. And a boyfriend."

"Who'd have thought?"

"Charlie, I keep telling you to stop stereotyping everyone you meet. You miss so much that way."

"Yeah, and she's totally cynical too," Kenny added.

Charlie'd learned a lot from this woman and had always thought she wanted to be like Luella if she ever grew up. They wandered absently along the footpaths, Kenny's big shoes crunching gravel behind them.

"Anyway, the skinny here is Judith not only went out for a cigarette after her gig, but she swallowed a handful of pills as well. Washed them down with bottled water and somehow choked on the bottle. It's strongly suspected she had some help with the latter."

"Legal drugs?" Kenny asked.

"Dr. Judy took drugs? Nice old Dr. Judy?"

"You know anybody who doesn't? Her assistant says she took them morning and night. She had them divided up in baggies and they were a combination of prescribed drugs, over the counter, and alternative. Her doctor listed an anti-depressant, anti-anxiety, hormones, blood pressure, acid reflux, allergy, cholesterol medications. And she had a sleeping disorder. He was looking through his records and sounded kind of stunned at the length of the list, himself. And then being a doctor herself—who knew what else she had access to with samples and all. Got a problem, take a pill."

"How did you get a doctor to give away confidential information like that and on another doctor?" Kenny the investigative reporter sounded impressed. "And over the phone yet?"

"He's my doctor too and his client has been murdered in one way or another, and I convinced him I could be of use to him should there be a lawsuit since I was also his patient's business agent and speaking from the scene of the crime. He has aspirations to become a celebrity doc on TV and will need representation. And I got to him before he'd had time to consult his lawyer. Toxicology won't be back with results for awhile."

"Man, you agents kick ass. I thought you were persuasive, diplomatic types."

Both women turned to look at him, shielding their eyes from the sun before continuing on their way. Charlie asked, "And the lawyer, did you know him?"

"I've dealt with him on estate matters, copyrights, residuals, that kind of thing. Her daughter gets everything, her ex and boyfriend nothing. She'd made that public herself recently, but not that it comes with strings, paid out in healthy yearly sums, forfeited if the daughter should give any of it to her father—trust fund kind of thing, I guess."

"Couldn't she have choked on the pills and sucked the water bottle down her throat and then fell in the pool?"

"Got me. That's your department."

"No, it's not."

Kenny brought them up short with, "Anybody know where we are?"

They were in a valley of ruins, the sound of the sea coming from three sides. Empty reflecting pools with crumbling columns and statues. Long dried-up vines and tipped-over fountains ran along what might have been where an old streambed eroded the rock, taking the rare storm runoff to the sea.

There had been a lot of less-than-useful building going on, on this bluff, and money squandered. The naked statue of a well-hung young man of the Greek or Roman persuasion tipped dangerously toward a fissure.

Charlie realized she was staring at the young Mediterranean while her companions tossed path pebbles into the fissure and listened for the reassurance of a landing. Maybe he'd had one orgy too many.

"Something about this place," Luella said, hugging her

arms. Her last pebble just kept slithering down in the crevice, rattling against one side, bouncing off to hit the other, the sound of its journey fading with the distance but still audible long after it should have been swallowed up by the earth. "Even without Judith's murder."

"Yeah, look at all this real estate—a bunch of it in ruins. There's gotta be developers salivating. On the way up here, there are houses stacked above each other and then on top where the view is worth zillions—there's all this unused," said the boy from Myrtle, Iowa.

"According to the VanZants, the state is trying to put a stop to shore developments cutting off public access, wants eventually to bring this cliff top into the park system. Right now there's no money for such a project, but they've been able to hold off developers so far."

Charlie followed the fissure to its end, maybe ten feet short of the cliff edge, and then continued on to peer over the rim, where there was no discernable beach but her acrophobia was relieved the drop was not as far as it had looked to be from the eddy-pool deck. Still, she moved well away from the precipice before turning around to look up at the Sea Spa's main building.

The fissure snaked jagged but true as far as her eye could see. So she followed it back again through the ruins, up slope until she reached a high point from which she could see matching tiled rooftops all in a row below on the other side. Those apartment houses must have been built after the earthquake that caused the fissure. And below them rooftops and commercial areas extended beyond the ribbons of the 101 and the 5 after that and into a mist of pollution obscuring less populated regions of the county inland.

She didn't realize her companions had joined her until they turned together to view the magic of the ruins and the unrealized promise of splendor offered by the Sea Spa against the backdrop of unending ocean and sky.

"The public would just ruin this," Kenny said. "There's too much of it—the public, I mean."

"If I were Arab-oil-filthy-rich, I'd buy it to protect it and to enjoy it all by myself." Luella Ridgeway took in such a deep breath she had to cough some of it back. "What would you do, Charlie?"

"I'd worry myself sick this sizable crack would open up and tumble me and all that's here into the sea."

"You ever consider Prozac or Zoloft or Paxil or Euphoria III?" Luella asked as they headed back to the Spa and the tinkle of wind chimes. "You're carrying too much stress, babe."

Two men stood in earnest conversation in the shade of one of the cottages, Warren VanZant and a shorter man who resembled the ferret. Had he followed them or was he just continuing his investigations for the *Union-Tribune*?

"Euphoria III?" Charlie came back to her own conversation, glad to see both men disappear before she reached them. "Is that a legal substance or something teenies think it's cool to take before dancing?"

But in the suffocating Victorian suite, Maggie refused to leave and the voice in the wardrobe swept away what little reality remained in San Diego County.

Charlie lost it this time and flounced out to find someone in this place who had retained an ounce of sanity. Instead, she found women with hair wrapped in towels, euphoric faces red from granite rubs, filing out the door to the parking lot with Sea Spa bags probably full of clay, cucumbers, packets of ship-bilge tea, and what all else Charlie did not wish to contemplate. But she did try to envision what an enema pack might look like.

Her cell tweedle-dee-deed in her purse and she was so stressed she answered it. Mitch was down at the Marina del Sol, thinking she must be at the Islandia in town. "No, I'm up at the Spa about ready to slit a throat, possibly mine. Maggie will not listen to reason."

"That's why she's there, right? I've got something you might like to see. And you can take a breath of fresh air, settle down."

58

She hated when he did that. But it would be good to get away for a bit. She explained she was without a car and Mitch would have to come get her, persuaded Kenny to go back to the conference and Luella to hang in for a while longer. Caroline VanZant assured her that her best friend was responding well to the therapies the Spa had to offer and suggested that it might do Maggie good to be alone a little, to find herself and not feel pressured.

"Have you talked to her about this?"

"Yes, and I know how protective you are, but I think she needs time to straighten out a few things. Ms. Ridgeway can go back to L.A. without worrying. I'll monitor Maggie during the night to see that she's comfortable and not afraid."

"Not Sue, or Raoul, or Dashiell."

"I promise. Give us a chance, Charlie." Caroline was using her sweet, caring voice. Her face, plump and pink as the tinted glasses, seemed to belie her mostly gray hair. Botox? "Give Maggie a chance too. In the end only she can deal with her demons and she must feel strong enough to make the right decisions."

"Makes great sense if there was anything normal about this situation, but there's been a murder here and she's offered herself up as a prime suspect."

"But she's still the same Maggie with the same problems as when she arrived and with the same desire to overcome them."

"What if the murderer strikes again? Strikes Maggie? Or she gets the blame for it?"

Eleven

"You all right?" Mitch asked when Charlie slid into the low, black, sinister rental.

"No. And I don't want to talk about it."

"Maggie?"

"Yes." The rooftops started just below the rim here too, descending in terraced rows on a curvy street that would lead eventually to the 101 or Pacific Highway or Coastal Highway—same road but the highway signs did not agree. Stucco houses in white, peach, sand colors. Wood bungalows in light grays, blues, and yellows. Small homes on small lots, known in real-estate parlance as "scrapers." Every third or fourth house spread over three or four lots where moderate homes had been excised, towering over their neighbors with setbacks of no more than ten feet, fifteen from the street. The setbacks were mostly filled with retaining or thick stucco walls, vines, trees, garage access, and heavy gates with "Armed Response" warning signs.

A wye in the street forked off to the Marina del Sol and on the opposite hillside the lowering sun glittered on the glassed-in fronts of lavish trophy homes the size of hotels, staking claim to an ocean view.

At the end of the wye, signs greeted them in a parade of warnings. NO PUBLIC ACCESS. PRIVATE PROPERTY BEYOND THIS GATE. MARINA MEMBERS, GUESTS, AND STAFF ONLY. TWENTY-FOUR HOUR ARMED HUMAN AND DOG RESPONSE. HAVE IDENTIFICATION AND MEMBERSHIP PASS IN POSSESSION AT ALL TIMES.

Charlie was impressed already. "What kind of heat do the dogs pack, I wonder?"

Mitch grimaced without even showing his beautiful teeth. They were capped and at one time insured by Lloyds of London. He presented a card for a machine to scan and about a minute later the gate opened. Charlie wondered what would happen if some partying "guest" was in a royal rush to get to the biffy but she didn't particularly feel like tempting another grimace.

Even through the tinted windshield of the black Stealth, the sun on the ocean glinted hard. This marina was a small town, the curved shoreline of the inlet lined with condos, the yacht club a rambling hotel with only two or three stories and just above the docks on one side of the inlet with condos terraced above that. On the other side, the shore accommodations were fewer and even more lavish. But the real difference between this marina and others Charlie had seen, here and on the East Coast, Long Beach, Oregon, and a few other places, was the size of these "yachts." Many looked more like ships, a few took up a whole dock by themselves. "Did I tell you I haven't had dinner?"

"We have reservations at the club, on the deck if the weather and wind are gentle, behind glass if not."

"Dinner with a view."

"Dinner with a view. But first, drinks on the *Mother-fricker*."

The *Motherfricker* was one of the ship-yachts, with its own dock across the inlet from "the club," and reached by a one-lane bridge at the head of the inlet.

"How many people does it take to operate something this size?" Charlie asked as they walked up the gangplank.

"There's a permanent crew of seven when she's underway, not including the chef who is on vacation for a month now to visit family in France, while the owner is at his home in Orange County. Probably has a resident chef there too."

"Is he a real Arab oil sheik?" Charlie had seen things like this only in the movies, as the *Motherfricker* was soon to be.

61

A master study and stateroom, a VIP stateroom almost as big. And two more smaller bedrooms, all with their own full baths.

"Car dealer." The master bath had a whirlpool tub and huge glass shower, his and her commode rooms, sinks in the shape of seashells.

"You're not going to use the name—"

"We're thinking of *The Cassandra*." Surprisingly large rooms, lavishly furnished and decorated. There was no crystal chandelier in the dining room, but the lighting consisted of an interesting array of recessed tiered tube lights in the ceiling molding, patterned to match the oval of the table.

"*The Cassandra* seems kind of lame for such a ridiculous story premise. At least the script's not a musical."

"There's actually talk of Harvey Piddle writing the music for a theater production aimed at Broadway or Vegas, smart-ass. All the great musicals have ridiculous premises, if you think about it. I don't know how I ever became involved with someone so cynical about everything."

The galley had white woodwork, stainless steel counters and appliances—two refrigerators and a spacious wine cooler. A "salon" with comfortable furniture and lush fabric on the mid deck, a "sky lounge" on the upper deck with great views and a bar, the seating in soft leather.

"I never dreamed I'd ever keep speaking to someone who'd made such marvelous films for years and then turned turncoat on all his values to endorse Hollywood shlock."

Something haunted in Mitch's expression reminded Charlie of Maggie. The dead look in his eyes was soon replaced with humor—but then he was an actor and Maggie was not. "It's simple, Charlie. I wanted to keep working. It's all I have."

Oh, Charlie didn't want to go there. Her work, crazy as it was, was all that kept her sane. She didn't want to end up on mood-numbing pharmaceuticals like Maggie.

A quick glance at the crew lounge and the "helm" cabin and then back to the sky lounge and bar, where they took glasses of the smoothest scotch she'd ever tasted out onto the "aft deck" and butter-soft leather armchairs under an overhang. Right now the crew, but for the steward who ministered to them, was off doing whatever crews do when they're not on board. The steward wore white like on *Love Boat*, and the yacht was white and all the buildings on the hillsides, the club, condos, and everything manmade. When she pointed this out to Mitch he in turn pointed to a seagull perched on a white railing not far from them.

"I have no expertise on this, but I expect if he shit black, boats and ships and marinas would be black too."

"Navy ships aren't white."

"They have young swab labor. We've got this for a month, my crew starts moving in tomorrow. We've got exterior shots of her running out on calm and rough seas already, some we'll digitalize. I've been offered a room at the club under special aegis, can run up to Long Beach for the wedding Saturday, and move into the club when I get back."

Across the inlet smaller boats rose and dipped gently as a remnant of the surf washed in clear to the bridge. The *Motherfricker* didn't seem to notice.

"We're addicted too, aren't we Mitch? Addicted to our work. Do you take medication?"

"Everybody does. I'm not on Viagra yet, if that's what you mean."

"It's not." But they were both grinning. Charlie preferred to think of their connection as a friendship rather than a relationship, although there had been occasional steam. But the warmth of the sun, the smooth scotch, and the luxury of the leather sort of molding to fit her, relaxed the tension, dulled the ache in her neck, put out the fire in her gut. That and the fact most of their expression hid behind sunglasses now. "I suppose this drink is self-medicating, huh?"

The lap of the water under the dock, the "scree" of the seagulls—and the sudden jarring of amplified guitars . . .

Mitch Hilsten, superstar, swore, picked their drinks off the top of a fancy metal barrel-like table between them, handed

her hers, and lifted the top to play with some buttons under-
neath. The guitars stopped, the lapping and screeing returned.
"Thanks a lot, Stanley."

"Who's Stanley?"

"The steward. Maybe it's Sidney."

"Maybe he wants us to leave."

"He's just sharing." But the result was the same and they
were soon driving across the bridge to the club.

"Thanks. Despite Sidney the steward, the *Motherfricker*
was beautiful, interesting, and relaxing. A good break."

"Thought you were strung pretty tight there. And the
evening's not over. Crab is the special at the club tonight."

At dinner they watched an older couple downing pill after
pill from baggies filled with them, one by one with water
between the main course and dessert.

"How do all those pills know where to go to do the job?"
Charlie whispered. "What happens when they mix with the
crab and the butter and the cocktails and the wine?"

"That's why you take the little silver football before bed,
Charlie. It takes care of the acid reflux, bloating, and
headache so you can sleep. Of course, there are certain sexual
side effects, but who cares if you can eat, drink, and be
merry? Who needs sexual gratification? Almost every
prescription drug on the market warns you not to mix them
with alcohol. Only teetotalers pay any attention."

"Don't forget about dry mouth," their waiter whispered,
bending lower than necessary to refill their wine glasses. He
was as tall as Kenny Cowper, but more willowy than muscular. He had a goatee and a shaved head with a five o'clock
shadow. He finally hunkered down between them and
squinted while rotating the raising of his brows. "Drugs,
which include alcohol, are simple. Rule of thumb. If it makes
you feel good, it's bad. If it makes you feel nothing, it's
good. So sex is bad by definition, so you don't need it
anyway, but if you do there's a blue pill. But if you do that
you risk stroke so why should you worry about dry mouth?"

"What if it makes you feel bad?"

He left them with, "You're overdosing."

"Jesus, that was brilliant," Mitch said. "He couldn't be over fifteen."

"More like twenty-five. Maybe he's auditioning. Clean up your wine like a good boy. I've got to get back to Maggie. And you have to take us to the Islandia, if we can budge her."

"Certain sexual side effects—that's the clincher."

"Mitch, what meds are you on?"

"Echinacea for colds, valerian root for anxiety, glucosamine/chondroitin for knee pain."

"Those are alternative meds."

"Right—don't have to give up alcohol, sexual gratification, or a reasonably juicy mouth."

Twelve

Charlie stepped off the elevator at the Hyatt Islandia weary, worried, sure she'd just made a whole lot of wrong decisions, and walked into a trap she should have seen coming when first invited to do this conference.

There are stories in the industry of waitresses handing superstars or producers complete scripts with the salad and seeing their baby become a hit film, of audacious manila envelope and/or CD attacks in elevators, subways, airplanes, bathrooms. Charlie, a mere agent, had an envelope dropped on her over a stall door at the Celebrity Pit during one of life's least convenient moments. To her knowledge only one of these myths had any truth to it, but the pent-up frustration of all those dreams, the hunger for fame and fortune and redemption is second only to the fantasy of gaining star status as an actor or actress. It's similar to the lure of publishing fiction and non-fiction, only many times worse because more people see films than actually read books. And now, with an Internet afloat in e-books, I-books, manuscripts, scripts and music—production companies, studios, stars, directors, and entertainment agencies were scuttling to maintain firewalls against unwanted submissions in order to carry on business at all, and this while battling to defend copyrights to published and produced properties.

Manila envelopes crowded against the molding of the hallway leading to Charlie's room door, where they piled in front of it. She had her card-key out before the five or six smug guys noticed her, so engrossed were they in perfecting the dominant sneer. Probably all under thirty, they were silent—the posturing one of expression, stance, neck and shoulder stretching, shifting, rolling eyes, sighs.

Charlie could feel it—the air charged with a dangerous mix of hope, fear, insecurity, and a nearly pathological need. It came in waves scary and suffocating. "Art" and the longing for others to recognize yours can be a terrible thing.

"Excuse me, gentlemen." Charlie edged between them, stabbed the plastic card in the slot.

"Miss Greene, could I speak to you a moment?"

"I have to fly back to New York on the red-eye so won't be able to see you—"

"This script won the Los Angeles Universal Script Contest last year, Charlie Greene. You can't tell me C & M wouldn't even want to look at it."

One stab induced the red light and Charlie knew panic as the eager "artists" closed in behind, jostling each other and bumping her against the door. She felt like a medic in a crowd of dying people pleading for help she couldn't give them.

The second stab got a green light and she shoved the door open as the jostling, panicking, desperate aspirants shoved each other and in the process shoved her inside, all slipping and tripping and falling over piled manila envelopes at their feet. The pitches, self-introductions, pleas, swearing became a crescendo.

There's always a crack under the door in hotel rooms so that your itemized bill can be slipped in on the last day of your stay and if it meets your approval you need only say so on the television checkout screen. But this time it left room to slip in still more manila envelopes and a few business sized envelopes that could hold short treatments and pitches.

"Please, Ms. Greene, it'll only take a minute of your time and—"

"Out," Charlie ordered in her tough-Hollywood-agent voice with what she hoped was a convincingly gutsy stare, more than a little aware of her vulnerability here and that when their frustration turned to anger her only salvation was that they were not at all united. Each was out for himself, dismissive of the talents of others.

"Bitch."

Charlie slammed, locked, and hooked the door closed after them, kicked off her shoes and headed for the phone to call the desk and request maintenance, security, somebody—get up here and remove the envelope deluge outside her door. "Some got in under the door too and when you get here I'll throw it out to you."

"We've been trying to reach you, Miss Greene. There have been complaints from other guests in that hall, but we were assured by the Film Institute staff that you would want to see it all when you returned tonight. We've got security and an extra-large rolling laundry cart on its way. What should we do with that stuff?"

"There was a long table, maybe two, outside the largest of the conference rooms across the hall from the bar this morning for selling books, magazines, sample scripts, mugs, T-shirts, hats, software, whatever to suckers. You could leave it there."

Charlie hadn't really seen Maggie much today, and now felt very uneasy. Her friend was no longer a reliably stable personality and no longer making her own decisions.

Charlie's gut burned and she fished out the Pepto-Bismol tablets from her purse, called her hotel voice-mail box so the red light would quit blinking at her from the phones—two in the room and one next to the commode in the bathroom. Her box was full. Full of pitches, invitations to breakfast, lunch, dinner, incredible sex, more pitches, pleas. Nothing from the Sea Spa or Maggie.

When Charlie and Mitch had arrived at the Sea Spa at the Marina del Sol Maggie Stutzman was in a serious hypno-meditation session. Against her better judgement, Charlie was persuaded to leave well enough alone and leave Maggie too. Caroline VanZant convinced Mitch Hilsten (who didn't really know Maggie firsthand) that she was getting what she needed and should not be yanked away from her treatment.

Charlie's cell was strangely empty of messages. But when the security officer arrived to pick up the offerings at and inside her door, he brought a gift basket of fruit and cheese—another of wine, chocolate, and a baguette. The fruit and cheese were compliments of the Institute responsible for this mess, the other from Keegan Monroe who got her into it. She'd earned them both just now. "Weren't you worried some of this stuff could have contained bombs or anthrax or something?"

"We've hosted the Institute's annual conference for the last five years and had a lot of this but nothing like now. Dr. Howard warned that there were some big names this year and it might get a little tricky. We had a bomb dog come in and sniff what was in the hall, didn't realize some had come in under the door, but it figures. Mr. Monroe's room got hit pretty hard too."

Charlie crawled out of her tuxedo and into a hot shower to wash away the tingly sweat of fear. The shower here was the size of a large tub and there was no tub. Those guys were not that dangerous—it was the situation, the emotion, the anger and helplessness that might have made them so. One testosterone spark could have ignited something she didn't want to consider. When she slid into her T-shirt and the Islandia's robe she heard a swish at the door and watched another manila envelope slide into the room. After kicking it back out she stuffed her wet towel into the crack, tore a hunk off the baguette, poured a glass of wine, and took them and a handful of grapes outside to the balcony. The chill felt good.

Okay, let's not blow all this out of proportion here.

Yeah, right.

You always get upset when things don't go as you plan. Which is most of the time. Take a few hundred breaths.

Charlie took three and drew in the decaying-fish smell on the breeze and the incomparable yeasty scent of a freshly broken baguette. The grapes were juicy and the wine even better. Where was Luella Ridgeway? She'd left a terse message on Charlie's cell that she had a lead on something and would get back to her tonight. And that Libby would too. About what she didn't say and Charlie's cell held no messages.

You can't control everything. You're a control freak. Settle down.

"Oh, shut up."

Somewhere down in the waters around the marina below, a sea lion answered her with an "ork." And the palm tree below her clapped its fronds. The bay splashed gently at the dock pilings, ruffled a line of captured boats. She could hear voices on other balconies, presumably talking to someone other than themselves. The balconies were triangles off each room and the building ribbed in such a way that you really couldn't see anybody from your balcony.

"That's what you get for being a star," Kenny told her the next morning at breakfast on his balcony. His room was just a few doors down the hall.

"You saw what happened when I came back?"

"Yeah, you kicked ass out there, man."

"Big guy like you didn't even bother to help me out?"

"Hell, you scared *me*. I may be big, but I'm not dumb." He dodged the half-peeled orange Charlie threw at him but caught the strawberry. "So how was dinner at the undisclosed, exclusive yacht club last night with that aging heartthrob?"

"Excellent, as a matter of fact. But how did you know?"

He held up the *San Diego Union-Tribune*. "Morning paper. But I scored the photo op this time, just like you promised."

He folded a section of the paper in half and handed it to her. A roar and a rattling of their dishes and then a jet appeared to soar out of a palm tree to make the moment even more momentous. The San Diego airport was in town and it was always a wonder as you flew between buildings to land that no major disasters, to Charlie's knowledge, had occurred.

They took off rather briskly as well and in the morning they appeared to top this particular palm every few minutes.

The headline read, *Hollywood as usual, ho-hum.* Two photos side by side, one of Moira staring adoringly up at Mitch, the other of Charlie staring the same way, way-up at Kenny. Damn, she'd been thinking about the fact she'd probably sold his book to Pitman's, was thinking triumph and ended up looking just as inane and silly as the Irish Jewish Bedouin princess. The caption under the pics read, *Speculation is that Moira Moriarty has come between Mitch Hilsten and long-time girlfriend, agent Charlie Greene, who does not appear to be inconsolable.*

The body of the article began with the fact that Mitch and Charlie were in San Diego for "supposedly" different reasons. She stopped there and put the paper down to pour herself more coffee and to find Kenny Cowper studying her.

"You didn't wake up to CNN, I take it."

"No, but to messages I should have gotten yesterday, after I thought to recharge my cellular. Why?"

He handed her the front page of the *Union-Tribune* and she nearly choked on hot coffee.

"They blew up the Celebrity Pit?"

"We could have made front page but for that, Charlie, you and me."

Most of the casualties were drunks, addicts, homeless who snuck into the enclosures around the closed-down colossus for shelter, privacy, and "street stuff." Congdon and Morse Representation, Inc. was only a few blocks away. That's why Luella raced back to the office.

The meteoric rise and fall of the Celebrity Pit, due to the enormous expense of building and maintaining such a place that close to the real estate tax reality of Wilshire and Rodeo Drive, had been the talk of the world. There had been attempts afoot for several months to resurrect, restore, reconstitute the place just because of its outrageous theme and audacity and because in its way it was a tribute to Hollywood. It was a hit from the get-go—irreverent, stupid, and campy.

It was fun. Reverent extremists consider unconcealed fun dangerous for the masses. Charlie loved it. "They bombed the Celebrity Pit."

"Hey, tough agent lady," Kenny reached for her hand over the small table holding the food and coffee, "innocent people died. And there was some major damage, but not much structural. Three bombs lobbed in from a pickup with a kludged backyard launcher—not dropped in the center from a plane or a nuclear missile from a ship at sea. Could have been worse."

Built much like a coliseum, and inside laid out in circular tiers around a stage and an extravagant bar, the Pit was arranged so that all diners had a view of the open pit in the building's center and whatever entertainment was provided below on the stage or staged shenanigans at the bar. They were given a table and level number upon entering from the street and took an elevator to the proper level. The wait staff all resembled entertainment celebrities and some "lookalikes," salted among the tables, would eventually go down to the stage and entertain. It was so much fun that real celebs enjoyed showing up on their own, often joining their imitators on the stage or staging bar fights at the "interactive" bar. Johnny Depp might be sitting at the next table. Or he might not.

The Pit had bouncers to keep the star-struck in hand and special hidden getaway exits for the famous. Too bad "Film Institutes" provided no such amenity.

Thirteen

"Two winners in consecutive years—men, early twenties, kidnap promoter of screenwriting contest when none of the advertised awards for winning—money, interviews with studio execs, and representation—materialize. They learn that they never do, but the great publicity of the contest draws so many submissions the promoter has grown rich on entry fees. They tie him to a chair, take turns reading aloud scripts stacked in unopened envelopes in his Tuff Shed, waking him with an electric shock when he falls asleep. Two weeks later they return him to his home, inert, incontinent, and incoherent. His family immediately dumps him in a nursing home—permanently. Kidnappers escape with hidden cash promoter tried to use to buy his freedom."

The young man—early twenties—stood for a moment soaking up the silence in the crowded room behind him. Charlie guessed there to be a hundred fifty to two hundred people in here. He faced the panel of three agents, Keegan, and Dr. Howard. Behind them a screen showed the audience what the panel of judges saw.

The tables outside this conference room were piled with a plethora of screenwriting contest opportunities. Charlie wondered what had happened to all the unopened envelopes security took from her hallway and room last night. Did they end up in a Tuff Shed? Magazines for budding screenwriters devoted whole pages to listing these contests. The pitch had come with the title, *Just Crime*.

Charlie was the first to break the silence. "So what did the kidnappers use the stolen money for?"

"To start up their own contest."

The other judges, even Keegan, were hard on this writer, Keegan admitting to having entered one of these contests, winning it, and never seeing any reward. But, he pontificated, it had been a good lesson. The other two agents and Dr. Howard were furious that anyone would suggest all such contests were out to swindle young hopefuls. Dr. Howard even offered, "What about the Sundance?"

"Which one?" The stalwart novice held his ground and his attitude.

As in most of the arts, entertainment, sports, modeling, publishing worlds more people make money on dreams than the "art" itself. It was no secret that the majority of voice trainers, writing, acting, locution, and dance instructors depended on "fees" from hopefuls who would never work in these dream fields. Charlie had always thought these classes added color to otherwise drab lives, until her daughter decided not to go to college next year.

But fees for contests that never paid the winners offered nothing and were well known in the industry's fringes. They just weren't dealt with, discussed. It was like special interests bribing congressmen and all the other injustices in this world that are too huge to get a handle on. You hope someone else will address the issue.

This young man's name was Brodie Caulfield. He was dangerous.

"As a pitch it needs work but I found the story idea intriguing and by the number of young faces gone suddenly pale out in the room behind you, I may not be alone," Charlie told him and the room.

Each judge offered a spoken comment and then wrote on a numbered card with the sacrifice's name on it. Charlie had cringed when Dr. Howard called this "giving notes."

Charlie wrote, *I'd like to see a treatment on this* and winked when she handed it to him.

Brodie was pretty much the bright spot of her afternoon, a long afternoon with a three-hour session. And only a twenty-minute break, during which Brodie slipped her an envelope and turned away to speak to nervous aspirants about the interesting mentality of the Hollywood fringe society. Charlie was earning her honorarium. Never again.

"They" bombed the Celebrity Pit, was her every other thought. How could all these people go on as if it hadn't happened?

And if she heard the words "segue," "back story," or "wrap" one more time she would throw up her late breakfast right there in front of the whole room. But she heard them and she didn't. Hollywood agents really are tough.

Her cellular had recharged overnight while she'd had a good night's sleep, and she'd returned calls from Libby, Luella, and Caroline VanZant, all of whom had been trying to contact her. Her room answering machine had refused to overdose on any more messages. Luella Ridgeway informed her there was no destruction at the office or the bank building in which C & M was housed. Some electricity and communications were out, but people still worked on laptops and by cellular. She could not leave now and come back to Maggie.

Charlie wondered if Mitch's new film would be jerked because distributors, theater companies, and customers might worry about a backlash from Muslim extremists.

"Nancy Drew meets J. Lo in outer space. And the universe will never be the same!"

Ohgod.

Hang in there. You can do this.

"Roman gladiator travels forward in time and runs amok in sorority house. He . . ."

Time to pop a Pepto.

"Hallucinating stripper . . ."

Okay, let's look at it this way. There seems to be no swelling of emotional backlash in this room filled with such desperate hope. Maybe dear Brodie defused it with his own little bomb. We feel safer than we did last night in the hallway, don't we?

Libby's message had been, as it often was, mind blowing.

"Mom, do not believe what you read. I am not pregnant. You are not going to be a grandma. Oh, that reminds me, Grandma wants you to call her. Mrs. Beesom OD'd on something but is fine and back from the emergency room. Jacob and I are taking care of her so I can't come to Maggie. Who the hell is Kenneth Cooper? You know how I hate to have my friends see your picture in the paper with some guy. You are my mother, don't forget. Oh, Kate came to clean up after Tuxedo and had a good talk with him. Gotta go, bye."

Kate Gonzales, bless her every breath, cleaned their little house, and had more sense than half of Long Beach and all of Congdon and Morse Representation, Inc. Jacob Forney was the only male other than Tuxedo who occupied the four small homes connected by an inner courtyard and surrounding high stucco walls, gated from street in front and alley behind.

Caroline VanZant reported in, that Maggie Stutzman had finished another day with no medications, alcohol, fat, sugar, or tears. She had, however, removed the lid from the toilet tank and used it to smash the screen of the television inside the wardrobe. It would, of course, be charged to her account.

Charlie wondered if it was possible to overdose on Pepto Bismol. But hey, at least she wasn't a grandmother—where the hell did that come from? Libby didn't read newspapers or watch news on TV so how did she know about Kenny Cowper? Probably from Jacob Forney or Doug Esterhazie or his father, Ed, of Esterhazie Concrete fame, who was about to marry his third on Sunday. Charlie popped another little pink Pepto and wondered if she'd live to see Sunday.

"Hi, Jerry Parks with the *Union-Tribune*. We met at the Sea Spa at the Marina del Sol the other day? Please don't run away this time. I'm investigating the murder there and understand—you sure don't look old enough to be a grandmother." He'd caught her slipping out of the ladies' room in the lobby which was in a separate building from her room and the conference rooms.

"What is all this grandmother stuff?"

Kenny was just coming out of the gents next door. "Charlie, there's a private bar, not far if you want to sneak away. Monroe's there already. Said I'd bring you."

"We'll have to kidnap him. He's press."

"Give me your cell?" Kenny asked Jerry Parks pleasantly. "Don't want to miss the action, do you? Where's your photographer?"

"Who are you? What's my cell and photographer got to do with—"

"Guess he doesn't want to go with us, Charlie. I'm her bodyguard. Let's step into the men's and I'll block you into a stall so she can make a getaway. Real reporters don't pass up chances to get on the inside of a story."

Jerry Parks went for his cell and Kenny grabbed it out of his hand before he could punch 911 or his photographer's number and handed it to Charlie. "You wanna hide this weapon somewhere in the ladies?"

"But that's against the law—you can't—"

By the time Charlie returned to the lobby after dropping the cellular weapon in the sanitary napkin bin's disposal slot, Jerry Parks had agreed that he'd rather go to the private party. But he squirmed when Kenny shoved him into a bright red car at the lobby door and they sped off to the Bahia close by.

"Photographer was in the parking lot," Kenny explained.

Brodie Caulfield, driving, winked at her in the rear view mirror. "Lots of budding screenwriters were too. Word's out you drive a metallic blue Dodge Ram, Ms. Greene, and there's only one of those in the parking lot."

"And it hasn't moved since you got here," the reporter from the local paper said. "But you have."

Kenny added, "Yeah, for somebody who doesn't want to get hassled, you sure know how to stand out."

The patio bar at the Bahia was deserted but for their little grouping. Keegan had needed a break from the aspirants too. "I enjoy adulation, but there is something else in the conference air back there. It's a little scary."

"Desperation." Charlie ordered a margarita with salt and dug into the nachos somebody had ordered placed in the center of each of the two tables, shoved together.

Chorizo, pintos, corn kernels, melted cheese, chopped green chiles, black olives, raw tomatoes, green onion, leaf lettuce sliced into strips on corn chips with a lime, and pineapple and roasted-chile salsa. A welcome and delicious dinner, sadists would consider an appetizer. Charlie would need it. "How do I get my truck back? I have to go to Maggie at the Sea Spa. I want to try to kidnap her and bring her back to my room at the Islandia."

Fourteen

"So who all is escaping, Jason North and the other shark? Sarah?"

"She's already here." And Dr. Grant Howard was already looped. "In the ladies. The rest of the faculty, Jason and Morrie, are at the Islandia cocktail party where they should be and mingling with the attendees as we all should be. I was abducted by Mr. Monroe and Sarah. Why do you not wish to socialize with the students you came to teach? Who are paying good money for it too." His voice deep and resonant, his diction dramatic, his thinning hair a comb-over dyed an innovative shade of dirty rust, his florid complexion deepening to rose when he felt thwarted.

"Not everybody feeds on desperation like you do, Doctor," Brodie said. "You an MD, PhD, Masters in English lit or psychology? What? Veterinary medicine?"

"You know, I always wondered that too, Grant." Sarah Newman returned to her chair and martini-up. It was that kind of day.

Grant Howard ignored the change of subject. "Have you no pity? Those desperate aspiring young talents are the future of Hollywood. We all have a responsibility here to encourage their endeavors in a very voracious and difficult field. I, for one, am proud of the Institute and all it stands for."

"I kind of liked the hallucinating stripper, myself," Kenny said, ignoring the subject too. "But then I'm not faculty."

"Who are you exactly?" Jerry, the ferret, asked Kenny. "You seem to hang out with the big shots around here."

"He's an investigative reporter like you," Charlie said and

79

ordered another margarita, "and my client, Kenneth Cooper."

"*The Last of the Manly Hardy Boys*? *Dead Time in Disneyland*? And you wrote for the *Miami Herald*." Jerry Parks had a boyish look about him, sideburns and mustache notwithstanding. "I thought you were a much older guy."

"And you thought I was too young to be a grandma. Where did that come from?"

Keegan Monroe pulled a folded newspaper clipping from his shirt pocket and handed it to her. "Was hoping, as busy as you are, you might possibly miss this." He was an odd man. Prison seemed to have given him more confidence than success had. "*Star Universe*."

The Star Universe, a tabloid actually not published in Florida, tended to concoct stories about Hollywood stars and their peccadillos and families. Rarely did they bother with mere agents. The picture was of Libby Greene dancing with (to Charlie) a total stranger at some outdoor venue and under lights. He had "predator" written all over him. *Libby Greene, daughter of Mitch Hilsten's agent-girlfriend, seen partying at producer Clint Melneck's estate with his youngest son, Gary, is rumored to be pregnant with Melneck's first grandchild*. It was this sort of unfortunate wording that had gotten Charlie in trouble before—she was an agent but not Mitch's. Congdon and Morse would be flooded with filmscripts for Mitch and they would get tossed unopened. Libby Greene, however, was her daughter.

Charlie took her margarita and cell out to the rescued sea lion garden next to the patio bar but concealed by palms and spiky things. Paths circled a series of connecting pools where the sea lions could glide over huge rocks and slumber still in the deepest part of the pool but not hide from the hotel guests wanting to stroll by and watch their every move. Today, Charlie could really identify with the sea lions.

She stopped to lean on the stone wall of an arched footbridge between pools, the fronds of some exotic swordlike thing clacking in the breeze, when Libby and not her cell's voice mail answered Charlie's sweaty panic attack. She nearly choked on a slug of salty margarita and relief.

When she returned to the table she was much settled down, even had some more nachos.

Kenny's grin was both satyrical and satirical though it showed little of his teeth and less mirth. "You should be listening to this, Charlie. Dr. Howard knows a few things about the Sea Spa at the Marina del Sol."

Jerry Parks, busy with PDA and stylus, apparently happy to have been abducted now, was so intent on the tiny screen, he had to keep blinking his eyes back into focus.

"Poor Judith. She deserved better." He teared up and shook his head. "She and Caroline VanZant were thrick as thieves, before the divorce. I, pershonally, do not condone divorce."

"You, personally, have a wife who'll put up with anything, even you." Sarah Newman was losing a few inhibitions herself. "My sister never did have enough starch."

"No amount of starch could straighten the spine of a female that rotund." Even with the slurs, his trained voice and perfect modulation would have made that last pronouncement a momentous statement. But if written, the period would have been drowned in an even deeper, yet still modulated belch.

"Married to you, she'd have to find something to enjoy." Sarah had an old-fashioned pageboy without the bangs and a good start on the wrinkles.

"Tell Charlie about the relationship between the VanZants and Judith Judd," Kenny said in a calming voice and signaled to the hovering waiter for another round.

Charlie waved a hand over the salt-encrusted rim of her goblet-glass and shook her head to be left out of this largess, and noticed the admiration in Jerry Parks' eyes as he stilled the stylus to consider Kenneth Cooper. She wanted to tell him that Kenny Cowper had not become rich because of his books. He was a trust funder. They were everywhere in the arts that paid only the top one or two percent and then often grossly. But trust funders had the money to appear, to a struggling novice, extremely successful in whatever field they chose. Talented trust funders, fortunately, could even afford to be book editors and live in Manhattan. Charlie knew more than a few who made grotesque jewelry instead and lived a lavish lifestyle that announced their jewelry was art, not grotesque. You can't argue with insured incomes.

"Caroline and Dr. Judy were thick as thieves before which divorce? They both were," Charlie said. "Divorced."

"Warren VanZant divorced Judith to marry Carolyn Hammett. Didn't you know that?"

How would I know that? I assume Detective Solomon knows that. "Dashiell Hammett. Wow. Well that opens a whole new docket. What happened to Mr. Hammett senior?"

"I've got to talk to my editor." Jerry Parks tried to stick his stylus behind his ear but it snapped back to his handheld on its bungie cord.

"You've got to read my treatment," Brodie Caulfield told Charlie.

"I've got to get Maggie out of that place." Charlie dipped her last nacho in the pineapple-chile salsa.

"I'll take Elmer Fudd here back to his conference," Sarah said and winked at Charlie. "Don't forget Uranus for *The Rites of Winter*, will you?"

Jerry Parks called in to his editor on Charlie's cell while en route to the Spa with Charlie and Kenny in Kenny's rental. Brodie and Keegan planned to go out to dinner somewhere in Charlie's pickup, after Sarah took them as well as her brother-in-law back to the Hyatt.

Libby and her cell had been at Mrs. Beesom's and Jacob Forney too, when Charlie called from the sea lion garden. They figured that Betty Beesom took all her pills and forgot and took them again. She had this plastic case with pills doled out for morning, noon, dinner time, and bedtime in little pockets. But it got tipped over or something and they all spilled out. She may have mixed them wrong. Anyway, they pumped her stomach in the emergency room and sent her home, telling Libby and Jacob that now her stomach was pumped she wasn't sick so she wouldn't be admitted to the hospital.

"I said if she's not sick how come she's taking all those pills and they said to keep from getting sick. All she can have is Jell-O and chicken broth. She's really pissed. And I wasn't even at that party with Gary Melneck. First time I even met him. He's a jerk. I went with Lori and some other cheerleaders. Anyway, you gotta get back here, Mom. Jacob leaves for his convention tomorrow. I've got more parties coming up."

"Sorry honey, Maggie's in real trouble too. I can't leave her now."

Charlie informed her daughter that anyone responsible enough to get a job and an apartment after graduation from mere high school could be depended upon to forgo partying and care for an elderly neighbor. That neighbor had come through for Libby on numerous occasions.

It was the second time in twenty-four hours someone had called Charlie a bitch.

"So, what story are you really covering? The conference, the Institute, or the murder at the Sea Spa at the Marina del Sol?" Charlie asked the reporter when he'd informed his editor of Warren VanZant's relationship to both Dr. Judy and Caroline, that he was safe but separated from Ted, his photographer, and on his way back to the scene of the murder.

"You, actually," Jerry Parks said. "And now I can honestly report and probably sue for being abducted and having my property stolen by a subject I was investigating." He produced a theatrical sneer. "Little guys always get the wrong end of the stick, right? Makes great press."

"You weren't wandering the halls of the Spa because of the murder there when I first saw you?" Charlie asked.

"Well, yeah, but I had already registered for the conference on my own and seen your photo in the brochure, so when I spied you at the murder scene I got assigned you too."

"You want to write screenplays?" Kenny turned from traffic to the backseat long enough to make Charlie nervous.

"Doesn't everyone?"

"In your investigations did you come across how Dr. Howard knew Dr. Judy? He seemed pretty upset by her death," Charlie said.

"Let's just say they go way back."

"Wonder who is the most likely person at the Spa that night who would want to murder Dr. Judith Judd. Or did someone from outside come in and do it and leave before the alarm was sounded?" Charlie pondered aloud.

Between the three of them, they came up with a list for each scenario and even a third. The guests and staff of the Spa, Judd's family and the staff of her production company who knew she would be there, and the owners of the Spa itself. Or a complete stranger looking for someone to kill or looking for somebody else and killed her by mistake.

"In murder mysteries," Charlie said, "the list has to be select and identifiable, but in real life the 'random' is as real as it is in the universe. That's why more murders go unsolved than not and why mysteries are so popular."

"God, you're depressing," Kenny Cowper said. "Okay, Parks, give your list and pick three candidates and I will too. Charlie will probably choose a wandering unidentifiable vagrant or something."

"Not so," Charlie said. "I pick Dashiell Hammett, Ruth Ann Singer—the dead doctor's assistant, or Warren VanZant. Or the pharmaceutical industry."

"Why the pharmaceutical industry?" Jerry Parks leaned forward to stick his face between the seats. "That's very interesting."

"Because I'm really, really pissed at them right now. How did Dr. Howard know about the VanZants and Dr. Judy?"

"Given that we don't know all the clients at the Spa that night or members of the film crew, I'd pick Maggie Stutzman as first choice because she found the body, the doctor's manager Ruth Ann Singer next because she knows everything about Judd's business, and Warren VanZant because he's an ex. And the movie industry because I can't sell them a screenplay," Jerry from the *San Diego Union-Tribune* said.

"So, you answer me a question for a change, discouraging agent-person. Did Margaret Stutzman mention seeing anybody else out at the Jacuzzi pools when Judd died? If she didn't do it, she might have seen whoever did."

"I'm sure she would have said. She's not that far gone." Charlie felt insulted, for Maggie's sake.

"I don't know most of the people there but I'd pick Dashiell Hammett any day, because he's a jerk with a loose screw, as my first candidate for murderer, Warren VanZant second because he's an ex, and that weird guy in the swimming pool with the aging musculature and dramatic presentation because he could be jealous that Dr. Judy gets on TV ad nauseam and he doesn't," Kenny said. "And Mitch Hilsten because I'm jealous of him."

"Raoul." Charlie had forgotten about him.

"He's another good candidate," Jerry said.

"How do you know that?" Charlie asked him.

"Research."

When they crested the ridge above the staggered and tight development to the open sea and sky, they found San Diego County police cars awaiting them. There had been another murder at the Sea Spa at the Marina del Sol.

Fifteen

Maggie Stutzman sat wrapped in spa towels looking rather exotic with the towel as a turban leaving only a dark curl dangling down her forehead, dark blue eyes sparking again instead of dulled. Which was not necessarily a good sign, but somehow made her beautiful. She sat with her legs crossed on the edge of the oversized swimming pool, one foot in the water.

Charlie tried to blink away tears and it only seemed to make her nose run. Indelicate for sure. Kenny handed her a cloth handkerchief yet. People still used non-disposable nose wipes?

As before, Charlie arrived too late to see the dead body in situ. Raoul Segundo had drowned in his pool. And while he was treating Maggie's addictive, suicidal, destructive, and capricious temperament with soothing water relaxation and hypnosis therapy too. Maybe he put himself to sleep.

Problem was, this time the Spa was filled with day customers, some of whom had wandered by the windows that exposed the pool from various sides and many were now being questioned by members of the homicide department of the San Diego County Sheriff's Office, Detective Solomon no doubt among them. And here of course sat a defiant Maggie Stutzman in the thick of another murder.

She used to be the most reasonable person Charlie had ever known. And now she defied reason like an out-of-control teenager. At the pool's edge Sue, of the ponytail and aging bounce, rose stiffly off her knees, one of which creaked.

"Am I glad to see you, Miss Greene. Could you take her

86

up to your room while I help see to the day spa clients? She's not to leave this building, you understand. I'll get back to you in half an hour, but it's situation-frantic right now. We've replaced the television up there but left the lid off the stool tank. She can plead insanity with no trouble." Sue cocked her head, shrugged on that side, and lifted her eyebrows into her bangs, rather eloquently pronouncing Maggie's condition unstable-extreme.

To Charlie, her friend seemed more in control than Sue Rippon. On first arriving Charlie and both her companions were kept at the gate until their identities could be checked inside, at which time Charlie was escorted directly to the pool area and Kenny and Jerry detained in the lobby. The enormous parking lot had been nearly full. The day spa crowd must be what kept so expensive a business venture afloat.

"Do you want Dashiell to help get her upstairs?"

"No way, absolutely."

Up in the room, there was indeed no lid on the toilet tank and the television in place in the wardrobe was smaller than the last. Charlie stood looking at the latter and then turned to Maggie. "Can you still signal for the TV to go on and off with the remote when the door's closed?"

"You have to aim it right for the slot there. Doesn't work as well with this smaller set. So I just turn it on and then close the door." Maggie shed her towels and spa tank suit and headed for the shower.

Charlie followed. "So why exactly *did* you bust the other TV?"

"Don't you mean why exactly *did* I kill Raoul?" Steam clouded the shower door and roiled up over it as the dark blue eyes did too. "Your priorities are weird, Greene. Now go away until I'm clean. Even crazy murderers need privacy."

Charlie did as she was told and took out the little black book with handy phone numbers she kept in a special pocket of her purse—handy but not used often enough to crowd the automatic dial. She'd had them all on her PDA and lost them for some reason only the wizards at Microsoft knew. She'd needed a defense lawyer herself a year ago and thought she'd ask Ernest Seligman for a reference in San Diego County for Maggie. Charlie hoped it wouldn't come to that and knew Maggie, as a lawyer, had contacts of her own but it wouldn't hurt to be ready for the worst. Boy, had she learned the truth of that in the last few years. Besides, Charlie had to do something about this problem.

She explained the situation to Ernest Seligman's assistant's voice mail and played with the remote and armoire door until she heard the shower subside and the hair dryer rev.

Maggie stepped out of the bathroom with that nervous giggle she'd developed, pulling a Spa T-shirt on over her bra. Waves washed at a watermelon pink sun with jagged yellow rays shooting out all around it. "Sea Spa at the Marina del Sol" in black squiggly letters intertwined rays and waves. Since she'd gained weight Maggie maxed out her cup size and the picture on her front made mountains on the sun and strange valleys in the waves. "I peed in Raoul's pool. I was just floating around while he did his 'Marrrgarrreett' thing, and trying to keep my butt up and all of a sudden he hit me in the head and tried to pull me under. I kicked him away and drowned him. Why are you looking at me like that?"

"Maggie, did he make any sound before he hit you in the head? I mean, was there something different in his tone, did he make a strange noise at all between the 'Margarrreett' thing and the blow? Did he just stop in mid-soothing word or sentence, drop your butt, and strike you, or—"

"I think he flailed around a little bit behind me while I swam for the edge of the pool after he hit me and before he grabbed my ankle—but I can't remember. I wasn't hypnotized, but I was drowsy. And the shock of coming out of it all—I don't know, Charlie." Maggie took a pair of white capris off a hanger. "I just know that even a take-charge female like you can't make everything right just because you want it to be."

"Well, I'm sure the autopsy will show it was an accident. Most sudden deaths are explainable—often for medical reasons or something—like a heart attack or stroke, aneurism."

"Some trouble just doesn't go away, Charlie." Another phony giggle and sudden tears.

A voice in the wardrobe said, "Are you feeling frazzled and out of control? Don't know where to turn? You may suffer from Apprehensive Ersatz Stress Syndrome. Studies show that the drug Pseudo Phren Pen may relieve symptoms and complications of this mind-threatening disease. If you think you suffer from AESS, tell your doctor about Pseudo Phren Pen! Side effects may include reduced libido, swelling, dry mouth, dizzyness, thinning hair, headache, facial rash and tics and tongue polyps."

"That's why." Maggie was one leg into the capris and tripping herself up trying to point to the closed door of the wardrobe and hop on one foot.

"What's why what?"

"The tongue polyps were just too much, so I busted the TV with the toilet tank lid. And you know, Charlie, it made me feel really good, so really good, I—Charlie, you okay? You laughing or crying?"

"Both. Get me a Kleenex?" Charlie had backed into the bed to sit on it while she convulsed and slid off instead, landing on the footstool. "You should have seen your face morph from inflamed to euphoric in a couple of big blinks, oh help." She was trying to hold her ribs—would they never heal?—and wipe her nose at the same time when a strange shuffling sounded at the door to the hallway and then a low whisper, "Charlie? You in there?"

Maggie, still looking like a madwoman with her hair all roughed up and sprayed to give it lift but not yet combed back down, stepped into huaraches and opened the door.

Kenny Cowper and Jerry Parks crept furtively inside, Kenny trying to lock the door behind them.

"Doors don't lock where murderous addicts have to be monitored at all times," Maggie told them and returned to the bathroom to bring order to her hair and apply makeup. When she emerged with rosy cheeks, nature's real blush applied by embarrassment or maybe a hot flash, Kenny was explaining how crazy it was downstairs.

"There're women running around with mud packs dried so tight they can't get their mouths open enough to answer questions, others demanding their money back because they're getting the sheriff's department instead of the treatments they prepaid for. And Jerry finally coughed up some of his research on good old Dashiell. He's got quite a history of drug and alcohol abuse, not to mention peeping Tomism."

And a voice in the armoire said, ". . . late-breaking news. There's been what appears to be another murder at the popular Sea Spa at the Marina del Sol. More on the evening news."

Another voice in the armoire said, "Trouble sleeping at night? Try Slumber X-X-X. It's worth staying up for." And then a giggle and heavy breathing.

Charlie had the weirdest thought—everybody in the room was staring at the closed door of the wardrobe. It was sort of haunting. If the ever-present TV screen had been visible, would any of them have taken notice of it?

Detective Solomon arched an eyebrow he didn't have—more like made a weird-shaped wrinkle where it should have been. Charlie looked again at his hair and wondered if he wore a rug. "So you kicked out because Mr. Segundo grabbed your ankle and you feared drowning. I know we've been over this, Ms. Stutzman, but I want to be sure I have it correct and thought you might be more comfortable answering further questions with Ms. Greene present."

"I would think there should be a lawyer present," Charlie said.

"I am merely questioning a witness about a death. Not accusing Ms. Stutzman of participating in its execution."

"I am a lawyer," Maggie said, "and that last is a very poor wording."

"Not that kind of lawyer," Charlie reminded her. "And not in the best decision-making shape at the moment. But right about the wording."

The phone on the desk bleeped and Caroline said, "I'm sorry, but there's no one on the lobby desk now, because of all the—well you know. Sea Spa at the Marina del Sol . . . oh, yes. Oh, I think we do. Just a moment." Solomon sat at the business side of the office desk and she pulled a large open appointment book away from him and toward her. He rolled his eyes and handed her a pen. Warren VanZant reached for a brochure and set it in front of her.

"For the day, yes. We ask clients to arrive by nine a.m. You know the way? And what type of treatments were you considering? Oh, all right." And Caroline began checking off boxes on the brochure. "Oh yes, that will be a full day. Any more would be two. And your name, home address, and phone number, please . . . splendid. We will welcome you tomorrow, Mr. Zeltow . . . I'm sure you will."

"That's the fourth one in an hour," Warren said. "Think they'll cancel when they hear of another death here?"

"Knowing Sou Cal, they already have and that's the draw," said his second wife and wrote Mr. Zeltow's name on the brochure. He took it and looked through schedule sheets on a clipboard. "We're filling up here. If everybody shows. We may be in trouble, especially with Raoul off the roster."

"Now, if we can get back to Ms.-Stutzman-on-the-roster and the question of where the two of you and little Dashiell were at the moment of uproar outside the pool gym this morning." But he was to be interrupted yet again, this time the bleating of Charlie's cell. "Oh Jesus, thought those things weren't allowed in here."

"We strongly discourage their use by overnight guests who are treated to a more deep and restful regimen than the day spa guests. But it's not always easy with such important people," Caroline assured him, her tone forbearing.

Charlie stepped out into the hall to answer. It was Ernest Seligman himself and not his snotty assistant. "Why can't you girls stay out of trouble?" he asked fondly. "And Charlie, you know I'm retired."

"I thought maybe you could suggest someone down here.

She's talking to the sheriff's detectives now, but I think her lawyer should be."

"Has she been accused in the deaths?"

"Ernie, Maggie found the first body and was present at the demise of the second. And to my knowledge there are currently no other leads."

"Jesus, get her out of there. Who's in charge?"

"Detective Solomon."

"He's a good man."

"That's good then."

"Not for Maggie, it isn't. Charlie, I want you to do two things. If they haven't charged her they can't keep her. Either way, she's going to need a lawyer and she's not to say another word until she does. Keep her away from cops and reporters until she's formally charged. Expect a call from either Wayne Hobbitt or Nancy Trujillo. I ought to be able to get a hold of one of them. I'll give them your cell number."

"What's the other thing?"

"Put Gordy Solomon on the line. Now."

"I hate lawyers," Gordy Solomon said when he handed Charlie's cell back to her. "My brother-in-law's a lawyer and I don't like him much."

Sixteen

The problem of course was Maggie Stutzman and Jerry Parks. Ernest Seligman warned Maggie be kept away from the press until she had a legal spokesman. They'd left Kenny Cowper and the reporter from the *San Diego Union-Tribune* hiding behind ruffles under Queen Victoria's tall bed when the knocking on the door called them down to the office for questioning. The guys were still there when Charlie and the chief suspect returned.

Charlie took Kenny aside in the only place possible and closed the bathroom door to explain the situation in whispers. "She shouldn't be around Parks. She'll say things we'll all regret. I've got some legal help coming."

"I could take him to the Islandia and then come back for you and Maggie. Where'd you put his cell phone—maybe I could sneak into the ladies and redeem myself by returning it to him. He's local press, could make things uncomfortable."

"Great idea, but I don't think so. I could maybe buy him a new cell? Well, you said to dispose of it. Seemed like a good idea."

He just stood blinking and squinting down at her, when she told him the destination of Jerry Parks' communication with his life. "You know, women are just really . . . unusual, huh? I mean you . . . uh, you really work at it."

But somehow Charlie's author got Jerry Parks out of the room, and she assumed the Sea Spa, leaving Charlie to wonder what she would do with Maggie until he returned for them and how to get her friend to leave willingly.

93

"What are you doing, Greene?" Maggie looked up from rubbing her hands and staring at the closed doors of the wardrobe, where the voices ceased only for music or sound effects.

"I'm packing your things. We have to leave here when Kenny gets back."

"But I'm paid up for three more days of treatment." Her face flushed as Charlie watched.

"It's not safe, Maggie. People are dying here." Would Charlie be able to handle her friend at the Islandia?

"People are dying everywhere. Get your hands off my stuff. You don't want me to get better, do you?"

"Yes, I do. Maybe we can get your three days back after things quiet down and someone else is found responsible for what happened to Raoul and Dr. Judy. It's almost like you're being set up here."

"Maybe I'm not remembering things right. Did you ever stop to think I might be responsible for all this? You don't really know me, you know."

"You've been my best friend for what, five years—what do you mean I don't know you?"

"What's my favorite color?"

"Blue."

"Is marketing prescription drugs first to the patient instead of the physician creating a sick society?"

"Will you turn that thing off?"

"Why blue?"

"Do mental health care specialists have a big stake in being indispensable, permanently? And why major drug companies don't want you to take aspirin to shrink inflammation."

"Because your car's blue and your eyes are blue?"

"All this and more tonight on *A Hundred and Twenty Minutes.*"

"Maggie, that sack of pills we brought in here when we came. What happened to it?"

"Haven't seen it. And my favorite color is red."

Thermacare heat wrap for lower back pain. An athlete's

94

foot treatment. Ensure—a drink for nutrition. A diabetic thing you suck on to test your blood sugar, Advil Liquid Gels for arthritis, Fibercon for blissful shitting and Beltone hearing aids touted by aging ex-movie actors. And finally the evening news. Jeez, no wonder Charlie felt buzzy. Those nachos hadn't held out as long as she expected. She put down Maggie's panties and sat beside her on the bed, little pops going off in her ears, tingles all over, decided weakness of the knees. And here she was in a place with no food and without a car. That cold sweaty feeling.

And the pain of a weather change in her neck where dwelt a titanium plate placed there by surgeons after a nasty auto accident on the 405 commute to work. Charlie was reminded of her own frailties and needs and terrors. Who was she to judge Margaret Mildred Stutzman, who had been steadfastly there for Charlie when she was losing it? Charlie had to be sure not to let her blood sugar get too low, or blood pressure too high.

The weatherman in the wardrobe began to describe an interesting weather front as Charlie's cell decided to tinkle in her purse. She stood up too fast and nearly lost what was left of the nachos looking for that purse. Maybe it was the lawyer for Maggie.

"Charlie?" It was Luella Ridgeway. "Watch your tush, girl. This is a lot bigger than we thought."

"The Celebrity Pit?"

"The Sea Spa at the Marina del Sol. Where are you right now? And Maggie?"

"You just said it. But we're expecting a ride out of here any minute. Heading for the Islandia. Where are you?"

"In my car on the way. I've booked a room at the Islandia, too. And Charlie, get Maggie out of there."

"Luella says we have to get out of here." Charlie turned to Maggie who was stuffing her underwear back into a drawer. She paused to stare over Charlie's shoulder.

"Did Ms. Ridgeway say why?" Caroline VanZant asked from the doorway to the hall. She hadn't even knocked.

"I think it's pretty obvious. There's a killer loose in this place and it's not Maggie. And Caroline, where're all the drugs you took from this room?"

"This was all I could find." She flopped down in a brocaded, fringy chair and held up a small plastic bottle. "It's Verapamil, a calcium blocker to regulate the heartbeat if it gets wacky. Probably the most benign drug in that bag we emptied on the bed there the other night. Somehow, I misplaced the rest. This has been a trying week. And we don't know for sure that these aren't accidental deaths. At least not yet. And if they are murder—your friend *was* there and she *is* unstable—"

"Yeah Greene, you sure you want to be alone with me at the Islandia?" Maggie made a ghoul face, difficult to describe but convincing. "Charlie, what are you doing?"

Charlie was hanging onto a bedpost. "You got anything to eat around here besides dirt? I'm getting giddy."

"Yes, of course." The Spa manager pulled a cellular out of her pocket and punched the pad. "Sue? Is there anything left of those fruit platters? Could you bring one up to the Victorian room? Thanks. Charlie, did you know a good colonic rinsing would give your food a better chance to feed you without having to go through all that sludge keeping the nutrients out of your blood stream?"

When Rippon brought in the platter there were, thank God, crackers and cheese with the strawberries and kiwi and melon squares set out for day spa guests who weren't on the gut-reaming program. Charlie would have loved a cup of coffee but didn't even hope. "Thanks, I didn't gauge my intake."

"Diabetes?" Sue leaned against the door jamb, considering Charlie.

"Appetite," Maggie said. "Only person I know who can forget to eat."

"My appetite is huge. It's my capacity that's trouble."

"Well, I'd like to say I don't envy you, but . . ." Caroline VanZant studied Charlie too and like Sue, in a strange sort of creepy way. As if they were zeroing in on the same thought at the same time without having to discuss it.

Oh come on, they're probably just planning a new weight loss treatment—not your demise, Charlie's inner voice cautioned rationality over paranoia. Charlie's inner voice was dead wrong more often than not. She didn't really trust anybody, especially herself.

Ruth Ann Singer, the snappy number, showed up to stand in the doorway and expose the glitzy stud in her navel above her low-rider shorts and below a halter top that barely covered her bosom, all in white including her earrings which didn't match her tummy stud. The voices in the armoire switched from Metamucil to the Celebrity Pit.

"Someone blew up the Celebrity Pit?" Maggie still stood over the open drawer, holding a pair of *her* drawers.

"You've been listening to the wardrobe all this time and didn't hear that?" Charlie said.

"Why doesn't she open the doors so she can see it?" Ruth Ann had to ask. "It's a TV, not a radio. It actually has moving pictures, duh."

"Don't you talk about Maggie like that." Charlie bristled, literally, her skin and hair follicles tweaking. "She's a practicing attorney and has even been a judge."

Three pairs of eyes now moved from Charlie to Maggie.

"Smarter they are . . ." Caroline said.

"Yeah," Sue answered.

This was getting creepier than a hotel full of testosterone-enhanced aspiring screenwriters.

"Deaths from the explosion at the once famous Celebrity Pit are confirmed at thirteen, with seven in critical condition and eleven with moderate to minor injuries," the armoire said. "Damage is less than at first reported and there are rumors of plans under consideration to re-create the popular venue, rebuild it as a museum venerating Hollywood and cinematography past and present, or to tear it down and replace it with affordable housing, heh heh—that last, of course, being a joke."

Charlie noticed again how much attention the voice in the wardrobe commanded when you couldn't see the picture. Because you were imagining what the picture would be or had to concentrate on that? It went totally against the common knowledge that one picture was worth a thousand words. Maybe that was just written words.

Charlie's cell beckoned. It sounded tinny.

"That's why we outlaw those things," Caroline said, unaware she was waving her own cell phone in the accompanying gesture.

It was the local lawyer, Nancy Trujillo. She sounded tinny too and Charlie's tweaking follicles were building to a painful rhapsody.

Funny, she'd never heard Maggie scream before. But she recognized who was doing it without having to think even. Way weird.

"I don't know," Charlie told Nancy Trujillo. And then wondered what the question was she'd answered that to. But it was Maggie she must protect.

Seventeen

"I'm not sure she should be released to Miss Greene's care. She's obviously under the influence of something—Miss Greene, I mean."

"Ask them who Raoul was." Charlie had meant to ask that herself but if she had, she'd forgotten the answer.

"Charlie?" Luella Ridgeway said. "This is a lot bigger than we thought."

"Tell me about it."

"Tell you about what?" Kenny asked. "Charlie, open your eyes."

"How did you get back so fast? Did you unload Jerry? Where's Luella? Why is Maggie screaming?" Charlie opened her eyes. "Oh."

Maggie stood there not screaming. Kenny held Charlie upright. And the female deputy of the clipboard stared at her hard. Caroline VanZant and Sue Rippon finished filling up a room already choked with furniture and fringe.

"Asking serial, unrelated questions without waiting for an answer is a sign of confusion," Sue Rippon of the aging ponytail said.

"Charlie always does that," Kenny and Maggie explained in near-sync, Kenny adding, "Have you had anything to eat or drink since happy hour at the Bahia?"

"Just fruit and cheese and crackers here from a platter. But I do feel sort of a buzz on." Charlie, embarrassed, pulled away from her client to stand on her own. "And I seem to have lost track of some time here. Did I pass out?"

"Are you on medication?" The deputy moved in to search Charlie's eyeballs.

"Just Pepto Bismol. And then only when I have to listen to the Rocky Horror Pitches Show or my daughter."

"Fruit platters. Like the ones that litter the lobby and halls downstairs in the late afternoons?"

"I didn't even know they had edibles here. In the dining room they serve dirt. On linen tablecloths."

"The fruit and cheese are compliments of the Sea Spa and offered to day clients to enhance their sense of euphoria after the pleasures of grooming, toning, relaxing, massage, being spoiled," Caroline VanZant explained, sounding like a brochure.

The deputy looked from Caroline to the chandelier dripping with beads, took a deep breath, and ordered them all to stay put while she stepped into the hall, closing the door behind her with one hand while punching the key pad on her cellular with the thumb of the other.

The marina slept under the balcony of Charlie's room at the Hyatt Islandia. The moon lit some things, shadowed others. Charlie felt like she'd been awake forty days and forty nights. She and Luella Ridgeway sipped hot coffee ordered up from room service, dined on strawberries and another fresh baguette from yet another gift basket left in the room. Maggie had a chocolate. And then another.

Kenny sat just inside at a dining table large enough for four, sipping wine and reading the contents of some of the manila envelopes that had been slipped under the door, groaning, chortling, sighing—but quietly. He and Luella apparently decided they had two nut cases on their hands now and were afraid to leave either alone.

A jet erupted from the palm tree and then relative quiet returned. Something disturbed some birds in the foliage below and they set up a chatter. Both Charlie and Maggie were taking deep breaths for some reason. They'd been escorted to a small clinic just off the coastal highway to leave blood and urine samples and then Kenny was allowed to drive them here. Luella had been waiting in the lobby.

Maggie's new lawyer promised to be here first thing in the morning. And the wardrobe in the room behind them remained blessedly silent.

"The unofficial word on Wilshire," Luella explained, "is that the explosions at the Pit were set up either by home-grown terrorists—read drugs and alcohol—who decided to make a statement and it went wrong, or local gangs decided to pick on the poor addicts camping out there and things got out of hand, or those invested in the property hired thugs to clean the place out. Whatever, it erupted into fire and gunshots and people died. The Pit came through it a lot better than did the outcasts camping there."

The sea lion's "ork" was answered by another on the other side of the marina. It startled him into silence. There was a good sized party going on over there with lights and music and voices—more of a wedding or relatively sedate gathering but with many guests. Not the kind Libby attended for sure. Probably more like the one Charlie was invited to on Sunday.

"Hey, get this. It's perfect for you, Charlie," Kenny reported from the other side of the screen. "Lost priest finds pot of gold at the end of rope hanging from a cloud and passes it by."

"Why?"

"Doesn't say. But there's more, want to hear it?"

"No." Moonlight cast long shadows from tethered sailboats below. Two sea lions orked now, but on the other side of the lagoon. "Luella, why did you tell me to get Maggie out of the Sea Spa right away?"

"Is your buzz off?"

"Pretty much. I'm just tired."

"I'm not really authorized to tell all, Charlie. Not yet. And I'm not positive that all I can tell is true, at least the whole truth. But there is, apparently, an investigation underway or just beginning, into the holdings, conflict of interest, and fraudulent accounting practices of Royal Pharmaca and Arthur Douglas, Inc."

"Which is?"

"Arthur Douglas is either an offshore holding company, a front for terrorists, or a scam to cover up the fact that research into the efficacy of Redux offered by Royal Pharmaca and touted by Dr. Judith Judd on her televised women's health series, and filmed at the Sea Spa at the Marina del Sol, found it to be little more than very expensive aspirin but with a lot more side effects."

"Who's investigating?"

"The SEC and FBI and I assume the FDA. FBI showed up at Congdon and Morse this morning and wanted to see all data on where Judith's royalties came from."

"Cooking the books?"

"Cooking the research results at least. I don't think Congdon and Morse is under that much of a cloud. Our books have been open and regularly scrutinized since you and Richard Morse got mixed up with Evan Black and your neighbor was found murdered with no recorded identification. Sounds like there's a scandal about to explode whether the VanZants know about it or not. It just seemed to me that since Maggie's under suspicion already, someone could find something else to blame on her so I wanted her out of there until we have an idea of what this is about."

"I don't want to hear false accusations about the Sea Spa or Dr. Judith. You're trying to turn me against everything." With that, Maggie Stutzman flounced off to the shower so Kenny came out onto the balcony. The chocolates were gone, Maggie was crying.

"I really can't see what all this would have to do with drugging a fruit platter." Kenny poured himself some coffee. Some of the sheriff's investigators had nibbled on the proffered fruit and cheese littering the lobby and reported weird reactions. It was thought Charlie might have suffered the same and they checked Maggie's fluids as well for good measure, or because she was a suspect—no one said, but that's why the side trip to the clinic before coming here.

"What are we going to do? Maggie's gone cold-turkey on

102

scads of medications and on nourishment altogether. She's simply not stable," Charlie worried.

A sweet flower scent changed places on a breeze with the slimy marina smell and decaying fish scales for a few seconds. A large fishing boat with lights glided into a berth below.

"What we need to know is the connection between Judith Judd and Raoul," Charlie said.

"Why?"

"They both were murdered presumably by the same person for the same reason."

"Well, Charlie's back on line. I'm going to bed." Luella gathered the food and drink receptacles onto one tray, then stopped to think a moment. "Kenneth, why don't you all change rooms for the night? They're close together."

"Thought the murderer was at the Sea Spa," Kenny said.

"But Maggie's here." Charlie looked at her colleague with even more respect. "And if someone's trying to pin the murders on her . . ."

"Exactly."

"So what difference would it make what room Maggie was in? If she wanted to murder someone she could come from any room." The proprietor of Viagra's Pool Hall in Myrtle, Iowa ran his hand through close-clipped hair and rubbed the back of his neck.

Charlie's neck got sore looking up at him. Did his do the same when he looked down at everyone else? "But if someone wanted to pin it on her and assumed she slept in this room—"

"Oh, let's just put big ol' Kenny in danger. He won't mind. Need I explain that I'm a big ol' wimp?"

Charlie and Maggie ended up sleeping in the same bed again, but in Kenny's and he in theirs.

Charlie slept hard again and woke to Maggie in the shower again, Kenny's shower this time. They'd moved most of their things with them, as women will. Kenny, Charlie happened to know, slept in the buff. When she stepped out of his shower in his terrycloth hotel robe, he sat on the balcony with Maggie, in a hotel robe from their room, hair still wet from a shower, but face in need of a shave. He'd left his utensils here.

"I've ordered you the seafood omelet special," he said with that smug look guys get when they think they know you. "And hold the cheese."

He'd brought the caffeinated coffee packet from their room and all three had a cup before room service arrived with a splendid roll-in table and a huge breakfast for all. More than enough to share with Luella when she knocked timidly and slipped in when Charlie opened it, relieved to see Kenny across the room through the sliding glass door.

"Thank God, how did he get away?"

"From what?"

"Your room. It's swarming with official type people—no one allowed near."

Charlie's hair was still dripping. Kenny hadn't been gone long from that room.

"So what all did you leave in our room?" Charlie yelled over the hair dryer.

He stood behind her putting on his shorts. "My dirty panties on the bathroom floor. Socks, shirt, shoes, and slacks is all."

"Oh, that ought to make a fun investigation."

"I have replacements here. We ought to get through breakfast anyway and I did bring out my wallet. Nothing in that room to identify me but fingerprints. Want a massage?"

"No." She avoided the glances under raised eyebrows as she took a change of clothes from his closet, threw it in the bathroom, shut the door on his smirk.

They soon sat at the table inside with extra plates to share everything. When Charlie took the metal lid off the seafood omelet and smelled the big pink shrimp and hunks of crab sticking out of it she couldn't repress an, "Oh my."

"I love the way she says that, don't you?" Kenny removed

the plastic wrap from the rims of the large wine goblets filled with orange juice, emptied a water goblet to divi it four ways and raised the latter in a toast, "Here's to good food, good drink, good living, and resolutions."

All three females automatically raised their orange juice to honor his toast whether they understood it or not and Charlie met the stares of the other two, responding with a, "Will you knock it off?"

Charlie ate a half of a very full omelet, one piece of bacon from someone else's plate, half a slice of toast and all her orange juice before she sat back with her second cup of coffee. "Can you hear that?"

Kenny had sliced what was left of her omelet in three pieces, put one on his empty pancake platter. Luella and Maggie finished it off along with muffins and sausage. But there was still toast no one could eat. "Hear what?"

"The quiet." Charlie blinked back at blank stares. "We're what—two, three doors away from my room? The door to this balcony is open. Luella, you said the hall, and I assume my room, was crawling with police. Why isn't there more commotion?"

Eighteen

Charlie took the last of the morning's coffee out onto the balcony to look or listen for any sign of commotion outside. Maggie dressed in the bathroom and Luella had turned on the TV in the wardrobe to morning news. No sounds from the other invisible balconies, no excitement on the walkway below either, where two groundsmen discussed something in Spanish while poking around the base of a bush with waxy leaves.

Luella called Charlie in for the local news. It began with the death of another burn victim from the explosion and fire at the Celebrity Pit. Then a quick clip from an interview with Mitch Hilsten about his plans for filming at a marina up the coast in North County and taking some clever camel shots out at the Wild Animal Park.

"Serious action, romance, great script, special effects— this story has it all," Mitch said with a penetrating squint leveled at the camera that brought a sigh from Maggie and a snort from Kenny Cowper.

Luella peered around into Charlie's face to check her reaction and then sat back. "He's learning to talk the talk."

"Has to if he's going to survive." Even Charlie heard the regret in her voice. She'd liked the old Mitch better. *She* must be getting old. An update on murder at the Sea Spa at the Marina del Sol, with the addition of Raoul Segundo. "Sounds like a stage name."

". . . another mysterious murder, this time at the Hyatt Islandia. Dr. Grant Howard, founder and president of the well-known San Diego Film Institute, was found this morning by housekeeping in his room—"

106

A rattling at the door startled them all and the impossible coincidence of a voice, "Housekeeping!"

Kenny grabbed the *Do Not Disturb* sign off the doorknob inside and explained, "I'm not ready yet."

"Hokay, I cumb back."

He slipped the sign over the outside handle, bolted the bolt, and put on the chain.

". . . shock from all who knew him. Details are sketchy at this time but Dr. Howard and his film institute," the voice on the TV in the wardrobe said, "was hosting screenwriter Keegan Monroe who penned the smash hit at Cannes, *Open and Shut*, starring Treat Devoe and Bella Burgoine, as well as the sleeper, *Phantom of the Alpine Tunnel*, several years ago. We'll keep you posted on this late breaking news. Now back to NBC and the current war—"

Luella clicked the war away. Charlie left them all looking at each other and took her clothes into the bathroom to dress and take time to think. When she came out the others had hardly moved. Maggie thumbed through a glossy magazine. Her cheeks were wet. Kenny wrote in a spiral notebook, looking up to stare inward.

Luella, out on the balcony, held up the inside of an index finger, extended outward, in a "just a minute" motion, and ended a conversation on her cell. "Charlie, shouldn't you try to get a hold of Maggie's lawyer? She's probably on her way."

All four of them glanced occasionally at the door to the hall, expecting the law to arrive any second. Charlie replaced Luella Ridgeway on the balcony to make the call and caught Nancy Trujillo at rush hour crawl, stop, crawl, stop on the 8, not far and indeed on her way. She'd just heard of the murder at the Islandia on her car radio. "Tell me Margaret Stutzman spent no time there alone last night, Ms. Greene."

"I've been with her since we got here, but we slept in a friend's room instead of mine and another friend told me my room, two doors down, is crawling with police this morning. I don't know if they'll even let you up to this hallway."

"I'll want a lot more questions answered but there may

not be time now if the police are two doors away. I'm going to park in a lot down the bay a ways and walk along the marina boardwalk. How many cells do you have in that room right now besides the one you're using? That aren't Margaret's either?"

"Two."

"I've got yours, give me the other two numbers, quick."

When Charlie had, the lawyer cautioned, "If any of you are being questioned and your cell rings don't answer it. If you are ordered to, say 'Yes?' instead of 'Hello' or 'This is Charlie' or whatever and I'll hang up and try someone else. Give my number to your friends and when anyone can get info out, call me."

"Can't you do anything now?"

"Not much until she's charged. Hang in, I'll be close."

"How did you know?" Charlie asked Luella. "How did you know Maggie and I shouldn't stay in our room last night?"

"How'd you know I'd get out in time?" Kenny had to add.

"I didn't, I swear. It's just my over-organized brain trying to cover all the bases. And everyone at the Sea Spa knows Charlie's sort of looking after Maggie. Somebody there who knew Charlie was here might figure Maggie would be in the same room like they were at the Spa. And there does appear to be an attempt to link her to the murders at the Spa—I don't know. It just seemed like a good idea."

Charlie sat on the bed next to Maggie, "How you doing, kid?"

Tears still welled in those beautiful eyes but her cheeks were dry. "I'm making it. Just missing my Nasonex. It was in the drug bag I never got back."

"Oh, I snort that," Luella said. "For my allergies."

"Was there any one doctor monitoring all the stuff you were on, Maggie?"

"Obviously not. Have you seen this, Charlie? The Sea Spa's in here. Sounds very legit in this write-up." Those eyes spit defiance again.

Luella took a nasal spray bottle from her purse, shook it

hard, and handed it to Maggie. Charlie took the magazine, *San Diego County Tourist Guide*, from Maggie's lap. It was a slick production touting all the things tourists and conventioneers might like to do to leave money in the area. The lead story was *"The Day Spa Phenom, Wave of the Future?"* The VanZants posed in front of the fancy wrought iron gate, Warren towering behind Caroline, Raoul off to one side, Sue Rippon the other—the latter two with arms crossed in front of them—and behind the four a good hint of the luxury accommodations and gardens. A professional head shot of Dr. Judy alone farther down on the page.

"Maggie, before or sometime during the time I passed out from drugged fruit and cheese in our room at the Sea Spa, I imagined I heard you screaming. Was that me hallucinating or what?"

"I went into the bathroom and the shower door was open and there was this hole in the tile. It had an eye in it. I yelled and the hole disappeared."

"Sounds like dear Dashiell, the handyman." Charlie's cell tweedled and she fully expected a cop to be on the other end, but it was Keegan.

"Is there any way you could sneak down here and help teach a course this morning? Natives are restless. I assume you've heard about Howard."

"Yes, and the hallway's full of investigators near my room at last report. I'm not in it, but close enough to be seen sneaking out of the one I'm in."

"My room was thoroughly gone over as well, but I'm told I have leave to carry on for the Institute. We'll be in the same room we used yesterday to hear the pitches and where your panel was, if you can make it."

"You know what would be cool," Kenny said when she'd explained Keegan's request, "is if you and I could go down to the conference where we belong, Luella could sneak Maggie out to meet her lawyer, and housekeeping could get into this room without drawing attention to it by banging on the door again."

It sounded good but too easy, still they took a chance. Kenny went first while the rest stowed all signs of woman's wear behind closet doors where Luella assured them housekeeping never looked. The only giveaway was the size of the breakfast and the number of towels used by one occupant. Maybe he had a lady up last night. And she stayed for breakfast and showered twice.

Kenny went first and called to say it looked clear if they turned the other way from Charlie's room and took the stairs instead of the elevator, while Luella set up a place to meet Nancy Trujillo. Luella left next, sent for Maggie, and Charlie escaped last. The housekeeping cart was just across the hall, the door to her room down the hall open, and she could hear voices in there, but hurried the other way to the stairs, head down. Had to be a trap. It was too easy.

Listen dufus, you know what's going on. The cops don't know the whole story yet—probably haven't connected people from both the Spa and the workshop yet. Probably other murders in town, you know.

Charlie had to admit her inner self made sense but still— the only thing she was totally convinced of was the expedience of having everyone armed with a cellular.

She stepped off the elevator to see two things at once, Detective Solomon talking to Keegan Monroe in the hall outside the conference room and a woman arranging a book display on a cleverly built expandable and foldable table with three levels. The woman and her display were way too close to the elevator and Charlie put a finger to her lips before she ducked behind a potted fern.

This put her in a dark corner facing the elevator's shiny doors that mirrored a good section of the hall. In fact she could see herself peering from behind the fern, more like a fern tree. She met the gaze of the startled woman she'd hoped to hush, and behind her, saw Solomon turn and walk into the bar which was directly across from the conference room.

At the end of the wide hallway the outside glass doors opened to the center courtyard containing a lovely garden and the pool, with curving walkways to the lobby building, business conference centers, a seafood restaurant, and yet more marina.

Mitch Hilsten had given Charlie CDs of the old Monty Python films and clips from the *Flying Circus* TV shows when she was recovering from her accident on the 405 and she was reminded of them now as the display woman kept staring back in the mirrored elevator doors, nodding and smiling at Charlie like an idiot. Her hair a shoulder-length brown shag with suspicious red highlights, her shape like facing parentheses between neck and knees, she wore small glasses and a big smile, a red checked sleeveless, waistless dress to midcalf and black rubber sandals. Charlie guessed her to be somewhere in her late forties, early fifties and probably fifty pounds overweight.

The woman looked around and then suddenly slipped over to hand Charlie a book. "Something to read while you hide. But you have to give it back. Or pay for it. But you can have it for author's discount."

She returned to her display table and unlike before looked everywhere but at Charlie and her fern tree. Mostly she smiled with a resigned hopefulness as the attendees filed past her to the conference room, avoiding her eyes and her display. Charlie would have pranced right on by her too if she hadn't seen Solomon in the hall first. She'd early on avoided her book authors' signings for this very reason. Charlie might be a tough Hollywood agent but watching hopeful authors embarrass themselves was more than she could stomach.

This one had the unfortunate name of Mary Keene and her novel was *Murder in the Midlands*. Charlie expected it to be a first novel and self-published but was astonished to find it the author's third in a series published by Simon and Shooter. Might as well have been titled *Murder on the Midlist* if she had to resort to this. Charlie looked up from a blood-stained piece of clothing and what might be an eyeball attached to something hidden in a ball of dirt on the book jacket to see Kenny alone in the hall with Mary Keene.

"Hey, Charlie, glad you could make it out from behind your tree, but you looked real colorful back there," Kenny said when she joined them.

Charlie glanced at the elevator doors to discover they showed her hidey hole plainly from here. Made sense if she could see here plainly from there. "I was trying to avoid Solomon. Did he see me? What did he want?"

"He was looking for Maggie. Told him she was meeting her lawyer. Did you know Mary here has my old agent?"

Charlie wondered if big deal agent Jeth Larue ever worked up the courage to attend any of his authors' signings, watch the baleful show of their attempts to swim upstream.

Both she and Kenny bought a book, at cover price—most likely the only two Mary Keene would sell this day.

Nineteen

I have published thirteen books in the last ten years, three of them bestsellers and written four prize-winning screenplays, plus I spend three months a year conducting workshops that provide concise and easy ways to break into markets of all kinds for beginning writers and how to break through the high income ceiling for publishing writers stuck in the midlist doldrums. One-day, ten-hour intense workshop with an editor and representative on hand to look at your material. All for $170 (lunch not included). Bestselling author Harry Wicks can show you how IN JUST TEN HOURS!

Harry's e-mail address and phone and fax numbers followed so that potential attendees could find out when he was speaking in their area. There was a picture included on the flyer of this amazing person in blue jeans and T-shirt who appeared to be a likeable everyday Joe with a friendly grin and short-cropped hair.

Other than the photo, the flyer was in colorful oranges and greens and they had been on every chair in the conference room this morning. The students arrived before a conference staff understandably in disarray with the murder of their leader. Belated attempts to gather up these advertisements for someone else's sucker scheme had been unsuccessful and many stuck out of the back pockets of denim jeans or front shirt pockets now. Kenny showed Charlie his. More grist for his exposé.

She sat at the back of the room with him as Keegan Monroe

113

talked about techniques of writing film scripts and made fun of his own success while writing in prison—somehow that experience tended to focus him. Kenny leaned over and whispered, "Scuttlebutt has it Howard was forcibly drowned in his tub."

"He's got a bathtub? All we have are showers."

"He has a complimentary suite because he brings the Institute workshop here and it has a Jacuzzi. But should anyone want to connect your friend Maggie to another murder—there does seem to be a pattern here. I think Luella Ridgeway may have had a point in insisting we get her out of your room."

"But who is connected with both the conference and the Sea Spa?"

"You, me, Maggie, Luella, Jerry Parks, and Mitch Hilsten, to name a few. Did we ever determine how Grant Howard knew the VanZants? I forget."

But it was time for Charlie to take the podium. The sharks had the afternoon shift. The last faculty member, Sarah Newman the story editor, was probably busy consoling her suddenly widowed sister.

Come to find out, Mary Keene was not only Jethro Larue's client, she was also Brodie Caulfield's mother. Charlie discovered this when she and Kenny had lunch with the two at the hotel's Baja Café just across the hall and through the bar from the conference room. They had saved a place for Keegan, who was surrounded by attendees with questions. Box lunches came with the registration for conferees so this seemed like a safe enough haven for now. Charlie didn't want to get too far away from Maggie who she hoped was busy planning strategies with her lawyer and Luella Ridgeway about now.

"So, do you want to see more?" Brodie asked Charlie and poured himself some margarita from the pitcher in the middle of the table.

"Excuse me?" She took a sip of the house merlot and tried to come down off the cliff of godwhat'llhappennext.

"You asked for a treatment, I gave you one yesterday. What do you think?"

"Brodie, I'm going to be honest with you. I haven't read it yet."

"Christ, she went from the Bahia straight to a murder scene. Get a heart, man," Kenny came to her defense.

"You haven't lost it?"

"I know right where your treatment is and first chance I get, I promise to let you know." It damn well better be in Kenny's closet.

Brodie's mother peered over her little glasses. They were rectangles on their sides and gray-tinted. "I know you now. You're Mitch Hilsten's agent."

"No, I handle writers. He's just a friend and with a different agency altogether."

"Anyway, Ma, you should have heard her take out this self-important smartass in there this morning. The jerk started challenging every last thing she said."

"There's one in every crowd, I frankly thought it was going to be you, Brodie, until this guy showed up."

"So what did she do?" Mary Keene shared some facial expressions with her son but otherwise there was little similarity.

"She just stood up there with her mouth shut, for five of the longest minutes. We were all embarrassed for her and the dork who made it all possible. Finally she says, 'We just wasted five minutes and more when you consider this gentleman's intrusions. My time is worth more to me than that, it's frankly worth more to me away from here. His time must be worth more to you than mine. Yours is apparently unlimited.'"

"You'll have to admit, Charlie, yours is a very unpopular message," Kenny said when the tacos arrived. "Anyway, Institute staff reluctantly escorted the offender out of the room. I think they agreed with him more than Charlie. I can't believe you didn't see it when they shoved him out the door, Mary."

"The Institute staff had already convinced hotel security to shut me down too."

"Contract up for renewal?" Charlie asked.

"Yeah, and the numbers aren't there. It's tough. I've done everything but mug Oprah. Takes a lot of energy and money. Nothing seems to work anyway."

"God, I can't believe it. I'd kill to be published by Simon and Shooter." Kenny put one of his tacos on a side plate for Charlie who'd ordered only a dinner salad after her heavy breakfast. "At least I used to think so."

"Numbers are numbers no matter where you go. Brodie keeps telling me I need a gimmick. I know lots of writers with great gimmicks and they're not getting anywhere either."

"From what I've understood from an admittedly quick review of the jacket copy, this seems to be a series aimed at older women, which is wise since they make up a large proportion of readers, but the market therefore is inundated with that kind of story. You'll notice younger males making up the majority of hopefuls at this conference—perhaps not the target audience for you." Charlie took a bite of the taco and realized it had the same filling with different spicing as her omelet this morning. This was a shellfish taco and simply wonderful, with a shredded cabbage topping.

"I know, but it gave me some quality time with my son so not all was lost, an excuse to come out here to be with him." Mary lived in Illinois, her son in L.A. and it was obvious he'd never move back to the Midwest.

Charlie wondered if she'd ever look at Libby with that kind of wistful acceptance. Nah. With Libby it was all scary dread. "You have other children?"

"He has two sisters. They moved to the East Coast."

Keegan arrived at last and Kenny poured him a margarita without being asked. "I wish I'd listened to you, Charlie, about not taking this thing on. Why didn't I?"

"Because you enjoy your success and being adored."

"Well, I'm all over the lust for adoration, let me tell you. God, do you think they'll call off the banquet? Surely they'll have to. I want out of here."

*   *   *

116

Charlie left the Baja Café through the marina-side exit planning to call Luella, but grabbed a moment to enjoy being alone, surrounded by quiet, sun, a cool breeze off the bay messing with her hair. Hard to believe Solomon and crew weren't after her by now. Maybe they'd rounded up Maggie and saw no need to bother with Charlie. But Maggie had never been near Grant Howard. Even though it was another drowning of sorts there was no reason to link her to this last murder just because she was in the building. The VanZants could have driven down and murdered the Institute's leader, or their son or any of the Sea Spa staff.

She walked around a sand patio with deck chairs—closest thing to a beach on a marina the size of this one—and turned up the walk on the other side of the Islandia that led eventually to the parking lot, but first to the area beneath her balcony and Kenny's. One message from Luella, they were at the Islandia Restaurant, a separate building across the courtyard from the café and bar in the building hosting the convention and Charlie's room, with Nancy Trujillo, the lawyer. Another from Mitch. He'd heard about Howard's death. Did she need help? Another from Libby threatening to take off for San Lucas in her car and never return if her mother didn't get back to Long Beach and take care of Betty Beesom. Jacob Forney had left for his mystery convention and she was there alone. "I am not a nurse and I don't intend to ever be one. Grandma's pissed too because you haven't called her yet."

And one from her secretary/assistant Larry Mann who had also heard of Grant Howard's untimely death and wanted details on that and on troublesome matters on the MacArthur contract. "I gotta tell the lawyers something and can't deal with this office alone, boss, because I have no clout and because Richard the Lionhearted has taken up roaring again."

Charlie stood on the walk, toeing at the roots of the waxy-leaved bush she'd noticed grounds keepers investigating earlier and deciding on the triage method. She'd return Luella's call first, but her scattered thoughts brought up something totally out of context with that even before a voice on a balcony seven floors above her said, "Here you are again, Ms. Greene."

Was there a similarity between the scam going on at the Spa and/or the pharmaceutical industry's persuasive advertising campaign and the Film Institute's misleading advertising of the odds for screenwriting success simply for purposes of profit? Was it so different from the promises of riches in the stock market, or vibrant health throughout increasing longevity in medicine? This is how a goodly proportion of people make a living—selling impossible dreams, Hollywood foremost among them. Is it necessarily evil? Excluding greedy CEOs, mass murderers, and sexual child abusers in powerful and respected positions, are dream merchants actually a necessary part of society? And wasn't Charlie actually a member of this group?

"What?" she asked the man without eyebrows leaning over her balcony rail.

"What is it you're looking for?"

"A little sanity would be nice about now."

"You won't find it in this." He held a tube or vial between thumb and forefinger, could have been a short pipe. It looked a lot like the ones under the bushes near to her foot. "I want you to stay right there, Ms. Greene, until I can join you. Deputy Saucier up here will watch to see that you do."

The clipboard deputy came to stand beside him, her expression both weary and wary. She took a revolver or whatever it was from the holster at her belt and leaned over the balcony rail.

Charlie didn't run off, merely punched Luella's number and knelt to look under the bush. There were several plastic medicine bottles there, all bearing the prescription label for one Margaret Mildred Stutzman. Just before Gordy Solomon arrived to show her that the one in his hand did too and that it was found next to Grant Howard's body, Luella informed her with a tone of panic Charlie had never heard in all the years they'd worked together, that Maggie had disappeared. She and Attorney Trujillo were in the midst of a frantic search.

Twenty

"I'd like to speak with Margaret Mildred Stutzman," Solomon said patiently, reading the name off the prescription label on the vial in his hand. The contents of which, barring evidence to the contrary from toxicology, he suspected was dumped into a glass of scotch, which was then imbibed in Dr. Grant Howard's Jacuzzi tub early this morning.

"He was pretty well sloshed the last time I saw him late yesterday afternoon in the bar at the Bahia. If he kept drinking into the night he could have died from alcohol poisoning or fell in the tub and hit his head and drowned," Charlie diagnosed through her hat.

"We also have reason to believe that when he was helpless for one reason or another, someone held him under the water until he drowned. We also happen to know there was a female in the room with him."

"Look, Maggie didn't even know who he was and there were all kinds of females in this hotel last night. Plus which she and I spent the night in the same room."

"We have reason to believe—"

"Will you stop that? Jesus, you sound like a corny TV mystery."

"We're fairly confident that you spent the night with a gentleman. A Mr. Kenneth Cooper who I believe you introduced to me at the Sea Spa at the Marina del Sol where there have been two recent suspected murders by drowning also."

"Maggie and I spent the night in his room and he in ours because . . . a mutual friend suggested it." Charlie would have continued but realized she was digging herself a hole here.

None of this made sense, so Solomon et al needed to connect dots any way they could. Housekeeping might never look in the closet but you can bet the police had. Someone obviously put that medicine bottle in Howard's room to implicate Maggie and connect the murder here to those at the Spa. Sort of ruled out the random theory. "Besides, Maggie is suddenly missing."

"How convenient."

Besides Detective Solomon and the deputy, Lydia Saucier, most of the officers about Charlie's room and Kenny's were city cops and homicide. She, Kenny, and Deputy Saucier (pronounced, she'd informed them, "saucy-A") sat on the balcony of his room now while who knew what was going on inside.

"You okay, Charlie?" Kenny reached over to knead her shoulder.

"No, I'm worried sick for Maggie. And now I can't even reach Luella. I don't know what's happening."

"How about the lawyer—what's her name?"

"Nancy Trujillo. Solomon's got my cell. And I can't describe her—I've yet to lay eyes on her."

When Detective Solomon stepped out of the room it was with another plainclothes Charlie assumed was city. "Luella Ridgeway's room is in order, all her stuff there except purse and car keys. Her car is not in the lot here. Could she have spirited Ms. Stutzman off the premises?"

"I have no idea. Let me try to call her again."

"Check your messages first." Solomon handed her cellular back. "She might have been trying to get a hold of you."

Another even more frantic message from her gorgeous secretary, Larry Mann. Another even more threatening message from her daughter who was not going to hang around a "bitchy old sick lady another minute if help doesn't arrive right now!" A guilt-trip message from her mother in Boulder, Colorado wanting to know what the hell was going on "out there" and threatening to hop on a plane and get "out there" if someone didn't talk to her "pretty goddamned soon!"

Three different well-known major banking institutions in a row wanted her to use the equity in her home to borrow money from them. Another shark wanted to consolidate her credit card debt to avoid bankruptcy. A dream vacation was hers, practically free, if she just "dialed" this number. Charlie was paying for all this crap, paying the bill for creeps to use her phone to harass her when she needed to contact someone on what could be a life and death matter. Luella still didn't answer and Charlie left a message on *her* cell.

The telemarketing slugs were dream merchants too, as bad as the pharmaceutical pushers. And God wanted us to spread this slime to the rest of world? "God, you sure about that?"

"She talks to herself," Kenny told the mildly startled officers. "She's also paranoid."

Charlie, still holding her phone when it tinkled, answered before Gordy Solomon could grab it. It was Nancy Trujillo wanting to know if Charlie knew where Maggie and Luella were.

Nancy Trujillo, a chunky blue-eyed blonde—go figure—stood in front of the Islandia Restaurant holding a purse the size of a briefcase to her chest like a closed book or file folder. Charlie would have walked right on by her if she hadn't been the only person standing right where they'd agreed to meet. And if the lawyer and Detective Solomon had not greeted each other by name and with decided reserve.

The breeze was a tad more insistent on this side of the tall hotel and grew distinctly chilly as a cloud blanket overtook the sun, just a friendly reminder that April is winter in Southern California.

The restaurant was in a separate building from the hotel and other adjacent buildings and at one corner of the property that curled around the marina and bay here. It served dinners and Sunday brunch at this time of year but was to open an hour early today for cocktails because of all the conferences being held this week at the Islandia. The lawyer, Maggie, and Luella were waiting outside for the doors to open, standing at the end of a line when Maggie disappeared.

"Luella and I got to talking about I can't remember what now and before we knew it Maggie wasn't in line with us. Luella rushed off to the lobby building to see if she'd headed to the ladies' room there and if not was going to check the parking lot. I was to search the pool and garden area here, the café in the hotel, and the ladies' room there. We were to meet back at this spot no later than fifteen minutes and check with each other every five. The last I heard, Luella hadn't found her in the lobby ladies' room and was on her way to the parking lot. That was nearly an hour ago."

"Ms. Ridgeway's car is not in the lot. She's not answering her cell phone. Everything but her purse is still in her room." Solomon arched the forehead over one eye and nodded knowingly. "What was Margaret Stutzman's mood like while you planned strategy? Cooperative? Grateful for your services? Worried?"

"Pretty much detached, compliant, nervous."

"Preliminary lab work on your and Margaret's bodily fluids indicate no drugs in her system, but enough in yours, Charlie, to confirm Deputy Saucier's suspicions about the fruit and cheese platters. Might explain your friend's nervousness, since she had a drug problem. Maybe she went off looking for some. Did she have any friends in San Diego?"

"None that I know of, but I don't know all her friends. She's fragile. We need to find her and Luella too." Charlie grabbed her phone from her purse before the first tinkle got a good start, praying it was Luella and that she'd found Maggie. But it was Larry Mann, her assistant.

"Charlie, I've just been cleaning the garbage out of your e-mail inbox and you are getting some scary stuff coming in here. It's even coded."

"Then how do you know it's scary? And have you heard from Luella in the last, say hour or two?"

"One of the FBI dudes running around here was looking over my shoulder. He says it's their code. I haven't heard from Luella since she left for San Diego again."

"Is the e-mail about Maggie or the Sea Spa?"

"No, it's about the explosion at the Celebrity Pit."

Charlie had managed to get her agency in trouble with THE agency several times and it was a given, after having had computer files screwed up by THEIR invasions, that she had her e-mail automatically downloaded to her laptop at home as well. Doug Esterhazie, son of Esterhazie Concrete who was going to marry his third this Saturday, was so adept at adapting computers that he managed to screen out most of the spam junk in the process.

When she called Libby at Betty Beesom's and got Doug instead, Charlie was glad and she was furious. She needed Doug right now and he shouldn't let Libby use him like this. But if anybody could break a code it was Doug Esterhazie. He already had her password because he and Libby had gotten her out of more than a few Internet jams before this.

"I can't leave Mrs. Beesom. Don't you have your laptop with you? Can't you access your e-mail with your PDA from there?"

There was no way to explain to the Dougs of the earth that Charlie delighted in getting away from the Internet, that she couldn't figure out how to use half the features on her Personal Digital Assistant, that she actually had a life, that as much as she'd appreciated it the last few days, truth be known she even got pretty sick of her cellular on regular occasions. "Look, Doug, just run next door and grab it. It's still at the desk in the dining room. Run it back over to Betty's. You can work on it there. You know my password. Larry thinks it's FBI." She could hear the disappointment in his sigh. "Look, they could have gotten a lot better at it by now with all the national security beef-up and all the available laid-off techies." His second sigh added impatience to the disappointment. "It's about the explosion at the Celebrity Pit."

"You were mixed up with that?" Now there was shock, but some interest.

"No, but they might think so—you know what a suspicious character I am. Call me back when you decode it. And if you see your friend Libby Abigail Greene, tell her I'm going to throttle her." Charlie came back to the visible world with a start to find Nancy Trujillo, Gordy Solomon, and Deputy Saucier gawking at her. Oh boy. She tried to replay in her head the pieces of conversation they had heard on this end.

Deputy Saucier had just arrived to inform her boss that Luella's car was spotted heading up the coastal highway not far from the Sea Spa at the Marina del Sol. And that Keegan Monroe was checking out of the Hyatt Islandia.

Twenty-One

The San Diego Film Institute Screenwriting Conference was in grave disarray, conferees leaving en masse, demanding refunds not forthcoming, Thursday's sessions and banquet called off. Charlie wanted only to pack her stuff and get out before the Institute officials decided not to comp her room after all. She doubted she'd ever see the honorarium. The important thing now was to find Maggie and Luella. Nancy Trujillo had gone to her office, prepared to return the minute a sign of Maggie turned up.

A sheriff's deputy sent to the Sea Spa at the Marina del Sol reported back to Solomon that there was no sign of either woman, nor of Luella's car. All their luggage was still here at the Islandia. What to do?

"What was that about the FBI?" Solomon asked Charlie up in Kenny's room. He rifled through Maggie's suitcase while she searched hers for Brodie Caulfield's treatment.

"Oh, Congdon and Morse had some trouble with them over a client who left the country while under suspicion, went to Spain to—"

"Evan Black, the producer? That was a great flick. And your friend Hilsten was in it. Black got out of the country with all that money, went to Spain to blow up Vegas on screen and get even. Man, the back story on that, what was it, um—oh yeah—*Paranoia Will Destroy Ya*, was as good as the film. They run that whole thing on E! every other month. And I hear it's out on DVD now. What are you looking at me like that for?"

"You're the law. And you liked *Paranoia*?"

"Oh yeah, cops love pyrotechnics—we're just suckers for it. You know what's really wild? I know a lot of firemen who do too." He looked off into the distance to recall a fond memory in his head—which he shook to come back to work. "So, this screenwriters' conference—do these things produce a lot of screenwriters? Why are you still looking at me funny?"

Well, for starters you have one of Maggie's bras dangling by a strap from your index finger. And you don't have any eyebrows and you wear a rug. And for the first time you seem like a real person somehow. But she said aloud, "If you're trying to come on as a lamebrain, I'm not buying in."

"Look, there's been a murder at this conference. I'm a cop and I'm curious, and got a right to be." He noticed the bra and shook it off like he'd surprised a cobweb.

"You're talking funny again."

"Well, I'm trying not to sound like a corny TV mystery."

"The odds against any of the attendees of this conference making headway in a career as a screenwriter, gaining contact with someone in a position to buy, recommend, judge, produce, make it happen are staggering."

"But there's four Hollywood agents here, as I understand it. Where else can you go and find that many in one place?"

"Two are crooks. The other two are here under duress— one of them a story editor or analyst, not an agent—neither looking for material but in fact drowning in it. The market is very selective."

"That why you're looking around so hard for that treatment? Seems like somebody made a contact here."

"It's just that Brodie's been helpful and useful and not pushy. He's inventive and he can pitch. I'm curious to see if he can conjure. Does San Diego homicide consider Maggie a suspect in Howard's death?"

"City guys seem to feel there's no connection between the murders at the Sea Spa and Dr. Howard's. He work at the university or what?"

"To my knowledge neither the Institute nor Grant Howard

are connected to anything but each other. Why do you see a connection between the Spa and the Institute?"

"You, Margaret Stutzman, Luella Ridgeway, your tall muscular writer Kenneth somebody, the fact that all three murders involved prescription drugs and drowning for starters."

"Those pill bottles were taken away from Maggie last Saturday night at the Sea Spa."

"Drug dependency does strange things to people and withdrawal can do worse."

Keegan arrived just as she found Brodie's treatment. "I'm out of here, Charlie. Brodie's going to take me up to Del Mar. I'll be at Les Artistes if you need me. Sorry I got you into this. But you were right about rogue film institutes. Never again." Keegan had taken the train down and would take it back to L.A. from Solana Beach. He rarely drove more than familiar paths around town since his stay in Folsom. She didn't ask why. Maybe because he'd been convicted of manslaughter in the drowning death of a novelist whose book he'd been commissioned to turn into a screenplay by a major studio. They'd shared a bottle of vodka and a nasty argument at a roadside park near Rizzi Reservoir. She'd driven her car into the water and he'd driven his back home. Keegan swore she was swimming to shore when he left. Her body was found floating free from the car.

Les Artistes was a dinky arty motel owned by friends of his, where he retreated now and then, especially after a blowout stint of writing or just to get out of town.

Charlie was about to open Brodie's envelope when Doug Esterhazie called her back.

"Already?" Solomon said. "Thought the FBI had all these safeguards now."

"Internet may be fast and effective but we're in real trouble to depend on it. These kids can outwit codes in minutes."

Betty Beesom was sleeping peacefully and Doug had more messages for FBI agent Green. "I'll get them all translated onto paper for you and then blow them away so no one knows you got them at home too. Charlie, this was a really dumbed-down code."

It seemed the information on the terrorist explosion was meant for an agent Charles Green. "But he wouldn't have my e-mail address."

"Well they have your password too now. Some screwup probably searched for his friend Charlie Green and your password came up. Happens. They got more information than money to pay someone to process it. What I'm getting so far is it was religious extremists who tried to take out the Celebrity Pit, supposedly for its symbol of evil influence on society. But these fanatics weren't from any third world country."

Charlie called Libby and left the message, "You get back home and relieve Doug Esterhazie or I'm selling your Jeep out from under you, sweet cheeks. And that will be just the beginning of my assault on your freedoms and privileges. And I mean instantly."

"Oh, that ought to get you a long way," the sheriff said.

"I know. It's just that she's so damn selfish." Charlie looked past him to see wind-driven raindrops committing suicide against the glass doors to the balcony. Not that Charlie wasn't selfish at that age. She expected better of her daughter. "I guess it's a generation thing. You got kids?"

"Sort of. The oldest is more your age than your daughter's. You wanna talk generation thing. Their mom raised them mostly. They don't like my present wife. What about your ex, he help out?"

"I've always been a single mom. My mom helped me raise Libby. And there's another generation problem." Charlie didn't know where to go from here, whether to continue to search for Maggie around the Islandia or follow her instincts to head for the Spa or what. What if she left and Maggie came back here? She closed the sliding glass door on a chilly wind. She wasn't dressed very warmly. "Maybe Maggie just got in a snit and she's sitting down in the bar now. Or she's over in the restaurant waiting for Luella and Nancy to come back. Or she's with Luella somewhere."

"Someone decides to get lost in Southern California, it's pretty damn easy."

"I wonder who all is home at the Sea Spa right now."

"Deputy Saucier's on her way there to report back on exactly that information. You think there's a connection between the deaths there and the one here too, don't you?"

Charlie didn't answer, but he was right. "I should be doing something. I just don't know what."

"Go on down to the bar. I'll call you the first I hear anything." He was really a nice guy. Too bad he was the enemy.

But Charlie did as he said, just went to the bar across from the conference rooms. And sat down on a bar stool next to Kenny Cowper who was busy writing on a tablet—so neanderthal. Without looking up he said, "Any news of Maggie?"

"You didn't even see me, how'd you know it was me?"

"I can smell you."

"Now don't start with that. I do definitely not need a massage. Jesus."

"That was a compliment."

"I do not wear perfume."

"I know." He crossed a t or dotted an i or placed a period, whatever, closed the notebook and turned to her with a theatrical sigh. "Good thing you don't live in Iowa. I'd never get any work done."

The bartender came over to them, looked between them. "Your sister, right? You got the same eyes."

"Cousin. What do you think?"

The bartender, short and cute, reminded Charlie of a younger Tom Cruise. He bent to search Charlie's expression. "Martini. Definitely in need of a martini. Up. Gin. Olive or lemon do you think? Bombay or Tanguray?"

Kenny swivelled his stool to face her. "I'd say olive and Bombay."

"You got it." The younger Cruise turned away and then back again. "We talking PMS, divorce, laid off from a job, here? What?"

"Murder," Kenny answered and raised his glass. "And I'll have another."

"Oh man, murder, that's two olives, guys, on the house."

"I hate it when men order for me."

"Hell, I'm buying it. And another for the lady on the other side of me."

Sarah Newman, Grant Howard's sister-in-law and story editor at Troll's New York office, returned to sit with them. The widow was with Sarah's other sister for now. "Boy, is this the time I'm glad not to be an only child. She's a mess. I sure hope he made some money selling dreams. June has no marketable skills."

"Do they have children?"

"A son who moved to Australia. Doubt if Rod will even come back for the funeral."

The bartender set Charlie's martini in front of her and a bowl of salty party mix, and another of pretzels. They all automatically watched the TV above and to one corner of the bar, the sound turned down so low it was like the opposite of the TV in the wardrobe, seen but not heard. A Dodge Ram spewed digested ecology from its tires crossing a meadow of wildflowers. In the next commercial at least thirty people walked across another meadow like zombies while the flowers around them turned into purple pills with chartreuse stripes.

The martini was wonderful. Too wonderful. It is almost impossible to drink half a martini but those zombies chasing the purple pills were a good incentive. She did eat both the gin-soaked olives though and grabbed a handful of pretzels to go and her purse. "Thanks, but I've got to look for Maggie. Make an effort somehow."

"Charlie?" Kenny Cowper stood to tower. "Keep in touch so I don't have to worry about you too. If I hear anything I'll let you know, okay?"

"Right. Good plan."

Charlie checked the dinner restaurant on the other side of the swimming pool to see if Maggie had returned. No one had noticed if she had and she wasn't there now. She talked to people at the desk in the lobby and was in the parking lot when her cell summoned.

It was Mitch. He'd just heard about the murder at the screenwriters' conference, wondered about her safety. He was at the Marina del Sol and had called to see if she could have dinner with him there again.

There was some excitement there too. Somebody had driven a car off the cliff above the marina. Divers were searching for the driver. The car had been a white one according to witnesses he'd talked to.

"I'm on my way. I'll let you know when I'm close so you can meet me at the gate and let me in."

Luella Ridgeway drove a white Lexus.

Twenty-Two

Y ou do not know that was Luella's car or, if it was, that she or Maggie were in it. You are driving a huge vehicle through heavy traffic, much of it pedestrian. Get a grip now. You are liable to be badly needed and soon. Don't cause other innocent people trouble.

"If I've let Maggie down, I'll kill myself."

No you won't. Others need you too.

"Detective Solomon? I'm on my way to the Marina del Sol. Thought you should know. There's been an accident." Charlie kept blinking away those zombies floating across that meadow in pursuit of purple capsules ringed with chartreuse.

"I just heard. Where are you now?"

"Heading north to La Jolla, on Mission, I think."

"I'll meet you at the marina. And Charlie? Be careful. It may well not have been your friends in that car. But there is something very scary going on at that Sea Spa. I can feel it."

Now it was tears she was blinking back. The enemy wasn't supposed to talk like that. Thanks for caring, guy. "Thanks. I'll be careful."

She navigated an area entering La Jolla where the street signs were purposely obtuse, too obvious to fake this confusion factor. And the deal was, it was confusing from either direction, as if the locals went out and changed the signs every other night to discourage foreigners. At least the concentration that required helped dry up the tear glands and return her vision.

She should call Kenny, but didn't want to encourage him to take off in his car after who-knew-how-many martinis.

Charlie didn't need to have to worry about him too.

When Charlie and the metallic blue Dodge Ram arrived at the Marina del Sol the gate was open and a car dripped from the end of a chain on a boom or crane of some kind. Every type of emergency vehicle with lights flashing parked along a central pier. Charlie pulled the truck into a no-parking zone in front of the yacht club and walked down to the excitement with her heart in her stomach—her panic on hold, in protective shock, but still buzzing in her ears. Her feet felt as if they weren't quite reaching the wood of the pier, as if she strode on a layer of air down the center between parked vehicles and shops of all sorts that fueled and serviced private boats of all sorts. There was even a hot dog/fish and chips stand.

"Charlie, I didn't think you'd get here this fast. But I knew the gate was open." Mitch put an arm around her shoulders and floated beside her.

There were two different TV news vans on the ground and a helicopter flying overhead. Two guys in wetsuits and diving gear climbed a ladder from a zodiac and two other divers replaced them. Her cell chirped in her purse and when she answered it, "This is Charlie," her voice echoed in her head. She cut off her daughter's angst, "Libby, they've just pulled a car out of the ocean. Luella and Maggie may have been in it. I can't talk right now, honey. I can barely even breathe."

She hung up on her only child and turned to Mitch, "Is it a Lexus?"

"Yeah." He pulled her head to his shoulder and patted her hair. "One door was off. There wasn't anybody in it. They're just diving to be sure nobody went down with it, just a precaution, Charlie."

"Wow, you don't waste time," Jerry Parks said behind her. When Charlie turned, his photographer blinded her with a flash. "If I stick with you I seem to get first to the breaking news." That eager boyish squint seemed almost theatrical and definitely silly. "Can you tell my readers who was in that car, Ms. Greene?"

"Don't let him bait you, Charlie," Mitch said softly and

led her away while Parks did his job by following and repeating his questions and his photographer came with him. The
very end of the pier was roped off. They were allowed past
the barricade which was backed by the San Diego County
Sheriff's Department and some marina security armed with
dogs. Jerry and friend were not. "Someone here you need to
talk to. Don't let him bait you either. What do you want on
your hot dog?"

"How did you know?" She hated when men did that.

"Heard your stomach rumble when we passed the Fins and
Fangs. Charlemagne Catherine Greene, I'd like you to meet
Charles Green."

"Mustard, pickle relish, catsup, and onion," Charlie told
Mitch.

"Make that two," Charles Green added.

"How about that, we're both Charlie Greens," Charlie told
the heavyset gentleman in Banana Republic khakis, "and
we're both agents."

"Excuse me?" He even wore a safari hat. Why would he
want to stand out like that? His surprise did appear authentic.

"I'm Hollywood and you're FBI."

By the time hot dogs, beer, and fries arrived via superstar,
the other Charlie had regained his voice and the car still
dangling from the boom on the barge pushed by a tug came
dripping closer.

"I'm getting your e-mail," Charlie told him.

"You can decode?"

"No, but the nearest teenager can." Charlie stuck her hand
in her purse as if looking for something, switched her phone
off, and managed to hook a tissue to wipe her nose.

"Your daughter?"

"Actually she's the farthest teenager at the moment." The
divers off the end of the curve of promontory were still down.
Oh please let those women be safe and dry and somewhere
I can find them.

The three of them sat on a bench with a backboard, Charlie
Greene in the middle, trying to keep dripping mustard and

ketchup off their clothes and squint around lowering sun glare against water. The other Charlie's glasses were untinted prescription and the safari hat didn't seem to help much.

"So what were these alleged messages about?" He held a french fry out in front of him to inspect with suspicion and before he could get it to his mouth a passing seagull swooped by to steal it on the fly.

"You're not going to like it."

"Tell me anyway," he said, instead of "humor me," like he would have on TV.

"He's investigating the Sea Spa up there," Mitch warned. "Is that what the e-mails were about?"

"No, they were about the bombing at the Celebrity Pit."

"Why wouldn't I like that?" the FBI asked.

"Won't play in the Bible belt or DC either. It was religious fanatics."

"Well that should come as no surprise." The other Charlie rolled his eyes and shook his head in ennui. "Who else do you think has been responsible for everything since 9/11?"

"They were our religious fanatics."

"Jesus," Mitch said softly, "is *your* computer about to become toast."

While Agent Green was processing this information, Charlie asked, "So what are you investigating at the Sea Spa?"

But he didn't fall for it. Instead he pulled out a pill bottle, shook a capsule into his hand, swallowed it with beer, paused, shook out another, swallowed it too, pulled down his hat brim, and refocused on her eyes. "What do you mean 'our' religious? Ours run charities and shelters and help the homeless. They don't bomb them."

"May not have been after the homeless and addicts who sheltered there. The Pit did have a reputation for saucy entertainment, fundamentalists would consider evil." Speaking of saucy, Deputy Saucier and her Detective Solomon came through the barricade and up to Charlie. "I wondered what happened to you." She introduced them all.

Solomon shook hands with Mitch but not the FBI. His

expression expressing a resigned, "now that's all I need."

"He's here to investigate the Sea Spa."

"The murders are my jurisdiction," Gordy Solomon said carefully if not cordially.

The white Lexus lowered onto the pier and the red sun touched the sea. While the FBI and San Diego County concentrated on each other, Charlie wandered over to the ruined Lexus with her tissue to her eyes, looked into the car and turned away to slip behind a shed. "Libby, you're at Betty's? That's great. Is Doug still there? Excellent. Anybody else? Okay, listen hard—you can ream me out later. I'm not kidding here. Right now there is big trouble descending upon our happy little compound. I want you and Doug to take Mrs. Beesom and your computer and mine and probably the damn cat and both your cars and your cells and disappear to Doug's house. Libby, this is seriously necessary. Don't let anybody know where you all are."

"Mom, you are so hopeless. Now what have you done to bring everything tumbling down on us? You need a keeper, girl. What about Maggie and Luella? What have you done to make *their* lives miserable?"

"Tell Doug it's about the FBI thing and hurry! . . . Hi, Stew? This is Charlie. Is Larry handy? I have an emergency . . . Larry, is Ruby still at the office? Good, you get back there and help her back up everything on the computer system, take the backups with you and hide them somewhere not in either of your houses. I've got the feeling they're going to get wiped tonight. It's the FBI thing. Gotta go."

"Charlie, you okay?" Mitch rounded the shed to hug her and she slipped her cell into his pocket while pretending to cry against his shoulder.

"Keep this for me. I've warned Libby and Larry."

"Gotcha." He raised his voice for public consumption, "We have to keep up the hope that the girls weren't in the Lexus, Charlie. That they got out before it went off the cliff. Be brave now."

*   *   *

136

Up at the Sea Spa at the Marina del Sol the VanZants and what remained of the staff were bidding goodbye to the last of the day spa clients and looking convincingly weary. Even Ruth Ann Singer and her navel stud was helping out, since her deceased employer no longer needed her services and jobs were tough to find these days. Charlie hadn't realized how large the day staff was—massage therapists, yoga, Pilates, contemplation, and meditation instructors, skin, nail, hair, and cosmetology experts. All being interviewed by the San Diego Sheriff's Department before leaving for the day.

"The permanent staff is much smaller but there's this incredible reservoir of unemployed woo-woo specialists down in Solana Beach to draw from, whenever we need them," Warren VanZant told Charlie in amazement. "And they keep multiplying and coming up with new specialties. They have a place to ply their wares and the Spa takes thirty percent of their take. It's nuts, and after two murders here we're turning customers away, there's so many. I don't under-stand people anymore. Perhaps I never did."

"What I don't understand is how you can combine a health and beauty day spa with a twenty-four hour clinic for addicts."

"Caroline, Judith, and I became convinced that the ambiance of a spa that coddled people would be more appro-priate for those working to overcome addictions. That less of a prison atmosphere would give the addicts a cause to accom-plish more and faster. The bowel cleansing and such seems extreme but many healthy non-addicts swear by it as well. And after three days your Maggie would have been massaged and coddled too. And we work with different drugs to help them, a combination of prescription and herbal, a balance if you will, once their systems are cleansed to accept the gentler but potentially more effective treatment. I am truly sorry about your Maggie and that Judith's agent was pulled into this misunderstanding through no fault of her own. It's a tragedy. They do happen, unfortunately. Unpredictable mentalities take a horrendous toll in this world."

Twenty-Three

The area where a white Lexus drove or rolled over the cliff to the Pacific below was on the opposite side of the promontory from the earthquake crevice. Charlie, Mitch, and Warren VanZant walked across the parking lot from the ornate front gate to the edge of the pavement and the tire tracks on the other side of the yellow police tape. The tracks showed clearly in the sandy dirt between weed grasses, in places digging deeper than others as if the Lexus had been periodically gunned.

"I have a very bad feeling about all this," Warren said almost in a whisper. They had stopped a short way down the slope to look back up at the Spa where the dazzling light show winked on in stages, traveling across the horizon. Steep enough here for an uncontrolled car to roll and eventually gain speed but not so steep as to make it impossible to control. Were the skid marks from braking instead of gunning?

"This place must eat money," Mitch said.

"It does, but makes money as well. Supports itself and us and a largely itinerant staff and the most recent extensive renovation to make it more inviting to the day spa clients. There's not actually an off season. The place has been pretty much under renovation since it was built. Caroline and I are but the latest in a long line of renovators. Problem is, each renewal never quite gets finished before a new owner starts another. There was an HGTV special on it a couple of years ago as a matter of fact."

Charlie shivered in the sea breeze and wondered if her missing friends did too. She couldn't bear to think of one or both washing around chilled by death at the bottom of the sea. Dreaded images floated around behind her eyes nonetheless and a foreboding hum surprised her breathing. Mitch put a warm arm around her shoulders as they set off again, Charlie too depressed to shrug it off.

"Won't Dr. Judy's death and her backing gone, affect the bottom line here though? That's got to be a hit," Mitch kept prodding.

Later, Charlie would think it strange that Warren VanZant hadn't answered that question. Now, it was all she could do to keep her feet moving toward the precipice.

By the time they reached it, it was too dark to determine the skid marks or lack thereof in the tracks. There was enough disturbance right at the edge to be noticeable in the waning light though, a breaking away of soil on the other side of more police tape. As if perhaps the Lexus had tipped over the edge rather than careened.

"You can lean over to look, Charlie. I'll hold onto you," Mitch offered.

She could see the inlet to the marina without even leaning over, and the surf breaking white farther out. "They could have been thrown from the car when the door came off and be caught up on a ledge and alive."

"There are actually some ledges and even a shallow cave along there, but rescuers sent down on ropes didn't find anyone. A news helicopter reported seeing no one either," VanZant said.

Charlie held onto Mitch's arm to grab a fast glance over the edge, dizzy nausea arriving on cue, the marina lights and their reflection about all she could see through it in the dark, the sea wind chilling the sick sweat coating her skin. She tasted hot dog and onions when her cell went off in Mitch's pocket.

"Thought you had this set to voice mail."

"I thought so too." She carried it well away from the precipice to answer. "Libby? Where are you?"

"I'm at Doug's and so is Tuxedo and Mrs. Beesom—and

poor Mrs. McDougall's trying to get ready for the wedding yet. Have they found Maggie and Luella?"

"No honey, I'll let you know when—"

"I'm coming down. Where do I meet you? Jacob'll be home tomorrow because he's mad at the convention or whatever it was. He's such a priss."

"No, you can't. I don't need one more person to worry about now. Just—"

"Listen up, lady, I have had it with you. You hear me? You are nothing but trouble. You are totally not trustworthy. This is the third run-in with the FBI, right? In how many years? And you have the nerve to judge me? You, who can't go anywhere but what there isn't a dead body or five? You, who get your family and friends in trouble. You are simply not a responsible adult. And you don't need to worry about *me* now? You with an ulcer always ready to pop and a metal plate in your neck? What is it with you? I don't know anybody who's got a mother who's such a big pain. Why can't you behave yourself?"

"Well, she does have a point," Mitch offered tentatively when he put the cellular back in his pocket.

"You stay out of this."

"Yes, ma'am." But he held her while she cried. "Your plate's too full right now. Maybe after you get some sleep, things'll—"

"Sleep!"

"Uh . . . some rest, timeout, you know—"

"It's useless to try to reason with an alpha female-thwarted," Warren VanZant said behind them on the way back up to the Spa.

"Excuse me?" Charlie whirled. He was showing some exhaustion too.

"Charlie or her daughter?" Mitch said. "Thwarted, I mean."

"Sounds suspiciously like both. I expect it dates back to the teens—usually does. The female expecting to dominate other females and thus impress males has to step back

140

because of some calamity. Loses social status for whatever reason— loss of looks, economic upheaval in the family, weight gain, illness, simply changing junior or high schools and finding the pecking order too established to breach, whatever. But it becomes a lifelong curse, unfortunately."

"Where'd you get that crap? For one thing Charlie's not a wolf, for another she's very successful in one of the most cut-throat professions known to man and in Hollywood yet where people are used and thrown away like Kleenex. And she may be alpha but she's sure not thwarted. She never had a big life-changing event in her teens. Why . . . oh."

"Nice try, Hilsten. But thanks for the support. I do appreciate you, you know." Charlie put an arm around his waist and hugged it. Even if I'm such a shit I hate admitting it. "So Mr. VanZant, are you a shrink, educator, biologist—what?"

"Let's just say I'm well-read and in constant touch with experts in many fields of creature mentality. And I've learned more about that at the Sea Spa at the Marina del Sol than I ever wanted to know."

"Was your ex an alpha female-thwarted?"

"He has an ex?" Mitch asked.

"Dr. Judy for one. I don't know if there are others."

"Judith was far from an alpha female, let alone thwarted. But your question is exactly that of an AF-T. Read catty. It's not your fault. Nature made you that way for some reason. How did you know about Judith and me?"

"Dr. Grant Howard—the latest dead body." How Howard knew, nobody had explained.

"Oh well, it would have come to light eventually, I guess. Judith and Mrs. Howard were sorority sisters years ago. Kept in touch."

"The *Union-Tribune* was present at the time so it will probably be soon rather than eventual. You, I take it, are the father of her daughter who will lose her inheritance if she shares any of it with you?"

"That's ridiculous—you know nothing of Judith's will or

141

finances—how could you? Will that be in the *Union-Tribune* too?"

"Jesus, heads up everybody," Mitch warned in a war-zone tone. "What is this, a firing squad?"

Lights and human shadow figures had lined the curve of asphalt parking lot above them. You couldn't make out faces, just the spread of their stance. They appeared at even intervals, and they all wore pants. Handheld searchlights swept the earth around Charlie and her companions, then moved up their bodies to blind them.

All Charlie could think of was that her daughter was right. Trouble just followed her around like a stray, homeless gorilla. A savage flesh-eating, homeless gorilla.

Oh let's just feel sorry for ourself, now when we need our cool above all else.

"Oh shut up." She sat in the Spa office, the FBI across the desk this time. "Oh, I didn't mean you."

"Who did you mean?" Charles Green asked. Without the safari hat he looked a lot meaner.

"I talk to myself. Myself says something and I answer it out loud by mistake."

"How can anyone in so brutal a profession as yours is purported to be afford such lack of discipline?" Agent Green asked.

"Well, it isn't easy. I guess it's because I'm an alpha female-thwarted."

"She really is, Mr. Green, a true-to-type if ever there was one." Warren VanZant appeared decidedly more uncomfortable with the FBI than he had the San Diego County Sheriff's Department and murder. Charlie wondered what there was here to interest Agent Green. Maybe, like Charlie, VanZant had a suspicious rap sheet.

He sat next to Charlie, Mitch on her other side. Detective Solomon leaned against a bookcase, where he could make sardonic expressions behind the federal agent's back and study the three facing them both at the same time. Caroline fluttered in and out behind them—Charlie could actually hear her, a sort of fluttery, busy sound with breath.

"And you, Mr. VanZant, or your wife never dispensed drugs at this facility?"

"Sometimes we monitored guests—particularly those with major health problems and/or addictions. We often consulted with the guests' physicians before we attempted any of the cleansing or physical stress treatments."

"You mean like, never administer an enema to someone with a bad heart?"

"Not unless you've checked with his or her physician."

"Then how do you explain the mix and strength of drugs found in both Dr. Judd and Raoul Segundo?" the FBI wanted to know.

"I can't. It's that simple."

"Many of them seem, at this stage of the investigation, to be consistent with the medications prescribed for the missing Margaret Stutzman, who now it appears is somewhere on the bottom of the sea off the cliff over there. How do you explain that?"

"Perhaps she felt remorse and drove her friend's car and her friend over the edge. She was not stable mentally. That's why she was here."

Both the agent and the sheriff's deputy looked to Charlie for rebuttal, but Solomon's cell rang. He stepped out into the hall, his "ummms" and grunts still perfectly audible. "Be right down."

He returned to announce, "We got bodies. I'd like all of you to come down to the marina and help make identification."

Twenty-Four

Charlie had left the truck illegally parked in front of the yacht club and ridden up to the Sea Spa with Mitch in his rental. FBI Agent Green insisted she ride back with him. The VanZants rode down with Solomon. Mitch drove himself.

Charlie's driver hadn't even started the car before he ordered her to hand over her cellular, which Mitch still had, and asked if she realized her laptop was neither with her belongings left at the Islandia nor in her pickup.

"I didn't bring it."

"It's not in your office either."

"No."

"Everyone in your house and your little development seems to be gone."

"We're busy people. There are not many of us. And one is probably lying dead and wet to be identified at our destination." Charlie still held out hope that it wasn't so. How could she not?

"You're obviously an intelligent woman of the world. How can you ignore the seriousness of your situation?"

"It's not as serious as Maggie's, is it?"

"What would you say if I told you, we have picked up your daughter for questioning?"

"I'd say be damned careful. That kid's lethal." Since she'd just recently talked to Libby, Charlie was fairly certain he lied. She couldn't imagine what she'd left at the Islandia. Her suitcase was in the back of the extended cab of the metallic-blue Ram as was her PDA.

He pulled over, turned on the overhead light, and asked her to empty her purse in her lap. Out came her wallet, tissue, lipstick, folded plastic hairbrush, plastic container of Tic Tacs, ballpoint, eye drops for her contacts, checkbook, sunglasses, two grocery receipts, a ticket stub, and purse lint. "What's next? A strip search?"

"Way you dress, you couldn't hide a peanut." His disapproval was palpable. The man had huge ears and tiny hair that formed a gray fuzz all over a knobby head.

"I was right about the fallout from exposing the identity of the fanatics, wasn't I?"

"You have no way of interpreting any information you may think you have. You've fallen for a spin that is not true. You are not a specialist trained to interpret it and should not be allowed to disseminate it."

Charlie knew she should be allowed to feel intimidated. But she was numb to the point of hopeless. The danger here was that, according to the rabid liberals, she could just disappear and no one would have to account for it. Her mind could only dwell on what Maggie might look like after drowning in the sea, being smashed around by tides and rocks and whatever. It was impossible to imagine Luella Ridgeway with more than one hair out of place.

The metallic-blue Ram still sat parked in the no-parking zone. She didn't see a ticket on the windshield. Mitch leaned against it, arms crossed, eyes and jaw bristling with anger and suspicion like when he'd played Artemis Bard in *Hell Hath No Pity* and grabbed a guard's super-duper bullet-spraying weapon and wiped out half a village in barely fifteen frames.

Detective Solomon and Deputy Saucier arrived to escort her to a makeshift tarpaulin tent set up in the parking lot. "What took you so long?"

"He had to be intimidating and convince himself my cell phone wasn't in my purse, upset because he can't round up my daughter, neighbors, laptop—you name it." She stopped at the flap to the tarp morgue. "I don't know if I can do this.

Maggie was my best friend and Luella sort of a mentor. I think I'm going to puke or something."

But there was only one body inside. And it wasn't Maggie or Luella either.

Warren VanZant stood holding his wife against his chest, staring at Charlie in what her mood interpreted as gloating. The body was battered and bloated and awful, one eyeball all but squished out of the socket, but definitely that of Dashiell Hammett.

"Good news is, it's not your friend, Margaret Stutzman," Gordy Solomon said. "Bad news is, she's in even worse trouble than before." When they exited the morgue tent it was under lights—Jerry Parks and his photographer, front and center. Jerry too seemed to be gloating.

"Why did Detective Solomon think Maggie was in worse trouble now that Dashiell Hammett is dead? Does he think she's still alive? That she murdered him? What?"

"I don't know, Charlie. But look at the bright side. Maggie and Luella weren't found near the car. So maybe they're alive." Mitch Hilsten had managed to smuggle Charlie away to the *Motherfricker* and escape an escalating media frenzy. The divers had come in, would search again in the morning for other victims. A large fish of some kind had been mistaken for another body initially, accounting for the original report of more than one.

They had brought the VanZants too and Warren tried to comfort Caroline up on the lounge deck. Mitch and Charlie stood on the lower deck with glasses of that satin scotch. It was chilly with night and sea breeze. What was it like for Maggie right now?

"What would old Dashiell be doing with Luella's car? How do I keep Libby from coming down here and walking right into an FBI trap? I'm so blown away I'm just not cutting it right now, Mitch."

"You know, time was, the Feds would have put a tap on your phone lines, known where you were calling from. I haven't heard they can do that with these, have you?" He pulled her cell from his pocket. "I'll keep watch for Agent Green."

She had two messages. Could someone tap into her voice mail? She'd never listed this number on her letterhead or business card. But it had to be on file in the office and the office had been thoroughly gone over.

The first was a cryptic message from Luella, "Charlie, Maggie and I are at the Sea Spa. Something's terribly wrong here. I'll get back to you as soon as I can."

Charlie plopped down on a narrow shelf bench and stared at the instrument of communication in her hand. Had she just heard the voice of a dead friend? A ghost of the once smooth scotch returned up her throat to burn her tongue.

She sipped at another scotch in the *Motherfricker*'s impressive dining room where she, Mitch, and the VanZants huddled at one end of an oval table that, with the room, rendered their little group small, insignificant, and dowdy. Sidney or whoever brought in a platter of crab salad croissant sandwiches and a carafe of coffee. He studied the mood of the huddle and left the room.

Warren and Mitch tried to discuss the scenes that would be shot in this room but their companions were so dismal they gave up.

"Was there a time on that first message?" Mitch finally broke the silence.

"Five? Five forty-five, I think."

"He'd finally gotten off the drugs and alcohol," Dashiell Hammett's mother said to no one and in a deadened tone beyond feeling. "He was clean for a year. My nightmares had all but stopped. There's nothing more devastating than an adult child you can't help and you can't help their hurt and they can't help but hurt you." No tears, she barely blinked, picked up her sandwich, set it down twice without taking a bite. "He'd worked so hard." Her melodious voice had flattened.

"Caroline," her husband said softly, "it's time for your medications."

*   *   *

147

The second message left on her voice mail had been from Kenny Cowper—both Maggie and Luella's luggage had disappeared from the hotel. "Hope you took yours because it's gone too. Hope you're okay. I'm on my way to the Spa."

Charlie had left a message that she was down at the marina and to call her back, but he hadn't yet. Her suitcase was still locked in the back of the extended cab of the Ram, she hoped.

"The press up at the Spa is going to be almost as bad as down here. What do we do?"

"My car is on this side of the bridge, give me your keys and I'll see if I can get someone to steal your truck and take it up to the Spa. I'll take you and the VanZants in my passenger-concealing rental. Just for the hell of it, why don't you try to get a hold of Luella?"

All Charlie got was Luella's professional voice mail. Even that was painful to listen to. Charlie left a message anyway, that she was heading up to the Sea Spa.

Charlie sat alone on the *Motherfricker*'s deck and watched the night, tried to make a connection between Dr. Judy's hyping of the product, Redux, as well as the hotly contested HRT treatments for women, and four murders including her own—between the Sea Spa at the Marina del Sol and the Film Institute—between prescription drug peddling and profiting from screenwriter hopefuls.

It was all about communication for profit, about misleading people—what was she missing here?

In Mitch's Stealth on the way up to the Spa, she asked the VanZants who Judith Judd's lover was and got one connection. She also noticed a new message on her cell. It was Libby telling her she was headed for the Spa because her mother hadn't answered her last message. Charlie called Libby to inform her daughter's voice mail that she must absolutely stay away from that place at all costs but to let Charlie know where she was going. "Keegan's at Les Artistes in Del Mar. A better place to head for because something very deadly is going on at the Spa."

But when Mitch's Stealth breached the promontory Libby's Jeep was already parked in the lot.

Twenty-Five

"Oh shit," Charlie said as the other Agent Green pulled up behind Mitch's rental. At least Libby's Jeep was empty and the people getting out of the low black Stealth probably didn't know who the dented Wrangler belonged to. Maybe Mitch, but she didn't think so. And probably not Charles Green, who worked so hard to imply he knew all, either. It sat at the end of a short line of cars, and Mitch *would* pull right in next to it instead of starting a new line.

Two San Diego sheriff's cars were parked there too so Charlie's daughter might be safe with them—but she didn't want Libby and Charles meeting up.

Charlie couldn't remember when she slept last. The crab salad croissants and scotch did help to keep the jitters at bay. A cup of coffee wouldn't hurt about now—wouldn't you know she was at probably the only place in Southern California where she couldn't get one.

How can you be thinking about such banal things when three of the most important people in your life are hopefully just in danger and not dead? "I don't know."

"Oh really? I thought you knew everything," the funny-haired agent in safari dress said pleasantly.

Kenny Cowper's flashy red rental pulled up to extend the line. Even so, there weren't an awful lot of people here.

"You don't know what?" the FBI man insisted, adding a touch of triumph to his pleasantness.

"I don't know where my friends are. Hi, Kenny, this is Mitch. Mitch, this is Kenny." And this has got to be a bad dream, right? "Oh, boy."

*   *   *

Charlie Greene decided she had a plan and was about to attempt an escape when she smelled the coffee. The VanZants, the Feds—three in number now—Charlie, Mitch, and Kenny, Sue Rippon, and Ruth Ann Singer sat in the Spa's kitchen at a long staff table. Somebody on the other side of a head-high partition was making coffee. Smelled like the real thing—as in caffeinated.

Dr. Grant Howard of the San Diego Film Institute had been Dr. Judy's lover. That was the connection between the Sea Spa and the Institute. And they were both murdered—another connection.

"So, Dr. Judith Judd prescribed medicines for your son's condition, is that right, Mrs. VanZant?" asked a man sitting next to Charles Green. He had a folder of papers he rustled through and tilted his head back to study them through bifocals. Neither he nor the gentleman on the other side of the FBI agent had bothered to introduce themselves. All three were so smug, intimidating, and patronizing Charlie would have been furious if she weren't so worried about her friends and her daughter, if she weren't so very weary.

"Judith was one of his doctors," Warren answered for his wife.

"He was addicted to drugs so you all gave him drugs?" Charlie asked. She'd always had trouble getting her head around that one.

"Just because you're allergic to milk doesn't mean you can't drink water. Dashiell was on medications to control his addiction to drugs and alcohol. The medications were for behavior control and cravings, not euphoria. It's possible to forget to take medications. They are definitely needed but one does not feel the need."

"There's a pill for everything." Charlie accepted a hot mug of the evil brew with a grateful sigh, refusing cream or sugar, wondering if there was a pill for caffeine addiction, vowing to flush it down the toilet if it was ever prescribed for her. This wasn't euphoria as much as an aid for getting through a horrible night. Right? Their server was Deputy Saucier of the San Diego County Sheriff's Department. She had a cute pug nose just right for her face. Where was Solomon?

Caroline VanZant wept softly into her hand and Charlie felt like a creep for questioning Dashiell's treatment. If she'd seen Libby in the condition Caroline had her son a few hours ago she would not have waxed flippant either. Did whoever killed Dashiell have Maggie and Luella, Libby even? The thought turned the coffee sour in her stomach and she set the mug down.

"And your daughter and her cell phone appear to have disappeared from the face of the earth, Mrs. Greene," said the smug Fed to the left of Agent Green. "I should think that would worry a mother." He was the youngest of the three but with only a fringe of head hair left.

"It's Miss Greene. I have never married. And I'm always worried about my daughter. How do you know her cell is missing?"

His scorn seemed triumphantly justified by Libby's father-less state. "I suppose you don't even know which one was the father."

"Kenny, leave it," Charlie warned the stud beside her as he threatened to bestir himself. "As a matter of fact I do and he's a creep."

"Next time your daughter uses her cellular, we've got her. Been having some trouble with the system, but it's all fixed now. You might as well tell us where she is. You are both suspected of interfering with a federal investigation."

Agent Charles Green asked to see her purse again. And again found no cell—not even her little address book, both having been hurriedly secreted in the crack between the front rider's seat and the gearshift console in Mitch's rental. Not that hard to find if they went searching for it, but all Charlie could manage in the time she had upon her arrival tonight.

"Your 'system' must be pretty crowded if you monitor all the cells in Southern California," Mitch said.

"Only selected frequencies or signals. And if you have nothing to hide it should be of no consequence. There will be some glitches, that's to be expected, but—"

"Yeah, like when I was getting your e-mail," Charlie said. "What?" bifocals said. "It wasn't in code?"

"Her daughter decoded it."

"Ahhhh well, we must speak to her then, mustn't we?" Bifocals relaxed back into his smirk.

Charlie, who'd studied no more history than the general required courses in college, tried to remember if it was somebody named McCarthy or something called the Inquisition where religious fanatics tortured witches or, under that pretext, anybody who got in their way. She often listened to NPR on her long commute, but spent many interruptions on her cell, talking to New York before her contacts went to lunch. She had assumed the government just listened in on foreign terrorists abroad or when found in the country.

Charlie rarely voted because she had all she could do to keep her head straight on work, personal, and family matters, so she rarely registered political stuff. A single mom with a scary teen, incipient ulcer, titanium plate in her neck, felonious feline, and a high-stress job can only compute so much without risking insanity. But, as often as she'd run into trouble with official types since her move to California, Charlie wished now she'd paid more attention. Not that she believed one person could make enough difference to change anything, but it is wise to be forewarned when the "rabids" are in charge of anything. Both rabid rights and rabid lefts drove her nuts. And then add the rabid religious and any attempt at reason was useless.

"Now I assume, Mr. VanZant, that you are aware of the vast wealth your previous wife salted away offshore." The Fed with the bifocals peered over them at Warren with a quick side glance at VanZant's present wife. "And that all the money is to be doled out to your daughter and granddaughter by a trust, with the stipulation that none of the money goes to you or the Sea Spa or several other individuals named."

"Judith was paid well to promote certain types of medications, but not brands, in her public appearances. I was not privy to exact figures, but was aware that our daughter and granddaughter would be well taken care of should something happen to their mother."

"She was paid a percentage of royalties for promoting types of medications, which is unethical but not illegal—hormones, anti-inflammatories, mood stabilizers—in other words, happy pills."

"To relieve misery, not to induce euphoria. There is a difference."

"Warren," Sue Rippon interrupted as Caroline VanZant rolled her head back and slid to the floor.

Charlie felt a lot like doing the same.

"Hey, my daughter, my best friend, and my mentor may be out here somewhere dead or alive in pain or in grave danger of one or all those things. Will you guys get real?" Charlie told the studs.

It's your own fault for getting involved with these types.

"I know. Now shut up."

The studs looked at her and then each other and shrugged, but still with proper squints of hostility, and said almost in tandem, "She talks to herself."

"Knock it off," Charlie warned.

They were wandering in the garden of pseudo earthquake Grecian, Roman ruins with two wimpy flashlights and a waning moon to light their way. One of them grabbed her as she was about to sprain an ankle, dislocate a knee, or bust her head missing a ruined step down into the cracked basin where the well-hung Mediterranean boy leaned over the crevice that snaked across the length of the promontory.

After Caroline VanZant did her fainting thing and brought the inquisition to a halt, and Detective Solomon arrived within minutes to report some matter of apparently grave significance—Charlie and "the guys" had the opportunity to slip away and took it. Actually, Charlie took off by herself and they chose to follow. If they got in trouble—it was their choice. She had people out here to look for and intended to do just that before she succumbed like Caroline VanZant had. Besides, she couldn't breathe without getting off that chair and taking action of some kind. Her head throbbed with the need to search for those most important to her.

Mitch fished a coin out of his pocket and dropped it down into the crevice. It didn't seem to ever land or to bounce off ledges either. "I don't see how they can monitor transmissions on selected cell phones in a place so crowded with conversations as Southern California. I mean . . . if you can't search out and destroy spam before it clogs computer networks . . . I don't claim to be able to keep up on technology, but it just doesn't ring true."

Kenny Cowper stepped up on a broken rock ledge so he could look even farther down on the superstar. Night light cast him a faint shadow. "So, you think those guys in there are faking it?"

"I think they believe what they are told to believe because they believe in their leaders and we all believe what we want to, doesn't make them all that different from the rest of us."

"Like assuming Middle Easterners are national, rather than tribal," Charlie said. Even she knew that, although she couldn't remember why. "Oh yes I do, a screenplay that never made it, *Wag the Camel*."

"Charlie, I think you should go lie down somewhere." Mitch aimed the business end of the flashlight into the crevice, walked toward the sea as far as the night and the condition of the ruins allowed, turned back and stopped to bend closer to the fissure. "Jesus, look at this."

Twenty-Six

"Friend of mine got an assignment from *The Times* to investigate the problem of government use of technologies that change faster than people can be trained for it. Lots of the bugs are discovered when the new technology is out on the market and by the time it's perfected a new and better product is developed by the same or a competing company. Government moves too slowly when retraining people and can't just fire the old specialists and hire new every time that happens because of seniority issues and those hired because of connections to congressmen, senior staff, and so on." Kenny Cowper sat on the ledge now and dangled his feet over the side, Charlie and Mitch on the base of a pedestal that no longer supported its statue. The pedestal leaned and they leaned against it. It was almost comfortable.

"Wow, how come you didn't get that assignment?" his agent wanted to know.

"She has better connections than I do."

Charlie was afraid to find her daughter and friends and afraid not to. Fear and fatigue had brought her to this impasse and she couldn't make a decision, couldn't risk making the wrong one. If any were alive, she could put them in danger of being located, if they were dead it didn't matter. They would all have normally pulled out their cell phones to locate somebody, but were afraid to now. Kenny was the only one who had his on him.

"So your point is?" Mitch insisted. "We worry more about Big Brother or less because the guys in the trenches can't keep up with the advances of spying on us?"

"I don't know. But now that we're trying to monitor communications all over the world it seems likely there'd be gigantic probabilities for error. A whole lot of innocent people could be falsely jailed and charged on inaccuracies in the information gathering. I guess that's already true some-what—but now it would be on a far grander scale."

They sat there in pretty much a state of exhaustion wait-ing for dawn and for an official in some capacity to track them down, tell them what to do or not to do, show him what they'd found in the crevice.

"I vote we take a chance. Do something. Before Charlie wigs-out on us."

Kenny drew his cell, flipped it open.

"I second the motion. Charlie, we've got to get something moving here." Mitch put an arm around her shoulders. "I'd sure be relieved if you'd just cry."

Charlie mumbled Libby's cell phone number, watched Kenny punch it, heard the improbable tinkle of a John Philip Sousa march. It came from the jagged fracture. She could hear her daughter's voice message explain that "Libby Greene" in Libby's voice was unable to get back to him but if he'd leave a name, number, and good reason—she'd make an attempt.

Kenny repunched the number twice and twice it rang from the crevice where Charlie and Mitch were pulling out an assort-ment of clothes and prescription medicine vials, CDs, and sheets of paper that could be records, too dark to tell. "Careful you don't dislodge it and send it to the center of the earth."

That's why they hadn't searched the stuff crammed into this section of the opening to begin with.

"Charlie, none of them can have gone down that hole. It's not wide enough for them to fall forever down there."

"They could be under all this though. Caught up some-where. Libby? It's me. Can you hear me? Maggie? Luella? They could be hurt or—I am not going to cry. I hate it when I cry."

"That tough-girl image is rough to maintain, huh?"

156

"Don't push your luck, Cowper," Charlie warned.

"Yes, ma'am."

"This it?" Mitch held up somebody's cell. He opened it and read the lighted screen. "This is it."

"Stick it in your pocket, Hilsten, and quick. Be sure it's turned off," Kenny whispered behind them. "Both of you get back to your pedestal. Company approacheth."

Charlie saw the dance of high powered flashlights before she heard the approach of authorities or reached the pedestal. Kenny was shoving stuff back into the crevice, but slowly and carefully, when he was yanked away.

"You will be happy to know that we have located your daughter's cellular telephone from satellite, Miss Greene," bifocals gloated. "Take them back to the lodge, deputy," he ordered just as he tripped on a shadow, misjudging his step down to something that existed only by moonlight and was caught by Deputy Lydia Saucier, the quickest, most agile, youngest, and probably strongest of those close by. He managed to fall on her nonetheless.

Kenny grabbed Charlie's elbow and had her started for the "lodge" before Deputy Lydia could squirm out from under the Fed and a fair way to their destination before Mitch caught up.

"You'd better have Libby Greene's cell on you, Cowper."

"Dinna worra, 'tis safe wi' me, man."

"Do you think the satellite found it when we rang it up?" Charlie asked.

"Don't know. How's that deputy doing on the catch-up?"

"She appears to be lagging," Mitch answered, irritation still evident in his voice. "Seems to be diverted by a conversation on her cell."

"Good, now heads up. We'll give her a chance to lose us by ducking behind the first shed or cottage we come to. Methinks she's not trying overhard there."

"Just who was it put you in charge, Steeplehead?" Mitch said in the low flat tones of Eddie Valance in *The Alleys Between Mean Streets*.

157

"Dinna get your back up, Shorty. Now!" Kenny dropped Charlie's elbow, lifted her by the waist, and she felt like she was flying behind this rundown cottage and then stuffed inside it.

"Charlie, we really don't think you should be doing this— we've pushed some pretty powerful people too far already and we don't know it was Libby driving—"

"Speak for yourself, Hilsten."

They'd ducked down beside Mitch's car, trying to hide from county and federal authorities and Charlie was leaning across the driver's seat groping for her cell and address book.

"What, you think she should try to run out now? How far do you think she'll get?" Mitch said.

Charlie had insisted upon getting out here and finding her phone to see if Libby had left a message on it before it was taken from her. Nobody seemed to be around to stop them. But just as they walked out the ornate gate, Libby's battered Wrangler sped off out of the lot almost hitting Charlie's truck coming in.

"No, I don't think she should take off now. Doesn't mean you can speak for me. You got a problem with that?"

"Kenny," Charlie admonished, stuffing phone and address book in her purse.

"Well, I get torqued, I start talking in clichés."

"That was Libby's Jeep that just took off out of here. Give me her cell," she told the tall stud and asked the kid who'd driven her truck in for the keys. "You want a ride down to the wye?"

"Charlie, you won't make it to the 101 and—"

"What are you, Hilsten, her daddy?"

"Will you just butt out, whatever-your-name-is?"

"You boys behave now. I'll let you know what's happening when I can."

"What are they doing?" Charlie asked the kid as the Ram roared out of there.

"Well, the tall one took a swing and the short one ducked

and rammed the tall one in the stomach. Last I saw they were both on the ground."

By the time she'd let him off at the wye to walk back down to the marina and made it to the 101, the sky was lightening, and she had no idea which way to turn. So she headed north, expecting to be pulled over at any minute. Rush hour hadn't gotten off to much of a start yet and most of the night life had made it home to bed. Her bag was still in the back of the cab. She had plenty of gas. The air came cool and pleasantly ocean-scented through the open window. It felt good to be taking some action, doing something instead of being done unto. The terrible ache brought on by finding Libby's cell in that crevice, had lifted some with the sudden disappearance of the Wrangler. It might not be Libby but it might be too and it was even possible she was obeying her mother's orders and heading for Del Mar—although that was a long shot.

Not as long a shot as Charlie and the Dodge Ram making it that far before being pulled over by a sheriff's car or highway patrol but nothing ventured—

She rested her elbow on the window frame and took the first really deep breath in hours, straightened grateful neck, back, and shoulders. "One thing at a time, one thing at a time, one thing at a time."

She was still repeating this mantra, inside her head at least, when she pulled into Les Artistes. It was right off the highway at the southern edge of Del Mar. It sat down from the highway and was easy to miss, which was curious, because it exuded color, perhaps because the color was real and not neon. Charlie had noted it in passing before because it was a favored spot of her prize screenwriter. She had to turn down the side street next to it and off that into a small setback parking lot in front of it.

It was a small motel, two-story with a balcony, maybe eight or nine rooms with an office down and nine rooms up, hard to tell because every last square inch was decorated with color swatches or cut-out lattice work, painted fish or butterflies or birds. Flowers hung in pots and rioted from earthenware and little patch gardens below. Wind chimes whispered, tinged, clanked, and clattered from every hook not dangling a bird feeder, from covered walkways below and above.

Charlie's first thought was disbelief that she'd made it this far without being stopped. The second was disappointment that Libby's Wrangler wasn't parked there. It was still early. The Amtrak or Coaster roared by down on the tracks near the sea, its horn bleating warning.

Worried, tired, hungry, thirsty, sore, and stiff, Charlie was still momentarily free to do what she wished. She couldn't face the thought that Libby Abigail Greene, Maggie Stutzman, and Luella Ridgeway might not be so privileged. Somebody else could easily have stolen the Wrangler and taken off with it, headed south where Charlie headed north on the Pacific Highway. But of all the cars in the lot at the Sea Spa at the Marina del Sol why would anyone choose the beat-up Wrangler?

On that more hopeful thought, Charlie slid out of the Ram to the cracked concrete. She could at least find Keegan Monroe. She needed a hug. She did not expect what she found inside.

Twenty-Seven

Charlie sidestepped a big man with a big smile, and an armload of used bedding on its way to the laundry room, and a couple bumping luggage on wheels across a mixture of decorated ceramic tiles and blocks of natural rock out to their car. In the process she ran into the carved figure of an Indian chief with a cigar and a low-hanging wind chime of colored-glass dolphins, and she'd thought the Sea Spa had a busy decor. If she hadn't been wearing sunglasses she'd have poked her eye out on that cigar.

The double doors to the office stood open and no one sat in the chair behind the desk but voices came over an open-topped partition and so did the odor of cooking. She walked around it instead of ringing the bell, as a sign requested, to see Libby Abigail Greene sitting at an ancient round pedestal table with Keegan Monroe and Brodie Caulfield.

"This is a motel, not a bed and breakfast you understand," said the man at an antique gas stove, "but any friend of Keegan Monroe is a—"

"She's my agent," Keegan said.

"Well in that case, she gets two eggs. Sit yourself in my chair, Charlie. I'll take the stool here at the bar." The man at the stove was bald with a fuzzy muzzle, plump rather than fat, and tall. A faint twinkle in his eyes softened an otherwise somber expression.

Brodie pulled out a chair for her, poured her some orange juice from a pitcher and said, "You look frazzled, lady. Did you park your metallic blue bomb out front?" When she nodded, drinking in the sight of her daughter whole, alive, healthy, and

161

eating with gusto, he said, "Give me your keys, I'll move it around to the side so it won't be visible from the road."

Charlie handed him the keys, took a sip of the orange juice, touched Libby's cheek with the back of her fingers, and broke into sobs.

"Mom, it's okay," the kid said softly and stroked the hair on top of Charlie's head like she did Tuxedo's. "What about Maggie and Luella?"

"You don't know?"

"No, you must have got my message. You're here."

"There, there . . . you'll be all right now. You're safe with us." Their bald host placed huge strong hands on Charlie's shoulders, digging into her lower neck with his thumbs and pulling back her shoulder bones with his hands. It hurt and felt good at the same time. "And so is your sprout. How about we feed you and then ask questions?"

Numbed by relief and exhaustion, Charlie ate the eggs benedict he'd just poached for himself. They sat on a bed of al dente asparagus spears instead of a muffin and with sliced fruit and banana bread. When she'd finished and sat back with coffee and the hiccups, Charlie decided she might live after all. "That's the best bearnaise I ever met."

Her host sat in Brodie's chair next to her with his freshly poached benedict and nodded his condescension. Brodie perched on the stool with coffee freshened.

"You did get my message, right?" Libby sat back in her chair so that a cat with a squashed-up nose and the size of a dog with big hair could jump on her lap.

"Oh Libby, you're so beautiful. I thought you were dead." The cat was suddenly on her lap now.

"No, Fluffy, she hates cats."

"Hates cats?" their host said, offended. "Well, I take back my welcome, agent or no."

Fluffy's cold nose moved from Charlie's neck under and behind her ear so her embarrassed sobbing was muffled in its fur. You went a long way into that fur before you came to cat.

"I've never known a kitty to offer sympathy before—

162

disdain, condescension, demands, but look at that. Fluffy, what's that Jezebel done to you?"

"It's because she doesn't like cats," Brodie said. "They have a diabolical need to snuggle up to those who can't stand them. Won't let me near her and I love cats. Watch. Come here, kitty, let me give you a snuggle."

Kitty moaned warning, hissed, spat, and jumped to the floor leaving Charlie with a face full of fur.

"Mom, about Maggie and Luella?" Libby said with a great show of patience Charlie figured would last about two more seconds.

"They weren't in Luella's car that went off the cliff— somebody else's body was—the son of one of the owners of the Spa. I don't know where they are. I thought you might have been with them and could tell me they're at least alive too. What were you doing up there?"

"Looking for you. I told you I was coming. You'd said I should come here instead and I did after those freaks started chasing me all over the place. I lost my cell and car keys— but I had an extra key hidden under the hood on that magnet thingy you gave me for Christmas. And I left you a message on your cell."

Libby had been snooping among the cottages and gardens behind the Sea Spa at the Marina del Sol, wondering where everyone was, when she heard the sound of women's voices somewhere and was trying to trace them when "this creepo came barging down a path at me with his arms full of file folders and I think floppy disks and maybe CDs and when he saw me he dropped everything and came after me, swearing and calling me a bitch and wanting to know who I was and he tripped and went down grabbing my wallet purse and I went down too."

"Were you hurt?"

"I'm fine, can't say the same for him—"

"You didn't—"

"Oh Mom, I got him so good—he wasn't expecting anything. He's gonna have bruised nuts for life."

163

The three guys stared at the willowy blonde in silence and Charlie couldn't blame them. That euphoria and triumph on the classic features—totally free of zits this week—the long fingers rearranging the platinum hair which fell back into place to cup her face when she let go of it. The combination of how she looked and what she said scared Charlie too.

"You enjoy hurting people?" their host asked.

"Just creepos. If I had my way they'd fall over dead at once, everyone of them and all over the world, just walking down the street or something."

"Do you think the voices you heard could have been Maggie and Luella?" Charlie asked, daring to hope again, and not as bothered by Libby's daydream of destroying "creepos" as the men at the table seemed to be. Maybe it was a female fantasy thing, but Charlie still dared to dream it sometimes. She didn't imagine herself "taking" them down like Libby did though.

"Why don't you try their cell phones?" Libby asked.

Charlie tried instead to explain the concept of satellites tracking cellulars. And how Kenny calling Libby's number made it ring in the earthquake crevice and all of a sudden the Feds showed up. She took it out of her purse. "But Mitch and I found it first and I got out of there with it. I'm afraid they could track Libby here if she uses it."

"I don't think that's possible." Brodie swooped in on the snub-nosed feline who'd leapt onto a cupboard shelf and held it upside down in one arm while reaching for the cell on his belt with the other. "Especially if your answering service got a message and then you accessed it later."

"So if I listened to my messages now, nobody could trace me here, right?"

Charlie asked and held out an empty coffee cup.

"You were both up all night. Eddie and Sang Waa have about got a room ready for you," their host, Wallie, warned but poured a refill anyway.

Obviously no one in the room understood the cell technology that well, although everyone of them had one and the very thought of the severance of this umbilical cord to life and the world as they knew it caused all but Fluffy to go silently inward and contemplative. This was an isolating and personal terrorist threat of silent but unimaginable proportions.

"What do we do if it rings, Mom?" Libby asked later when they stood in the newly vacated and now restored Georgia O'Keeffe room. "Couldn't we at least listen to our messages?"

"I don't know, honey. I'm afraid to and afraid not to. I see they didn't confiscate your backpack. There were all these clothes stuffed into the crevasse with papers and pill bottles and your cell. I thought some of them might have been yours."

"I don't think so. It was in the Wrangler when I took off out of there." But she unzipped what she considered luggage. It was a large backpack with a pull-out handle and wheels to be towed as well as shoulder straps so it could be carried on the back. It actually held an amazing amount of stuff. "This is a weird place, huh?"

"It's certainly artistic." How could they let Libby dash off in her car that way, and Charlie too? Something funny about this whole business.

Copies of colorful paintings and smaller practice drawings of the artist, a lone voluptuous flower blossom with curved petals in bright colors standing out on a dark background on a large canvas where a lesser artist would have painted a whole tree.

"A rustic southwestern mission look to the decor," Libby said when Charlie stepped out of the shower. It actually had a curtain.

"How do you know that? Are you into interior design now?" Anything would be better than the model, movie star, hopeful, waitress, retail clerk reality pit.

"There're little signs everywhere explaining this room and the 'artiste' who designed it. Let's take a nap and then decide whether to check our voice mail. I'm taking the couch. You can have the bed."

"I'll set the alarm for two hours."

The room was divided into sitting room and bedroom by a shoulder-high partition that had art nooks and shelves. Charlie opened the front door and locked the screen, drew the curtains over the front window. Outside, across the narrow cobbled general walkway to the lower floor rooms was their own little outdoor breakfast arbor with a small yellow and blue inlaid tabletop on an iron pedestal, chairs, and a tiny splashing fountain in the wall, sheltered from the parking lot and highway above with bougainvillaea, potted plants and vines, hummingbird feeders, and latticework.

Inside, on the wall opposite the queen-size stood an armoire in brushed mingled tones of faded turquoise and blue, a large mirror over a sink, small fridge, and corner cupboard with a TV on top. She opened the backdoor for ventilation too. Here, a tiny rock patio looked out on a narrow garden running the length of the motel like an alley, but filled with potted plants and small trees as well as planted ones with an occasional flowered bush. Two wooden chairs nestled in among the vegetation. Someday when she wanted a getaway—this might be fun. But they hadn't even bothered to unpack. Their world permitted little peace or leisure now.

She was reminded of that thought when they awoke suddenly to the shrill pandemonium of sirens, an indecipherable message on a bullhorn, thundering engine noise on the street outside, and a helicopter flying low overhead.

Charlie's grownup, independent, tough, testicle-mashing daughter flew out of nowhere to land on the bed.

Twenty-Eight

"We better get on the floor in case they start shooting in here, Mom."

Charlie's heart was still in shock when she hit the bristly rug with Libby on top of her. Just when it seemed the noise began to let up it got worse instead, shaking the funky little chandelier and tilting a Spanish cross on the wall.

"Those guys are really mad at us, huh? What do we do, wave a white flag or what? We didn't even use our cells."

Frenzied shouting in the parking lot, moaning and groaning and screaming—

"Is it an earthquake?" Charlie ventured. "Maybe they're not after us, maybe—"

"I gotta pee!"

"Well don't do it here." Her slender daughter was taller and chestier than Charlie, surprisingly heavy. Charlie tried to squirm out from under but Libby slid off and slithered on her stomach toward the bathroom. Charlie started after on hands and knees.

"Mah-om."

Charlie locked the door behind them and pulled herself up to peer out the small window. All she could see was the back of a man's neck but she recognized it. She widened the crack and whispered, "Keegan? Is it the Feds? Have they found us?"

"You guys up? Come on out and watch the show."

"What do you mean show? All the sirens and shouting and traffic and helicopters?" But Keegan's grin got her out there, where Wallie, Brodie, and Eddie stood out in the open entryway in front of the office, two of them with cameras and Wallie trying to keep a terrified Fluffy from climbing his face. Triage

167

people strove to diagnose possible survivors in the parking lot, one dead man giving them the finger when their backs were turned. The hovering, sinister helicopter was clearly marked as at work for a television news station instead of the black, low-flying types Charlie once encountered near Groom Lake in Nevada. It was a scheduled, federally mandated, emergency response drill, that local officials and emergency and medical types must participate in today. Charlie vaguely remembered reading or hearing something about it.

The sound of the alarm back in the room managed to pierce the din out here on the rough stone slabs leading to the entrance of Les Artistes. Libby slipped in to turn it off. She'd regained her composure a lot sooner than her mother.

A San Diego County Sheriff's cruiser pulled up almost in front of Charlie in the separate parking lot between that of the motel and the Pacific Highway. She slipped behind the stalwart Wallie, but Detective Gordy Solomon didn't even look her way. He stood with cell to ear, gesturing at the emergency pandemonium drill as if describing it to someone at the other end of the conversation and shaking his head, appalled and frustrated by what he saw. Where, Charlie wondered, was his saucy sidekick, Lydia Saucier? And why wasn't he at the Sea Spa at the Marina del Sol helping out the Feds and looking for Maggie and Luella?

If Charlie had been in a less troubled mood and time she'd have found the scene hilarious. A couple of young boys with huge grins and some kind of futuristic laser-sword weaponry slashed through the fallen dead and wounded, squealing, and escaped from sight around a stranded semi across the side street. But a couple of belly dancers were herded off by stern-visaged plainclothes before they could get properly wound up. Charlie slipped quietly back to the Georgia O'Keeffe room and out of sight—she was most probably on a wanted list about now—only to find lovely Libby sprawled across the bed on her stomach, Fluffy stretched across the small of her back, Libby's feet and her legs in the air from the knee and crossed at the ankles.

"Libby, I told you about using your cellular and being traced. What—"

"Mom, chill. Okay? Oh, my mother's blowing fuses again. So—they really can't trace cells that well yet? What's the deal on the wedding and is Tux behaving himself, and dorky Jacob back to take care of Mrs. Beesom? Um . . . yeah . . . okay. Sounds like you better keep the laptops and the cat hidden for awhile."

Charlie stepped out onto the tiny back deck/patio, expecting Solomon to come pounding on the door any second. So what difference did it make now if Libby used her phone? In fact, if Charlie was about to be taken into custody or something she'd better get busy checking some of her own calls.

She ignored the first four, listened to one from her boss wanting to know what had happened to Luella Ridgeway, but didn't return it. The narrow backyard was a jungle of palmy, ferny, swordy, spiky leaves and fronds—all making scratchy whispers in a light sea breeze. Was it that sheltered back here or had the exercise in chaos out front and above ended suddenly?

The next call was from Detective Gordon Solomon. He needed to know what she knew about Sarah Newman, the murdered Grant Howard's sister-in-law. Charlie didn't answer that one either. She'd be seeing him any minute anyway. The next from Maggie's maybe lawyer, wanting to know if Maggie had been found and in what condition. And then Mitch's call—where the "hell" was she? Charlie was about to answer that one when she thought better of it—what if "they" had forced him to send that message and were ready to trace her here? But then Solomon was already here. Still, she sensed they were two different sets of "theys."

There was lots of ratty, jagged bark, three foot canoe-shaped leaves down here, poofs of piney spines high overhead on ends of monstrous branches. Some leaves like swords. Even a potted bamboo tree, about ten foot high. She knew that because a sign sticking in the pot told her so.

"Mom," Libby snuck up behind her, "here. Hilsten, your elderly creepo, wants to talk to you. He's been trying to get you."

"Libby, he's only forty something. They could be using him to get to us." But Charlie took Libby's cell. Mitch was at the marina. He didn't know where Kenny was. Neither had any more trouble driving away from the Sea Spa than Charlie or Libby. "What do you think's going on? Mitch, did Kenny hurt you?"

"No, I hurt him. And I think there's a hell of a disconnect happening at the Sea Spa and I'll bet elsewhere. You and Libby sit tight until I—"

"Mitch, Detective Solomon's out front in the parking lot right now."

"No he's not," Libby said behind her. "They've almost all left the fright scene."

Then Mitch explained the "disconnect." According to a local news "leak" the federal government had mandated a search into the financial files of the Sea Spa at the Marina del Sol and conscripted local county officials to aid them, while another federal agency had scheduled months ago many of the same departments to conduct the Emergency Response Drill. "The ease with which we all drove out of there tells me most of the sheriff's department chose to honor the previous commitment."

After the disdainful attitude of those people sitting across the coffee cups from Charlie at the Spa in the wee hours, Charlie didn't blame them. "So no one's even looking for Maggie and Luella? What if they're alive and tied up somewhere and—"

"Charlie, don't go there, leave it alone for a few hours at least. Things are too unpredictable and volatile right now. I'm going to see if I can wrangle a way up there on the sly and—"

"Mitch, you can't go anywhere on the sly. Everybody over thirty knows you on sight."

"Okay, I'll wrangle a disguise then. Just sit tight till I call."

Charlie wondered, considering all the "wrangle" talk, if he'd scheduled an upcoming Western project—the man was on self-destruct. She returned Libby's phone. The kid was splayed majestically across the other wooden chair and onto the wooden deck railing with ankles and feet, like a graceful wet noodle, the whole effect ruined by her jaw movement.

Hey, she's alive, remember? So she's chewing gum. That's one thing she doesn't do gracefully, but yeah, you're even right for once.

"Ma-ahhmm, don't get all googly-eyed again," Libby warned. "You're creeping me."

"He wants us to stay here, let him snoop around the Sea Spa to find a trace of what's happened to Luella and Maggie. I don't want to have to start worrying about him too."

"I think it's time you started worrying about you. So does Grandma."

"She called again?"

"I called her."

"Ohgod. Tell me she's not coming out. I can't take anymore."

"She will if I call."

"Is this a power play? Remember your grandmother is up against semester exams and whatever about now and she's no longer a young woman."

"Yes, this is a power play and you remember she has grad assistants to handle that and the lab work now."

"And a desert rat manuscript due soon."

"And a daughter who's losing it."

Pine needles dried to brown stuck out of the ends of the tiles in the roof overhang, washed down from upper tiers of tiles when it rained. The lot across the alley-garden had humongous trees not quite hiding a good-sized house and . . . Charlie woke to the Coastal, warning all that it was roaring through on tracks down by the sea and by a hummingbird fluttering up to some kind of bell-shaped flower above her head and then down to check on her face. It was so peaceful out here she felt drunk with it. Her back hurt, her mouth was dry, only Fluffy occupied the other chair out here now. Her watch said she'd slept for two hours more. Where was everybody?

Out front two men picked up trash left by the homeland "disaster" and threw it in the back of a pickup. The front parking lot didn't belong to Les Artistes and was home to craft fairs and farmer's markets on weekends, Keegan explained. He and Brodie sat at the little table across from her window in the shade of all the hanging debris. Libby had walked up to the local convenience store/deli within sight on the corner.

She brought back a tuna salad sub to split with her mother, a six pack of Diet Coke, and a newspaper, the *San Diego Union-Tribune*.

"Libby, you don't read newspapers—what's the deal here?"

Libby set it down on the crowded table and the men had to lift their beer bottles. "I saw it on the counter up at the little store. That's the guy whose nuts I did my best to crack last night."

"It was dark on that path, honey. How can you be sure?"

"We got up close and personal."

"Wow, he was so incensed at my pitch," Brodie said. "Didn't want to hear the truth about the real profits to be made on starry-eyed hopefuls. How could anyone in his profession live so close to Hollywood and not know that? It's hardly news."

"You don't understand, Brodie," Keegan said. "You know it's rampant in other professions, even those related to your dream-wish one, but you don't want to believe it true in yours so bad, you won't listen to reason. It's like a wish fulfilling drug or something—I could probably rewrite that better but I'm too relaxed."

Charlie wished he'd rewrite it for Libby, tried to ignore how long her own mother'd had to support her and her daughter until Charlie could make a living as an agent.

It was front page but not the headline story. Small picture and article about a reporter receiving a national award for an exposé on drug companies handing out enormous amounts of sample drugs to local doctors and therapists. It was Jerry Parks. He'd been carrying records and whatever toward the chasm at the Sea Spa at the Marina del Sol. Helping the VanZants hide evidence of something?

Twenty-Nine

"Mom? I hate to do this to you but, I've got a confession to make. Actually two."

Ohgod not now. Why was it when Charlie couldn't take any more there always was some? They'd walked downhill toward the tracks and the ocean, just to keep from going crazy. It was a few blocks and sometimes there was sidewalk and sometimes there wasn't. Keegan and Brodie had gone on and on about the difficulties of writing and the unfairness and stupidity of the industry. Charlie loved writers and made a living off their talents, but had to admit when they talked shop they were the most boring people on earth. "What is it, honey?"

"I love it when you hyperventilate like that. Sorry, can't resist it, you're so—"

"Vulnerable."

"Yeah, you're a real—"

"Wuss."

"Nobody says that anymore, except old people. But . . . well, Doug and me are going to—"

"Doug and I—"

"WE are going to stand up with Ed and what's-her-name at the wedding."

"Certainly unusual, but I guess it's their wedding and he's paying for it and it's at his house. I actually have bigger things on my mind right now. We going to need to get you a dress on short notice?"

"I've already been measured—it'll just have to do."

"And Tuxedo's going to be flower girl?" Their families

had a strange relationship. The Esterhazies lived in a mini-estate on some of the most valuable property in Long Beach.

"No, what's-her-name actually has a niece or something." Doug Esterhazie had called the new fiancée "what's-her-name" for so long the Greenes had trouble remembering her real name.

"So what's the other thing you have to tell me?"

"Grandma's plane gets in tomorrow."

The Greenes avoided profanity and/or violence only because Charlie's phone tinkled. It was Richard Morse. "Charlie, I just listened to a message from Luella."

"Where is she?"

"I don't know. But she's alive or she was when she made the call about two hours ago. Tried to call her back but got no answer. You still at that spa or marina?"

"No, I'm in Del Mar. But it's not that far. I might try to get back there. Did she say anything about Maggie?"

"Not a thing, but if she was alive today to make that call, she didn't go off the cliff with her car."

"So what did she want?"

"Wanted to talk to you. But, Charlie, she sounded like maybe she'd been drinking a little much. You know?"

"What did we do before cell phones, Mom?" They hurried back up toward Les Artistes.

"I don't remember, but we must have been totally out of touch with reality, life, everything, huh? I mean, like . . . cordless wouldn't get you down the street even. You could be all alone in the world."

There had been any number of times Charlie'd wished they had never been invented and this was one of them. She checked her own voice mail and also got a message from Luella, "Sharly cotsh, cotchja, helpshus, cotjachas—"

She'd received it about fifteen minutes ago. She tried to get Mitch. He didn't answer. She was afraid to leave a message.

"She didn't sound much like Luella to me, but she did kind of sound like she was in a bar someplace, Mom, like, you know, the background noise?"

Charlie listened to it again and didn't hear the bar scene. "Maybe it's traffic. And voices too. But I do think it's Luella."

"Sounded like a slurry, 'help us,'" Brodie Caulfield offered when he heard the message, "might mean your friend Maggie's still alive." He sat on the footstool facing her and Keegan Monroe in the other chair out in the tiny back deck garden of the Georgia O'Keeffe room among the humming-birds and a few butterflies. Libby sprawled on the bed inside talking on her cell. It bothered Charlie. What if the author-ities got it right this time? Doug Esterhazie couldn't know everything.

"Mitch is supposedly up there, could be him she was talk-ing about. I still don't know where Kenny is." Charlie so longed to enjoy the peace here, but knew it was not to be. She had to do something soon. Problem was, how to shed Libby?

"Gotcha," Keegan said, listening to the strange message on Charlie's cellular. He sounded a tad slurry with beer himself— but nothing like Luella—if it was Luella. "Gosh you cha. Cots ya. Gotch ya. Cots ya hus. Cots ya jus. Cot ah jus. Gotta jud-ges. Cottages. Charlie, mean anything? Cottages?"

"Detective Solomon? This is—"

"Charlie? You're alive—I mean well? Jesus, that's good news. Where are you? I've been really worried."

"Why?"

"Because you and a few others seemed to have disap-peared from the face of the earth all of a sudden and I felt some responsibility there—"

"Who?"

"Well, I hate to tell you this but we have some evidence that your daughter is up here."

"You're at the Spa? Libby's fine, she's with me. Who else?"

"Well, we haven't been able to locate Mr. Hilsten, or your tall author, Cooper, either. Are they with you too? Where are you?"

"Detective Solomon, I just got a call from Luella—I'm coming up there. I may know where she is."

"No, Charlie, I appreciate your mistrust of authority after that odd grilling you got last night and your worry for your friends—but please trust me on this one, okay? You keep you and your daughter safe and I'll do my best to find Ms. Ridgeway and Ms. Stutzman too if she's alive. I don't know what's going on but I don't want you and your daughter in danger as well. Please trust me, I know it's hard—"

"Gordy, let me tell you something. Luella said that she and at least one someone else were in the cottages and asked me to help them."

"Cottages . . ."

"Those little buildings behind the Spa and, Gordy, she sounded drugged."

"Drugged . . ."

"You know exactly what I'm talking about. That place is so full of drugs if they were nuclear and somebody detonated them we wouldn't have to wait for the big quake to take out California."

"Are you alone, Charlie?"

"No, I'm sitting in a room full of witnesses—and I'll tell you and them that if you betray my trust and tell the wrong people what I've told you and something happens to my friends because of it, I'll devote the rest of my life to making yours miserable and I'm very resourceful. I'll wait one hour for your call and then I'm on my way. Oh, and watch out for Jerry Parks of the *Union-Tribune*. He was hauling files, vials, and tapes out to the quake pit where you found Libby's purse."

"What say we all go someplace else for an hour—just in case they can trace us here," Charlie said to the roomful of witnesses, namely Libby, Brodie Caulfield, and Keegan Monroe. And Fluffy. Even the cat looked tense.

"Think we should move the vehicles?" Brodie said.

"Why don't we take them downtown? There's a mall of sorts with a shadowy parking barn where you could lose Air Force One. Not park them together." Keegan wiped his brow with a tissue. "Sometimes you scare me, Charlie."

"Yeah, me too. And she's only your agent. I got me a lotta trouble for a motha."

"You're very intense, Charlie," Brodie added when they were ensconced in a small bar with an hors d'oeuvre bar set up to take care of dinner too, should they decide to stay the evening and drink. There were inviting outdoor or "court-yard" tables in the open but they chose a semi-enclosed corner where they could see outside but were still under-cover. It would be lusciously warm in summer, but a chill breeze that smelled of rain reminded them it was still April.

Charlie munched on carrot, bell pepper, jicama, and celery sticks, tomato and cucumber slices, corn chips and guacamole, and sipped at a beer. She ate more to prepare for an uncertain evening and night than out of hunger. When she felt this stressed, nothing really tasted very good. She checked her watch. This had to be the slowest hour she'd ever endured. It was the guilt thing. She was as bad as her mother but what if she'd let her friends down in a life and death situation by reading the signs wrong?

It was, selfishly, just as much about her having to live with the guilt of a bad decision at crisis time as it was about them losing their lives altogether because of it. Libby came by her selfish streak naturally.

"Look," Brodie said, "why don't you give him two hours? I know you don't trust anybody, but what difference will it make if the damage has already been done while the detective was trying to get a hold of you?" Since he'd left the conference Brodie had reverted to wearing a baseball cap with the bill at the back and eyeing Libby Abigail Greene at every opportunity. Charlie estimated he had four years on her and Libby had two inches on him. One would think that after what she'd done to Jerry Parks, Brodie would have lost interest fast. Libby appeared unaware of his interest, which her mother thought highly unlikely.

"I'm not letting you out of my sight anyway, Mom. You go up there, I'm going up there."

"Libby, there are government officials up there who think it was you who broke the code on the message accidently sent to my computer and not Doug. Think about it. They don't seem to need much justification for hauling people off without giving them a chance for legal counsel these days. You could just disappear instead of graduate you know, not to mention all the parties you'd miss."

"I promised Grandma I wouldn't leave you alone till she got here. Besides, they only do that to Middle Eastern types."

"Yeah," Keegan said. "What could you do if they handcuffed your knees?"

Charlie was still trying to figure out how to detain her daughter here in Del Mar so she could go up to the Sea Spa at the Marina del Sol when her phone tinkled in her purse.

"Charlie," Deputy Gordy Solomon said, "we've looked everywhere, every crook, cranny, crevice, cottage, and closet. We didn't find a trace of Ms. Ridgeway or any of the others. I'm sorry."

Thirty

"So, who all is 'we?' You said 'we didn't find anybody.'"
"Deputy Saucier and myself, the VanZants, remaining staff."

"That's a lot of area to search that fast."

"Well, there's also the federal officials you met yesterday," Solomon said.

"And the satellite in the sky that traces cell phones."

"I don't know anything about that, Charlie."

"One thing you do know. When you showed me Dashiell's body, you said if Maggie was alive she was in worse trouble than before. What did that mean?"

"Simply meant that she was the last person seen with him alive. She didn't have a car, he didn't have a license or a car because of his drug background. She was also dependent on drugs. They got to the Sea Spa from the Islandia. Obviously, neither were stable. She could have been responsible for his death as well as the others."

"Somebody else could have driven them both. So why is Luella missing too?"

"I have no idea. Perhaps she drove them in her car which ended up in the drink."

"She was also Judith Judd's agent and had access to much of her private as well as public financial information. Ask the Feds and the VanZants about Arthur Douglas, Redux, and Royal Pharmaca and Dr. Judy. Watch for reactions. This is much bigger than you and me, Gordy, Maggie, Luella, and Dashiell Hammett, Raoul Segundo or Grant Howard."

"Ever noticed Dr. Judy's picture right next to the Redux

179

display at Long's Drugs? Rite Aid too I think," Keegan Monroe asked the atmosphere in general or maybe the ozone. "Been seeing that probably six months anyway. Just now connecting her to the murdered one."

Charlie broke into whatever Gordy Solomon was saying to keep her away from the Spa. "Oh, ask around up there about Judith Judd's picture appearing in the Redux ad at Long's and Rite Aid for the last six months while you're at it."

"So, are we going up there? Or not?" Libby ordered another beer in defiance. Well, that's how she came about— a six pack and a dare.

"I might. You are not. I don't care what you promised your grandma. I'm almost getting up the nerve to call Mitch back. Doesn't sound like the satellite tracking thing works that well, like Doug said."

Mitch's voice mail asked her to leave a message. She did. It was, "You okay?"

"You know, Mom, I just thought of something. How come they can trace people calling from plane or hiking or skiing accidents by tracing their cells?"

"Why couldn't you have thought of that before I returned his call? Maybe you have to be calling 911."

"Isn't it interesting how little we know of the technology we depend on so completely?" Keegan Monroe said, pulling out his little pocket spiral notepad and presumably writing down that authorial thought.

"You tried a PDA?" Brodie Caulfield whipped out his. "It's a cell too, all in one, even a camera."

"Brodie, my life and career are complicated to the max the way it is. I do not desire yet another gadget that I do not understand." He stared off into the artificially lighted potted plant life tossing animated shadows in the increasing sea breeze that wafted uphill from the Pacific. The breeze still carried the scent of rain if not the reality.

Libby and Brodie disappeared for a few minutes, return-ing with shrimp and bowls of creamed spinach and cheese dip for all and other fattening grazing goodies Charlie couldn't identify. Sirens screamed by on the Pacific Highway. No one in Charlie's line of vision even paused at the sound. After this morning it would take a whole lot to make a credible emergency in Del Mar. Great time for terrorists to blow up something with no one paying attention.

Just as Charlie pulled the Ram out of the parking garage, her cell beckoned. It was Mitch returning her call. He was at the Spa.

"I'm on my way. What's going on up there?"

"I'm not sure. But don't drive up into the lot. Park down at the marina. I'll call Sidney, the steward, to drive you up just below the crest and drop you off. I'll meet you there. And, Charlie, don't bring anybody."

He hung up before she could explain the Libby problem. Or how long it would take her to get there. Seemed odd he didn't ask, hung up so suddenly. She had visions of him being tied down and forced to say what he was told. At least he didn't sound drugged. And what the hell had happened to Kenny Cowper? She didn't have his cell number in the memory, but she did have it. Somewhere. Rush hour traffic again, and constant tourist traffic, and beach bum traffic. Where could Mitch be waiting forever, not knowing how long it would take?

How long could Keegan and Brodie keep Libby from jumping in her Jeep and heading for the Sea Spa? Short of hog-tying her? That could be dangerous for all three of them. Brodie was strong enough to subdue her long enough to tie her up. She really shouldn't be asking her friends to do any of this. They could end up in jail for attempted sexual abuse or something. And her mother was flying in tomorrow. Now all Charlie needed was to run out of gas. What if her stopping at the Marina del Sol was a trap?

She couldn't find Kenny's number but was pretty sure she remembered it now and punched it at the next stop sign. Through all this she kept seeing Maggie's face in the old days when it was perky and mischievous and sharp and funny. And Luella's half-lidded look with one eyebrow raised slightly that told you the battery on her bullshit detector was fully charged. Funny how you don't appreciate the little things until you think it's too late.

Heads up, Greene. You can't see anything through tears. You decided to venture out here, ignore all the warnings. You either get strong or turn the truck around and control your daughter yourself.

"This is Kenneth. Charlie? Where are you? I thought you were dead."

"Where are you?"

If any satellite was tracing her phone calls it must not know where she was or everyone wouldn't be asking where she was. Wouldn't there be a lot more important legal deviants it would be using its time looking for?

"I'm at the marina—they won't let my car out the gate."

"Well you walk through and around the curve out of sight and I'll pick you up. I'm maybe ten, fifteen minutes away."

"Then what do we do?"

I haven't the foggiest. "Tell you when I see you."

"Jesus, I'm glad somebody knows what's going on." He sounded so relieved she wanted to laugh. No, maybe cry.

This was all suspiciously easy. He was waiting for her when she got there. She drove into a residential cul-de-sac, turned off the engine, and leaned back against the headrest. "I want to know what's happened—no bullshit, no macho— just the facts. I don't care what happened between you and Mitch. Kenny, I want to know what's happened to Maggie and Luella. Focus for me, okay?"

Two little boys chased each other, one with a toy rake, the other a toy shovel on a tiny front lawn. Two cats squared off in the middle of the street.

If Mitch had hurt him, none of the damage showed. Dark half-moons showed under his eyes though, the rest of his face a little gaunt. If she remembered correctly he was a year or two younger than she, but in the current light she could see an occasional gray hair hiding among its short dark cousins. She wondered if there were any in hers. She'd had a couple a few years back and plucked them, hadn't seen any since.

The guard and his dog at the Marina del Sol would not let him take his car out of the gate because he had no pass for getting it in there.

"So you just drove off after I left?"

"No, I scuffled with your inflated manfriend awhile and then drove my rental down to the marina and hiked back to see what was transpiring up there. By that time it was light and so I wandered around the grounds. Most of the activity was down by the earthquake crack or along the path to it. I stayed out of sight near the buildings where they had to walk by—the trio of government guys that tried to grill us last night, a female deputy, couple of staff women. Finally crawled onto a dusty couch in one of those cabins and slept for a couple of hours."

"What were they doing?"

"Talking on their cells mostly. Sheriff's department all but disappeared. I figured everybody was looking for you and Libby and I was going to hang around if they brought you back. And finally I thought why would they do that? And also got hungry so I hiked back down to the marina. Didn't have any trouble buying food at the restaurant but my car was parked illegally because I wasn't a member or something."

"Did you try to call me?"

"No, I was worried I'd help them trace you. So I lounged around the dock, watched CNN in the bar. That's when I figured out what had happened to the sheriff's department. They'd had prior orders from another part of the government to participate in the Emergency Response Drill and nobody in the bureaucracy ever talks to anybody else in the bureaucracy if they can help it so—"

"We watched part of it in a parking lot in Del Mar. It was a hoot. Kenny, I got a call from Luella this afternoon. She said she was in the cottages. And she said 'we.' I'm hoping that means Maggie is still alive and they're together. She sounded drunk or drugged so I'm not positive that's what she said. I've had a call from Detective Solomon who says he's back up there now too. He insists I stay away from the Spa. I've talked to Mitch who says to park down at the marina and have the steward from the *Motherfricker*, that's a yacht he'll be shooting on in a few days, drop me off just below the crest of the promontory where he, Mitch, will meet me. And I have connived to get Brodie Caulfield and Keegan Monroe to forcibly restrain Libby Abigail Greene from coming up to the Spa as she has threatened to do because she has promised her grandmother she wouldn't let me out of her sight until said grandmother arrives at LAX sometime tomorrow."

After a long pause and a longer stretch, a deep yawn, a shake of the head, Kenneth Cooper/Kenny Cowper blinked his black eyes at her black eyes and said, "That's what I've always liked about women—they lead such simple straight-forward lives. But having met Edwina, having your mom here is not that bad an idea."

"And the call from Mitch sounded funny. If he were being forced to have me be picked up down at the marina so I wouldn't get up there to begin with—I don't know—but there was something funny about that call."

"You really sure you were talking to Mitch Hilsten there?" Kenny said in Mitch's voice. "See, he's famous enough to be mimicked pretty easy, sweet little Charlie. And you're hearing this from an amateur at mimicking."

Thirty-One

"So you figure they're going to be waiting for you just below the crest of the cliff top?"

"Either that, or down at the marina where I was to leave the truck. Or it was Mitch waiting to meet me there like he said." She kept a pair of crummy running shoes in the truck for emergencies she never had. Until now, maybe.

"Might have known any woman who'd drive a Ram would pack sensible shoes. Stands to reason." But Kenny shook his head in bewilderment to negate his words.

They'd parked the Ram in a construction zone located several cul-de-sacs closer to their destination than their first stop and where a modest home, in the process of being scraped off its lot by a bulldozer, hunkered injured among several trucks, machines, piles of debris that overflowed onto the street. The mostly open lot gave them access to a social trail snaking up the side of the promontory for a way at least. Best they could do without knowing the lay of the land.

"I still don't know what you think we can do if your daughter shows up. Or what we can do about anything, frankly."

"Do you want to just turn around and go back? Well, go." She slipped her wallet and keys in her pocket, stuffed her purse under the seat. Her neck ached again. This time the weather change was for real.

"No Charlie, I want to know what the plan is."

"The plan is to sneak around any welcoming committee waiting on the crest of the whatever-it-is and the main building of the Spa to the cottages behind it and rescue Maggie and Luella."

185

"Oh well, that's easy. Why didn't you say so? One little problem I can think of though is that there's no cover. Unless we crawled on our stomachs and then—"

"Kenny, that's a wonderful idea. Why didn't I think of it?"

"I was being either vacuous or facetious. Man, I'm too tired to sort out which."

"I really do appreciate your doing this." She put an arm around his waist, which with the uneven terrain and his height was a stretch. "Tell you what, we get out of this all right, I'll give *you* a massage."

"I'm holding you to that, Greene."

"I know." The climb was getting serious. He was in shape and she wasn't. That wind in Del Mar had followed her and tried now to push her over. So much for sensible shoes. Charlie finally called a rest stop—a real bruise to her ego but it took her three steps to match one of his. "Get down, way down, flat. Now."

"I'm not really in the mood for my massage right—"

"No, I think I see someone." A big rock would have been nice. But there weren't any. There was someone walking toward them though, and in a crouch.

It was Mitch. And the closer he came the angrier he looked. "What the hell you two doing? Charlie, I thought you were meeting Sidney down at the marina. You didn't say anything about bringing him."

"Trying to sneak onto the Spa property without being seen," Kenny said with a touch of sneer-like tone. "What are you doing?"

"Waiting for Charlie. Saw you guys for miles. What the fuck stupid trick is this, Steeplehead?"

"Sorry you're so vertically challenged, Hilsten." That sudden draining of all expression in the black eyes, the flattening of voice tone men exhibit when they're recharging the testosterone level in preparation to do something stupid. The world would be a lot less interesting without men but it would make a lot more sense.

"Now stop that," she ordered, but wasn't about to step

between them. "How did you expect to get me in there without being seen if I'd been dropped off by Sidney?"

"By approaching the Spa from the other direction. There's a lot more cover."

"We'd have to cross the road." Kenny straightened taller, just to rub it in. "You know the terrain over there?"

"Houses, backyards, dogs, and cul-de-sacs. Better than crossing the promontory, wide open to all the big-view windows of the main building."

A very temporary truce evolved and they took off for the road heading up to the Sea Spa, pausing before crossing it to let Charlie catch her breath—another grudge she had against guys. No sign of Mitch's rental, the wind building even here, but no official types peering down at them that Charlie could see. Suddenly, they were in a neighborhood on a path along a dry drainage ditch lined with rocks and then on a sidewalk. Mitch led them down a street to a cross street and then up another cul-de-sac where his black rental was parked. He motioned them inside and drove to the end of the cross street—where it dead ended at a permanent concrete barrier, on the other side of which jagged a ditch filled with deep darkness instead of water. It meandered downhill out of sight and uphill it made a cut through the cliff top where sunlight spilled through like in a religious movie.

Charlie stood looking up at that inspirational beacon, feeling distressingly creepy.

"You made it this far, Charlie. This last little bit shouldn't be all that difficult." Mitch Hilsten had some bruising under and along to the side of one eye.

"I could carry you," Kenny offered.

"I know." Charlie turned around so they could see her tears—part actress, part overwhelmed responsible person here—before they could make their own remarks into a reason to strike out at each other. "I'm just so afraid of what I might find up there."

Whoa, we're not too manipulative here.

"Yeah, but it's for their own good."

"What's for who's own good? Oh—" Kenny shrugged, embarrassed for her.

"Well, she's under a lot of stress."

"I know that, Hilsten."

"Okay, I'm ready to go up there now. This is really serious stuff here. I wish you guys would grow up."

"Well, you're the one talking to yourself."

"Are you intimating Charlie's losing it, Cow-per?" Mitch did his highly offended rage thing.

"See you guys later. I have more important things to deal with right now. Like life and death?" Charlie took off at a pace faster than she could ever maintain, hoping anger and dread would give her the extra energy the cocktail hour in Del Mar had not. She was halfway to the divine light when a firecracker, car backfire, or gunshot sounded above her. She couldn't tell how long surprise stopped her in her tracks before the males in the trio had raced up behind her and flattened her to the ground.

Charlie could barely catch enough breath to release a stream of invective that should have flipped-off the heavenly finger on the light switch above.

There was a dead man staring at them when they peeked over the crest's edge. But his eyes didn't follow Charlie as she pulled herself up on crumbling earth with the help of a butt-shove from the guys below. When she stood finally he stared at her sensible shoes instead.

"Christ, get down, Charlie. The shooter's still up here for sure."

And she was pulled to earth once more and it was beginning to piss her off. She had half a mind to turn Libby and her famous knee loose on the other two stooges in this pratfall of an endeavor.

"I've never seen him before. Shot in the back of the neck. Looks real surprised." Mitch.

"White shirt and tie, sleeves rolled up. East Coast maybe." Kenny.

The guys continued the crime scene investigation dialogue in whispers, looking around for the person with the gun. All Charlie could think of was that it wasn't Maggie or Luella lying dead there. Maybe they were alive, still in the cottages somewhere. Hiding, waiting for her to come and help them.

The wind ruffled the guy's hair and the back of his shirt except where blood from his neck had stuck it to his skin. Charlie wondered if they'd try to pin this one on Maggie too. There were all kinds of different agendas stacking up here. All the deaths did not have to have come about by the same people or motive. But blaming it all on Maggie could be very convenient for both the killer, killers, and more so for overworked authorities trying to resolve the murders.

"This is a real dangerous place to be," Kenny reminded them. "How do we get to the cottages, Hilsten, without getting picked off by the sniper? Your call."

"That's somebody's son, husband, dad, brother, boyfriend, meal ticket," the actor/producer said righteously.

"Look at it this way, he won't ever have to linger in a nursing home." Kenny pushed her to move away from the dead loved one and crawl after Mitch toward a fake foundation of a fake stone ruin of antiquity. The whole place was like a planned copy of a ruin rather than the ruin of a copy of an ancient ruin, when you looked at it while slithering along on your belly—sort of a snake's eye view of man's folly.

When the going gets tough, Charlie gets philosophical, herself reminded her, and totally useless.

Another shot pinged off the fake stone next to Charlie's head and her contact lens went painfully crazy so fast she just removed it—all her eye paraphernalia back in her purse in the metallic blue Ram. Her tears provided the eyewash to move the offending speck of fake foundation rock to a corner where she could snag it out.

"You think that was a rifle or a pistol, Stretch?"

"I don't know the difference from this end of it, Shorty, but the guy's a good shot."

While they argued over sound and velocity and whatever, Charlie snuck a peek with her one good eye before one of them pulled her back to earth.

"Jesus, Charlie, will you—"

"It's a girl."

"What's a girl?"

"The shooter." Knowing she wasn't supposed to do this, Charlie stuck the lens on her tongue to clean and lubricate it the only way she had now, not even a bottle of water to rinse it, and stuck it back in. If she got shot, this sin and probably all the others wouldn't mean much.

"Okay, stand up, all of you, with your hands behind your head," Caroline VanZant said above them. "Believe me, I have nothing to lose by killing all three of you."

Thirty-Two

"Why didn't you just shoot them too?" Snappy number, Ruth Ann Singer, snapped. "Might as well, you're shooting everybody else and now they'll rat on us."

"For what?" Caroline's eyeglasses magnified her sadness and the redness.

"For what we're doing to them right now." Ruth Ann was talking tough but looking terrified.

They herded Charlie and the guys into a side door of the Spa, ground floor at this level, which varied with the terrain. But this was the pool level and they were guided by Caroline's rifle into the exercise-machine room, forced to sit on the floor where Sue Rippon tied their wrists with elastic exercise cords to some of the heavy equipment Kenny had thought so cool.

"Caroline, please tell me what you know about Maggie and Luella," Charlie pleaded.

"Let's just say they're feeling no pain." She and the rifle turned to go. Sue and Ruth Ann couldn't leave fast enough. They were definitely not comfortable with this.

"Wait. Are they alive?"

"Not for long. Or you either."

"And she'd seemed like such a sweet little old lady," Kenny whispered when Caroline had closed the door behind her.

"I knew it. They're still alive. We've got to hurry." Charlie set to squirming. "Watch to see if anyone's coming back."

"Careful, Charlie, these things are tight. Now's not the time to break something." Kenny pulled, pushed, and grunted against the restraints too. The three of them were attached

191

too far apart to help each other and the machinery was attached to skids bolted to the floor.

"Relax, Cowper. She can fold her hands nearly in half vertically. And she's highly motivated about now."

"He's right, Kenny, save your strength for later. We may need it."

The walls seemed half glass with the show windows into the hall leading to the pool. Part of the pool was even visible. And then another wall had windows to the outside where a few shrubby things tossed in the wind off the Pacific.

When Charlie folded her hands, they were barely wider than her wrists—the right one particularly collapsible—and it took less time for her to free herself than Mitch and the two of them to free Kenny because they had to pry the knots loose.

"You know, Charlie, what Caroline VanZant implied about the girls being alive may not be true. I mean don't give up— but consider the shock and stress she's under."

"She's going around shooting people with a rifle, probably not in her right mind," Kenny agreed. "Nice old ladies don't usually do that. Which doesn't mean she isn't to be feared. Maybe more so."

"Okay, what do we do now?" Charlie asked to hurry things up. They spoke in whispers behind a large compressor of some kind at the back of the main building. It in turn was hidden by a boxed-in enclosure of redwood.

"Hell, this is your show."

"Yeah, what do you want us to do?"

"I want Mitch, who can duck behind things better, to sneak out the back way and figure what and who are going on between here and the earthquake crevice and to keep a low profile—just watch, no heroics. Kenny, I want you to do the same between here and the parking lot. I'll snoop around the cottages. We meet back here in thirty minutes to compare news and decide further what to do. We've all got cells. Set yours on stun and move out—"

"Wait just a damn minute, I didn't mean—"

"Yeah," Mitch agreed. "We were talking about guarding you, not—"

"My show, remember? You both said so. I want information and help, not heroics." She didn't know about setting cells on stun—but she left their faces that way when she took off. Whether they decided to follow her wishes or not, both had the good sense not to follow her openly. Charlie's aching gut knew there was little time to waste arguing with them.

It had been threatening on and off to storm for a couple of days, which usually meant nothing would happen. Charlie hadn't had much time or inclination to check TV or newspaper for weather. She could probably check it on this freaking cell phone—they did everything but inject plasma these days, but she frankly did not want to deal with it now. Still, she was aware that it was very dark for this time of day— that there would be no colorful sunset and that the wind still smelled like rain.

Why hadn't the sheriff's department or the Feds rushed to check out the shot that killed the man in the tie at the ruins area or noticed Caroline and the girls hustling three unarmed people back to the Spa's main building?

Charlie dropped to the ground between a cottage and a shedlike building at the sound of muted throat-clearing and the hesitant crunching of gravel and with no help from the boys. They would have been proud. The person passed very quietly otherwise and on the other side of a porch, gone before she could push herself up far enough to get a look so she moved, crouching, around the building to see a man bent low, skulking off toward the crevice, arms wrapped around something she couldn't see. She stepped out further toward the path to get a better look and something crunched.

He turned and she dropped. Everything but her heart and the wind gone silent.

Charlie lay still as stone, trying not to breathe—which was pretty stupid even for her. The titanium plate in her neck ached. The contact she'd washed up with germy spit decided

193

to be irritated, but worst of all was the incipient sneeze joyously demanding her attention. All she needed now was gas.

Concentrating on stifling all body functions, she took awhile to register the presence of yet another soul creeping about at this particular area on the grounds.

And then aware of a quiet struggle, but still noisy enough to apparently cover the "skinx" she made to thwart the full blown sneeze because the scuffling and muted grunting continued on as if she'd made no sound at all.

Charlie turned her head to peer at the struggle through one painfully watery eye and saw only shadowy shoe soles as the coupled combatants scuffled flat-out on the sharp grit of the small stones lining the path. Two men, she either didn't know or couldn't recognize in her present condition, finally tore apart when one banged the other's head down on rough pebbles so hard he let out an honest-to-god "arga" and lay still. The other man then picked up an overturned box and gathered papers and other things strewn about to fill it up and carry right past Charlie but on the run and in the opposite direction from which it had come.

Charlie had no idea how long she and the downed man lay silent before she got up the nerve to lift herself far enough to explore what she had tripped over. It appeared to be a laptop computer that had been viciously treated even before it met her. Somebody trying to destroy a hard drive?

The man still on the path jerked and whimpered. Her cell vibrated in her pocket. "Charlie, nix the meeting place. Somebody's there. Stay away from the path. What's happening at your end?"

She crawled away from the injured man, the ruined computer, and the path before answering in a whisper, "Sneak along the back edge of the row of cottages along the path on the left. I'll watch for you. Is Kenny with you?"

"Yeah. You hide. We'll be there," Mitch whispered back.

The man on the path gurgled, then lay still. Charlie stood to peek around the corner of the last cottage on the left of

194

the path at the man on the ground. Her vision was not good right now, but by closing one eye and staring hard she thought she recognized the other Charlie, Charles Green. This she deduced by the eyeglasses flung to the side of the path and what appeared to be safari shorts.

But it didn't make sense that he would be skulking toward the earthquake crevice with the box instead of away from it. He lay very still. She rather thought he might be dead. Would Maggie be blamed for this death too, if Charlie found her before Caroline VanZant? She had no proof but held to the fantasy that Maggie was hiding from Caroline. If not, why was she still alive? Or had been when Caroline and company tied Charlie and the guys up in the exercise room.

There were new footsteps on the path and Charlie slid away for her rendezvous, startled by a lightning flash that blinded her rather than revealing anything. She froze to get her bearings and blink contacts back in place. Her titanium implant responded to the lightning in a really weird way, her teeth tasted metallic—sort of. Odd-colored spots swirled on the inside of her eyelids.

"Charlie?" someone whispered in her ear. A warm arm around her shoulder eased the tautness.

"Why was he running away from the Spa with the evidence, Kenny? He should have been trying to save it." She opened her eyes to find both guys snuggled around her, shushing her.

"We don't know what's going on either," Mitch whispered close to her ear. "Other than a lot of highjinx. You sure that was the FBI's Charles Green?"

"No, but he dressed like him and wore glasses. What have you guys been doing?"

"I was watching the path farther down, closer to the body. It's still there. I saw one guy racing up toward the Spa with a box that appeared to be heavy." He'd snuck back behind the cabins looking for Charlie, apparently passed her and met Kenny just short of the redwood compressor cage.

"That's when we called you, Charlie. I've got bad news."

"Christ, Cowper, you don't have to get brutal here. Poor kid's had enough stress."

"Charlie's a big girl—she can handle the truth. This is getting very serious here, Hilsten. Just because you're old enough to be, doesn't make you her father."

"You found Maggie? And Luella? Dead?" Charlie didn't even have to try to whisper now. She thought she'd choke.

"No, Charlie, I found Libby's Jeep Wrangler. In the parking lot."

Thirty-Three

The light was poor, nobody had a flashlight. Charlie wanted everyone to split up and search a cottage to save precious time, but the guys refused to leave her side.

"I really don't think I was struck by lightning."

"You were close enough to the strike for it to have had some effect. You were in shock when we found you," Mitch whispered behind her as they entered another cottage, this time by prying open a side window with Kenny's pocket knife. Some cottages were locked, some not. So far, all were deadly quiet—except for creaking floors, thunder, and wind-driven rain. All three were soaked just sneaking between them, almost refreshing after the lightning bolt.

Charlie, already a basket case, trying to keep her cool and the guys' testosterone levels in check, now had the added fear for her child thrown into the mix of all the other stuff eating up her guts from the inside out. Maggie and Luella for instance.

"Stop," Kenny ordered. "I hear something."

All Charlie saw were shadows, some of them made by wind blowing plant life around outside, and the white basin of an old-fashioned sink. All she heard was her breathing and heartbeat and desire to scream. And then a faint groaning.

"It's coming from under the floor. Do these places have basements? I'd kill for a flashlight right now." Charlie crawled on what felt like boards instead of vinyl or carpet, feeling for a seam that cut across the fit of boards—some idea of a metal ring that would lift a trap door in the floor, like in historical films, worried about picking up slivers instead.

And then the groan became a word, "Help me. He-lp me. Ohhhh, oh."

"It's coming from outside." Mitch crawled back out the window. Kenny followed.

"Oh, Jeez," one of them said and Charlie, still on hands and knees, peeked up over the sill to see three men suddenly illuminated by lightning, lashed by sheets of rain. Charles Green minus his eyeglasses and safari hat staggered up to Kenny and groaned something. His clothes sagged, dripping water, his scalp and the fuzz of hair left on it did too. He swayed toward Kenny.

"What'd he say?" Mitch yelled over the storm.

The stricken man moaned something else and reached for Kenny, started to go down.

"I thought he said he needed a pill and something about his pocket. His medication must be in his pocket." He began groping in the man's clothes.

Safari shorts being mostly pockets anyway, Green went down, nearly taking Kenny with him. Mitch knelt to feel his neck. "I think he's past the need for pills."

Charlie was about to climb out the window to join them, in the process of deciding which foot to stick out first so she could sort of roll out sideways, when three new figures raced out of the rain haze and off the path, stopping to spread their legs and hold handguns out in front of them, ordering both men to put their hands behind their heads. Charlie slipped back to the floor and tried not breathing again.

She lay very still for a long time after the voices quieted outside, heard no footsteps, heavy breathing, throat clearing. Only the storm and the water running in the eaves trough. And that faint groaning sound again. Had they taken Mitch and Kenny off at gunpoint and left poor Agent Charles Green out on the path?

She tried breathing deep and slow, holding the air as long as she could before exhaling, then pushed herself to the windowsill again. Even after blinking her contacts into focus, the path looked and sounded completely empty of people. So, who was doing the moaning? On the heels of that thought there was a faint coughing. It was female. And it came from beneath her. Not outside.

She yearned again for a flashlight.

Think, Greene.

Charlie sat back on the floor under the window and closed her eyes as long as she could stand to, then opened them squinting into the room and toward the floor, hoping a lightning flash wouldn't blind her night vision again. Shapes—a white sink lay on the floor—a double sink without its faucets, drain pipe, or cupboard. An overturned table of some kind. An upright wooden chair. A closed door to another room or a closet. But the human sounds, faint though they were, were coming from under the floor. A crawl space?

Charlie crawled across the tiny room to the door, reached up for the old-fashioned glass knob. It turned, but the door wouldn't open. She went back to the window and peered out along the side of the building. There couldn't be another room over there. It must be the backdoor, or a closet or an entry to an underground room. She climbed out the window and to the back of the building. There was no door here.

She crawled back in the window—and sort of identified the odd smell of this place as a combination of old wood and campground outhouse—to that inside door and pulled and pushed and shoved and yanked. She was thrown on the floor on her back when it came off its hinges, well one of them. It hung into the room so she could crawl over it—into pitch darkness—with a musty smell added to the one upstairs and the sound of water dripping. Probably rats and spiders and—

"Hello? Anybody there?" *There* had to be below her, but she didn't know where the steps were. A muffled groan and maybe a sob, cut off? It sure wasn't rats.

Charlie reached for her cell, punched 911. As she settled down on the door to explain the emergency it gave way and she reached out with the other hand in an automatic grab, sliding down on what was indeed a set of stairs, her hand finding a light switch. And it worked.

She described in detail where she was and what she saw to the operator who soon had her connected to paramedics as well. Charlie tried to relay the urgency and the fact that there might be those who would try to stop them.

"We got paramedics not paratroopers. How do we know you're not a nutcase, lady?"

"I have three people in this room in awful shape—one of them is Gordy Solomon of the San Diego County Sheriff's Department. We need help and we need it fast."

After a long pause—"We've got people on the way. I want two things of you. Your name, and put Detective Solomon on the line."

"Charlie. They've been drugged, but I'll try. Detective Solomon, try to talk to dispatch on the phone."

"Sharlee?" he said. "Good girl."

"Tell them I'm not a nutcase and we need help fast. There have been two more murders. We need police as well, Gordy."

"Right. Dishpatch? Thish Gordon Solomon and we need the Nationalll Guard too. Lotsa bodies. Shtep on it—fast. The She-eye-aye hates the FBI who hates the IRS and everybody hates the San Diego Sheriffsh Department. Ee-eye-ee-eye-oh. How'd I do, Sharlee?" And then he started throwing up, again.

"What's happening now? I'm tuned in to you. I'm a nurse."

"He's vomiting. His eyes are rolled back. All three have vomited before. Please hurry."

"Turn him over so he doesn't choke, Charlie. We're just turning off the Pacific Highway. We've got another ambulance and sheriff's deputies on the way."

"Be careful. There are men with guns here and Caroline VanZant has a rifle. She killed a man wearing a tie and they kidnaped Mitch Hilsten and Kenny Cowper, just now. And there's a dead FBI agent up here. And my daughter's up here."

"You getting this, Lloyd?" the female nurse asked someone who answered—

"We read. We're on our way. You better wait and let us lead."

"Okay. Charlie? I'm going to talk you through keeping those people alive until we get there. Please don't panic. We need you as much as you need us. Now here's what you do." And the calm voice with the sirens in the background talked her through reading the pulse rate on all three of the captives, describing skin color, breathing, checking the eyes by pulling up the lids, feeling for muscle rigidity, describing the smell on their breaths, had them all turned over on their stomachs, mouths checked for vomit blockage.

"Charlie, what's happening?"

"Now *I'm* gagging. The smell down here is so horrible."

"Take your cell with you and go up the stairs till you can get to fresh air. Don't overdose on it too fast. Tell me when you can control the urge to vomit."

"I'm sweating all over."

"That's a normal reaction."

"They're going to turn you away at the gate you know. And then we're all dead here."

"Miss Greene? This is Lloyd. I'm vaguely familiar with the layout there. Can you tell me which of those cabins you're in?"

"How do I know you're not a kook? What's that racket?"

"Well, how do we know you're not a kook? And I'm flying a helicopter. This is costing somebody a lot of money. I'm going to try to drop some help to you, but with the weather, I'd kind of like to get in close. You going to trust us, or what? We got lives on the line up here too, you know."

"Only because you've got a great drawl, Lloyd. And you'd better get your guy down here fast, because if someone's listening in on this, my patients and I won't be able to greet him."

Lloyd laughed. Probably because the incoming was a she. Charlie and the nurse were busy on the phone figuring out how to triage until the ambulances arrived. Charlie tried not to think about Libby. About Mitch and Kenny. She concentrated on helping those she could at the moment, increasingly aware of the non-human inhabitants of the room, which was actually a one-room apartment.

A futon bed and a small tattered couch, a computer table, with office chair and computer, bookshelves filled with CDs and tapes and videos instead, television, DVD player, small one-compartment college dorm refrigerator producing an unhealthy hum. Small sink and bathroom stool behind a folding screen. Too bad none of the patients had had time to reach either. Amateurish photos on the walls of women in the shower, disrobing, preening, stretching, slipping into tanksuits, sitting on the bathroom stool, etc. One of Maggie Stutzman almost stopped Charlie's heart.

"I'm in. She's here with the wounded," a woman said behind Charlie and started her heart back up with a rush. "Situation as described and moderately under control. Noticed funny lights scurrying every which way on the way down."

Thirty-Four

"How ya doin', Charlie? My name's Roy," the apparition said, walking among the victims, holstering her flashlight, drawing her own cell. "Hello all, especially medics, we need you bad here, a female sheriff's deputy, a male, and another female. I'd say things are critical. There's a graveled maintenance road off the southeast side of the parking lot, wends its way around the east side of the main building. Follow the winding road to the third outbuilding, hang a right, stay focused for the second row of cottages and you want the next one left at the turn. My gut suggests you run minus sirens and lightbars and with as little notification as possible. Read?"

"Read. How do you know all this?"

"I used to work here."

"Roy as in Rogers?" Charlie asked the apparition, so grateful to have some help, there were tears running down her face and the term "weak-kneed" took on a whole new significance. "And where did you leave your parachute?"

"As in Roylene and the chute's up on the porch, wadded. Sort of figured you wanted me here in a hurry." Roy looked as little like a James Bond movie as you could imagine—short, pudgy, dressed in black pants and hooded windbreaker, an interesting utility belt about her middle. She swept the hood back to reveal a short no-nonsense cut and brownish hair.

"You used to work here?"

"Cleaning lady. I got a kid. It don't pay the bills. I ask myself what else could I train for, that might even be rewarding, fun, and keep us off welfare? And here I am, Roy-to-the-rescue. Panache or what?" All the while Roy-to-the-rescue

203

was taking in details of the room, checking pulses with her wristwatch. Then she stopped to study Charlie. "On a scale of one to ten, ten being the most severe, how close would you say you are to losing it?"

Through a giggle, some tears, and a shrug Charlie answered, "Two? Now that you're here."

"Good. We all may need each other before this night's over." Roy's face was blotchy, maybe from parachuting down in a storm, her movements brisk, her voice tone measured and reassuring. They found wash cloths and hand towels in a drawer, wet them at the sink, wrapped them around the wrists of the suffering trio, bathed foreheads hanging over the bedsides and couch too. Roy described the progress of the patients' condition to the ambulance nurse and asked if she should try to administer water, and was told to wait till the ambulances arrived.

Roy found time to study the pictures on the wall. "Somebody got their jollies peeping, looks like."

"You used to work here. Ever meet Dashiell Hammett?"

"Maids don't get to fraternize with guests and not much with the rest of the staff either—wait, he the owner's son?"

"Yeah, I think this was his little secret hiding place."

"I was gone by the time he came, but word had it he was an addict and they barely got him off the street before he zoned on meth. Wouldn't allow him off the premises. Heard he died recently."

Roy worked for a private company that contracted out trained professionals—emergency, security, whatever—to law enforcement agencies strapped for money. "We cost more but local governments don't have to pay all the benefits— medical, retirement, training costs, social security. So old Dashiell was a peeping Tom too, addict *and* pervert?"

But they both fell silent at the sound of gravel crunching— didn't sound like the vehicles they were expecting, more like footsteps, furtive, tentative. Roy put a finger to her lips, pulled a handgun from her utility belt, motioned Charlie to crouch, and climbed the stairs far enough to switch off the light.

"I saw a light in here, I tell you."

"Well come back out, there's not one now. We've got to find Libby."

"Keegan? Brodie? What?" Charlie tried to push past Roy on the stairs, but was shoved back. By the time she made it to her feet and to the stairs the whole world lit suddenly. It wasn't lightning either.

"Hello ladies," a sheriff's deputy said. "I better be talking to Charlie and Roy, here." The blinding searchlight/flashlight made the room light unnecessary. "Oh, Jesus. Get the ambulance up now. It's Solomon and Saucier. Roy, are they alive?"

Charlie hid again. This time in the crawl space under the porch of the cottage in which Dashiell had kept his dirty little secrets and someone had drugged Luella Ridgeway, Detective Solomon, and Deputy Lydia Saucier nearly to death. One ambulance hauled them out with sirens blasting and to hell with the higher authorities. Several deputies and Roy-to-the-rescue hung around trying to find Charlie who was to be hauled out fast too and questioned at the station in Encinitas. Someone had shone a flashlight under here twice but Charlie lay in a trench up against the foundation that apparently hid her.

"Charlie, please come out wherever you are," Roylene could be heard whispering in a widening circle around the cottage. "We want to help you, get you out of danger and find your daughter and friends. We need you to help us do that. We're on your side."

Yeah, right, the San Diego Sheriff's Department is going to take on the FBI, the CIA, and the IRS. You're just going to be sandbagged and helpless, and you know it, while higher ups figure out how to handle all this and control the spin so that "righteousness" overshadows a possible PR scandal. Meanwhile my daughter and friends will be held hostage, drugged, or killed by whoever is doing the kidnaping and murdering around here. I don't think so.

Charlie had heard plenty of speculation going on among those looking for her and this end of the cell contact with headquarters. At least it didn't seem as if there'd be a delay in racing the sick to an emergency room. The other ambulance pulled out quietly to wait in the parking lot for more wounded. As far as Charlie could determine there were about four deputies and Roylene out there. If she thought they'd help her locate Libby and the rest she'd have shown herself. But she'd heard the orders. Get Charlie Greene out of there and those left were to wait for further orders and keep a low profile until headquarters could determine what was going on.

Charlie needed to search for Brodie and Keegan as well as Libby and Maggie now, not to mention Kenny and Mitch. In all the excitement over the drugged trio and conjecture about the shady people deputies might go after, she'd managed to disappear this far.

Now she needed a moment or two to disappear again, away from here, skulk somewhere else out of sight and sound. Check her cell which was vibrating itself silly in her pocket. At first she'd been so freaked she hadn't recognized the feeling. She was used to having it in her purse, tweedling, thought it must be ants or spiders or a muscle spasm.

Her chance came when they began searching for her further, discussing radius and pattern and, as it stretched out and away, one of them found the dead man wearing a necktie.

There was something else under here with her and it was a lot bigger than ants or spiders. It stopped to sniff her nose. It had whiskers. It scurried off and Charlie rolled out of the trench on the goosebumps it had created, scuttled out under the porch steps and crawled between shadows as those looking for her, she hoped, headed for the body near the crevice.

As would only make sense in retrospect, they'd left one of their own behind, but the search radius had spread so far she was able to slip behind one cabin after another until she spotted him and then behind the compressor in the redwood enclosure. She thought it might be safe to listen to any messages on her cell now but there was a dead man here too.

Charlie huddled on the concrete platform with the compressor and the late Charles Green when Roy whispered on the other side of the redwood wall, "You see her? We got to get her out of here and someplace safe. Poor woman's been through too much to think straight."

"She didn't come this way. What about the dead man down there?"

"He's not talking. Roger's going through his pockets. He didn't buy his suits at Wal-Mart."

No way they wouldn't check out what was inside the redwood fort. Too good a place to try to hide. How to avoid her well-intentioned but clueless saviors? It all felt so hopeless, she turned her head away from the Fed's corpse. He didn't smell that bad yet, just strange in a way that didn't encourage introspection.

"I see something over there. Just past that window, a shadow."

"I see some*one*. You work around to the side, I'll go straight in. Don't frighten her."

Charlie felt something against her lips. Something warm like a finger. It wasn't Charles'. She lay in a thin puddle of water with her cheek on the concrete next to the redwood wall. He was on the other side of her. There was, it appeared now, maybe a six-inch space between the concrete floor and the base of the redwood. There was someone on the other side, shushing her with an index finger. Charlie could feel that someone's breath as she spoke.

"Mom? You got seconds to worm your way out and around to this side, before they come back. Think you can save your unneeded comments for later?"

Charlie did as she was told, actually kicking Agent Green's head at the last minute, as she slithered around the barrier into the deeper shadow behind it, furious and relieved, building up questions and admonitions for her daughter every second of the way. She could and would not condone this behavior. Putting herself in danger was the absolutely last thing Charlie wanted from Libby Abigail Greene. Now and forever.

Her maternal rage nearly overcame her fear for them both and her own reason, but by the time she'd scuttled around the barrier, there was no one there. Everything in her deflated. The world had gone mad. This was the ultimate. She was going to lose it.

No you're not. You're just feeling scared and thwarted. And do not tell me to shut up aloud.

"Psssst." What might well be a human hand beckoned from under a shrub not two feet away.

Charlie scuttled some more, the skin of her stomach and thighs in full revolt. She was suddenly yanked forward, rolled over, and had her mouth covered with a hand. It smelled like cocoa butter. Damn kid. This might well be the ultimate insult.

"Stuff it, Mom, you can change your will later," the kid whispered ever so softly in her ear but did not remove the hand barricading Charlie's mouth.

Who'd have thought cheerleading could make a teen this strong? And it was even wetter under the bush.

"Sorry, I thought I saw someone or something," the male deputy whispered, very close by.

"You did, and so did I," Roy answered. "Let's call in the others and figure out what to do next. Maybe they have instructions from headquarters."

"Shit, what's this?" And somebody's flashlight let there be light.

Charlie was sure either her feet or Libby's were sticking out in the path somewhere and she tensed to defend her child, who tightened the grip on Charlie to two minutes to murder.

"Another fatality it looks like. Way dead, this guy," Roy proclaimed. "We've really barged into a mess here, haven't we? Get through to your chief."

When he had, the deputy told Roy, "They say to stick tight and quiet until it's determined whether or not foreign terrorists were involved here."

"Crap, they're going to try and bury this in *that* hole?" Roy said. "Maybe our friend Charlie had the right idea after all."

Thirty-Five

"You barely passed the dummy track in high school. What makes you think you know how to handle all this stuff?" Charlie whispered.

"Hell, I live with a madwoman. I gotta learn survival skills, big time. I'm the only responsible adult in the family, except Grandma and she doesn't live here. We ought to get together and have you committed. You have any idea the parties I've missed this week?"

They crouched in a towel closet off the pool area because that was near where they'd found an unlocked outer door when shots fired somewhere, heavy footsteps, grunts and groans, and the smashing of glass drove them away from their shrub outside the compressor fort. Maybe there *were* terrorists in on all this, besides the bunch of lunatics Charlie'd already met here. And Libby was right. Anybody who worked in Hollywood who could be surprised by lunatics was not operating on all cylinders—whatever they were.

"And I have to get my hair done tomorrow for the wedding. But no, I'm here trying to get my mother out of one stupid jam after another. I'm even beginning to sound like you. I hate this."

"Libby, we're surrounded by dead bodies, friends rushed off in an ambulance who could well be dead by now, others being held who knows where or by whom, who may have already been killed or soon will be, plus we may soon join them in that fatal situation, and you have to get your hair done for a wedding? God, what have I spawned?"

"Someone who just now saved your tush. Like for the second time. But then I'm still young."

"They weren't going to kill me. They were trying to get me out of here because it's so dangerous. But I couldn't go because you, Maggie, Mitch, Kenny, Brodie, and Keegan are here. Why did you bring them?"

"Because they wouldn't let me come alone. You set them up for this. And I had to save you from your stupid female hero fantasies. I promised Grandma. Mom, I think you've been in showbiz too long. You've lost your perspective."

They whispered in such intense angst at close quarters they were spitting on each other—is that how the noun "spat" evolved? In the real world where people lived normal lives, Charlie would have blown her cool and let the kid have it. But the kid was one more person here who would not have been if it weren't for her and for Maggie. Poor caring Maggie who rescued bees trapped inside window panes, for godsake . . . How could all this crazy be happening? In the context of the last week, Libby almost made sense.

Okay, Greene, get a grip. You can't let Libby's involvement throw you off. You could well be responsible for a whole bunch of people who may still be alive. We settle family feuds when we know we're still going to have one, right?

"Okay, we've got to figure out how to find some of these people, Libby. Tell me what you saw and heard when you and Keegan and Brodie got here. Didn't anyone try to stop you from coming in?"

"We didn't see anybody when we parked. Didn't see your dumb truck even. That really jerked me. The guys wanted to turn and get out of here the minute they noticed, but I wouldn't do it and I had the car. Told 'em they could walk back to Del Mar."

There'd been no problem entering through the wrought iron gate. Most of the lights inside and out were not on, which made it easier to sneak around. "It was like nobody was home and then you'd hear somebody like clear his throat or sniff. We'd freeze. And people with flashlights would go racing around like they had a rabid Doberman biting their

butts. And then everything'd go quiet. There was some shooting and some screaming and everything went quiet again and
you could hear cell phones, people talking on them, and then
quiet again. Where's the Ram?"

"Down the hill in a cul-de-sac."

"So you came up alone?"

"No, with Kenny and Mitch. What else did you see? I
heard Brodie and Keegan talk about looking for you but the
sheriff's department and ambulance arrived before I could
get out to them. Hope they haven't been captured too. I saw
Mitch and Kenny get caught."

"Do you know what's going on?"

"Sort of, I think. I have a hunch it's more than one thing
and that there's going to be some heavy damage control
applied here. Seems to be a lot of drugs around."

"You mean like meth?"

"Prescription drugs like Maggie was on and Mrs. Beesom
and somehow about off-shore money laundering and different government entities either not aware of what the others
are doing or simply unable to modernize fast enough to keep
up with technology and graft and crime—"

"Mom, you're whacking at too many trees at once. Just
relax and think things through. I mean, why would anybody
want to wash money?"

"Hey, Brodie-man, what you doing up here?" a male voice
said aloud on the other side of the door and Libby grabbed
her mother, held a hand over her mouth. What was with this
kid? Jeez.

"Wish I knew, man. Hey, read about your award in the
paper today. Congrats."

"Oh yeah? I haven't seen the paper yet. You a Fed in
disguise, man?"

"I wish. Then I'd be armed too."

"You got a problem there, man," Jerry Parks said in a satisfied tone.

Charlie was in the midst of the irrelevant, irreverent
thought-flash that this was not the first time she'd questioned

the progress of human dialogue when there was a crunch and a grunt and somebody's body hit the floor.

"Jesus, where you been, Monroe? Took you long enough."

Libby let go of Charlie and opened the door. "Hi, guys, like what are you up to? I got Mom here in the closet. Is he dead?"

They left Jerry Parks in the closet, tied at wrists and ankles and gagged with hand towels in case he wasn't dead. Brodie had the gun when they crept to the stairs instead of the elevator.

Keegan was the only one protesting. "What if he's hurt?"

"Of course he's hurt, but *I'm* not dead. Makes up for a lot in my book. That reminds me, Charlie, did you ever read my treatment?" After the long silence, Brodie continued with a Broadway sigh, "I know. You've been too busy. Now what do we do?"

"Try to find Maggie, Mitch, and Kenny, and get us and them the hell out of here before the murderers and different authorities-that-be stop us." Even their whispers echoed in the stairwell. They had checked out the exercise gym and therapy-pool room where no one was floating or tied to a machine and then headed for the stairs rather than the elevator.

"You ever doubt yourself, Charlie?" the aspiring screen-writer asked.

"Always and ever."

"Yeah, right. Now Mom's into parables. How do they force people to take medicines?"

"Good question. Offer them drugged water or food? Knock them out and give them a shot? Not a lot of finesse involved—people in that basement room were really sick."

"Looks like whoever got to the fuse box didn't finish the job," Keegan said when they reached the main floor. Some rooms were lit, others not.

One lit up as they passed it and they flattened against the wall of the hallway, Charlie leaning around to peer into the kitchen. It appeared empty until a shadow moved from behind the partition where Deputy Saucier had made them coffee.

"You realize, do you not, that you are helping the bad guys here? Obstructing justice by your actions? Have you no loyalty to your great nation and your church and your flag and everything we all hold dear?" a male voice said, seemingly from several different directions at once. Charlie ducked back away from the door to see Brodie holding the gun out in front of him in both hands swinging his head from up the hall to down, trying to determine which way to open fire and Keegan slipping down the hall toward the office and auditorium, head and upper torso bent forward as if following something he saw or maybe heard.

"Careful, VanZant," a different male voice said. "You can't reason with the righteous. They know the only real truth is what *they* believe in—whatever it may be. And that only the weak and the evil waffle." That voice sounded a lot like Mitch Hilsten in *All The President's Buddies*, a flick that deserved to go nowhere and achieved that destination, even in straight to DVD.

At least Brodie had the gun aimed at the floor now. Libby nudged Charlie and pointed up to a round ventlike thing—the light was too poor to be sure. No, it was too small for a vent, more like a PA system.

Raoul's was the next voice. "Butt up, Margar-r-r-eet. Now looooose yourself in the floating, warma universe." Then a gargling, gagging, choking—a slapping at water and Maggie's scream which tore at what little composure Charlie had left. She shouldn't have left Maggie here in this place to begin with. Just like Libby said, everything was Charlie's fault. Had Dashiell recorded Raoul's death?

"It's time for your medication, Caroline," Warren VanZant said softly, tenderly.

"What every woman needs is a fighting chance against the ravages of menopause and estrogen is the answer. Countless supposed scientific studies blame everything from God, Mother Nature, the devil, and drinking coffee for the debilitating sickness of hot flashes and the misery of sleeplessness and memory loss that affects mood and appetite. The right dosage prescribed personally by your doctor for you and without the progesterone will keep you happy and safe, sexually active, and free of breast cancer. But there is a conspiracy to keep you or any woman from ever becoming President of the United States." Startled laughter from a captive audience. And Dr. Judy said, "I can't say that, can I?"

"You're doing fine, Dr. Judd," Ruth Ann Singer snapped, condescendingly. "Please continue with the script as written. We will edit out that last line."

Charlie peered around the door once more. None of the shadows moved this time, as if the whole place had paused to listen to the voices on the PA. It reminded her again of how illogically riveting were the voices hiding behind the closed doors of wardrobes.

Charlie turned to find Brodie and even Libby looking at her as if for direction. It was a strange mix of messages on the PA. Charlie put her finger to her lips and nodded in the direction Keegan Monroe had headed. Someone was sending out mixed messages from either the office or the control room in the auditorium.

But they'd gotten only a few steps before Margaret Mildred Stutzman said, "Charlie? Please help me. Please? Hurry."

Charlie was at first awash in helplessness and guilt. But then she rejoiced in the fact that her best friend in the whole world *was* alive, as she'd been stubbornly maintaining all along. Yes! But then she'd heard Raoul's voice too. She had no reason to think she'd been lied to about his death and the next voice on the PA further dashed that brief hope.

It was Dashiell's voice. And Charlie knew that he *was* dead.

Thirty-Six

"**Y**ou going to make it?" Libby whispered in Charlie's ear.

And the gruesomely dead Dashiell Hammett said from the grave and the PA system, "I love my mother, God is my witness. She will protect me from my cravings and from those who try to steal my sanity. For her I would kill, but for no one else. I'm recording this so—"

"Because she loves me. The only person in the world who can say that," he said after a pause as if the other person in the conversation was talking to him on the phone.

The sounds came from the direction of the auditorium where Judith Judd had taped shows for worried, aging health nuts and pharmaceutical companies anxious to pitch to them. They sidled down the hall toward it, Charlie of two minds about Brodie packing a gun. He seemed to be too and uncertain whether to cover their front or their rear. She worried he might shoot his foot or Charlie and Libby by mistake if startled.

Charlie shivered in her clammy wet clothes and hair. Even in the intermittent and dim light Libby looked as if she'd been dragged through a drain pipe—smudged and soggy. Keegan seemed to have disappeared. The office was dark as they passed. How could she persuade Libby and Brodie to take off for the Wrangler so she'd have two less to worry about? Probably about as easy as Roy-to-the-rescue had in getting Charlie out of here.

"What does Washington say about this? We have to do something soon."

"Which part of it and who? My instructions say the White House gave us the authorization here and you and your bean counters can come in for the cleanup."

"Right. After you've removed all the records we need to investigate," the second voice said. "Leave us to take the blame for the coverup."

"I thought I made myself clear. There is nothing to cover up. You people just don't listen."

"You people just don't read the papers."

Dr. Judy looked a lot better on the big screen in the auditorium than she had in person. She never turned her back on the audience or the cameras so her hump didn't show. She merely highlighted points on the small screen with a clicker and turned her head toward it as she spoke. She wasn't glamorous but she was compelling and convincing—at least when you couldn't hear what she said. It was disconcerting to be hearing other people on the sound system instead.

"We happen to know that you, as her Hollywood agent, had intimate knowledge of Dr. Judd's financial dealings, Ms. Ridgeway. If you cooperate we could perhaps—"

"You'll have to take that up with her lawyer, her accountant, and financial advisers. As an agent I have knowledge only of her performance contracts and commitments and am not permitted to discuss such unless subpoenaed in a court of law."

"Oh, come now. Hollywood is hardly known for its integrity, morality, or sincerity. You can't expect us to—" This was the guy who'd dripped condescension at the coffee gathering in the dining room last night. Okay, one of the guys.

All the while Dr. Judy motioned, stepped from side to side, nodded and squinted knowingly, tilted her head, mouthing words with studied lip, tongue, and teeth coordination you probably wouldn't have noticed had there been sound.

Libby nudged Charlie's arm and pointed down into the auditorium seating where a shadow man sat, with his back to them, not watching Dr. Judy. By the exaggerated tilt of his head, he

216

was either asleep, unconscious, or dead like the doctor.

Charlie feared it might be Keegan but was afraid to slip down and take a look because she didn't know who else might be in the fringes of shadow left by the flickering of the screen on the stage or who was running this show from the control room.

"So, Charlie Greene, what do you think of the show so far, humm?" Ruth Ann Singer asked and if you looked closely at the window of the control room you could see blonde hair in the colored glow of flashing monitors and blinking consoles. There had to be another door into it from outside the auditorium.

Didn't there? The one behind the screen wouldn't hide traffic to and from and would be a distraction for an audience being filmed. Of course they could edit the videos— still, it would be very handy to have direct access. There had been so much money lavishly wasted on this place, hard to believe that would have been overlooked. Symmetry didn't appear to be a high priority.

Charlie backed out of the auditorium tugging Brodie and Libby with her, then putting her index fingers on each of their lips as her daughter had done to her a short time ago. Her inner voice was not so easily stilled, however.

Do we have a clue what's up? That anyone is safer out here than in there? I have the feeling that wasn't Keegan Monroe slumped over in the theater seat, don't you?

Charlie wasn't about to answer herself at all. Someone could be picking people off or out of the halls one by one. If it was the federal types why was snappy number running the show from the control room? Charlie so wished she had the mind of a detective and at the same time so wished she didn't need to. Her calling was not danger and weirdness, violent people doing unexpected things.

Which reminded her of her vibrating cellular. What if Kenny or Mitch was trying to contact her? She should be able to listen to her messages without making noise. She motioned to Libby and Brodie with the cell in hand that she wanted to hide behind them to reduce the glow of the screen.

There was a message from Kenny. She slid her shirt up over her head to hide any sound. He was lost in the walls someplace, trying to get out. "Stay away from the main building and Jerry Parks, the reporter. Try to get out of here and get help. Don't know what happened to Hilsten."

She couldn't return the call without making noise. How did he get lost in the walls? Had he been drugged too, didn't really know what he was saying? He'd sounded tired, but not slurred or incoherent. The other messages weren't worth opening now.

Charlie came out from under her shirt to hear the PA system over the exaggerated drumming of her heart and to see Libby walking down the hall into the shadows.

"You do see the futility of refusing to cooperate with the full might of the United States Government, surely," some guy said from the speaker overhead.

"I don't see the United States Government. I see one dumb-ass bureaucrat where last night I saw three," Kenny Cowper said. "Things aren't going so good for you guys either, huh?"

Charlie followed Brodie who had crept off in the same direction as had Libby. They mustn't get separated. But they did. When she caught up with Brodie, he'd already lost Libby.

"Did she say anything?" Charlie whispered.

"She wondered why the PA system wouldn't be in the office instead of mixed in with the auditorium sound system. What we were hearing came from speakers in the halls. I don't know if I can take much more of this."

"Charlie? Why did you leave me?" Maggie said. She was crying.

"I'm not sure I can either, Brodie." About the time they reached the office, the lights came on. Everywhere. It was blinding. Somebody must have found the switch.

"Caroline, come out now. Stop this madness," Warren VanZant pleaded with his wife. "Just leave the rifle and come to the office. We'll help you, I promise."

Charlie saw no sign of a PA system but there was one shoe in the air above the desk with a pant leg attached. Charlie walked around to see the rest of the Fed sprawled across the tipped-over desk chair instead of Warren VanZant. Charlie wondered if he had been part of "we" with VanZant. Hard to tell which of any of the broadcasts were new or just pre-recorded. If they were both, there must be two systems or two or more accesses to the one.

"Oh God." Brodie turned away from the body on the floor. "Who's that?"

"A federali. If my hunch that the guy slumped over in the front row of the auditorium is one of them and is dead—all three that questioned us last night are dead plus one way out back I'd never seen—you'd think they'd send in the marines by now. And at least two members of the San Diego County Sheriff's Department were real close to being fatally poisoned. There are deputies on the premises and last I knew an ambulance sitting out in the parking lot. Seems like every-body's waiting for word of what to do and meanwhile sweet little Caroline VanZant is running around killing people with a rifle and my daughter's here somewhere."

"Plus your two boyfriends. And your star client, don't forget. Me even."

"I didn't forget all you guys, it's just—"

"I know, it's the mom thing. Sure glad my mom's back home. If we get out of this alive, will you—"

"I promise I'll read your treatment."

"She talked, Warren. I know who killed Dashiell. You thought she was dead but she talked. Where is he?"

"I don't know where he is. I thought you killed him already. Caroline, please stop this. Meet me in our room. But don't bring the rifle. I swear everything will be okay."

She was on the PA. He was yelling from somewhere close. Charlie's phone vibrated in her pocket again and she pulled up her shirt to talk in it again. "Mom, where are you?"

"In the office. Where are you?"

"I'm in the walls with Kenny and Mitch. Have you seen Keegan and Brodie?"

"Brodie's with me. I don't know where Keegan is. How

can we get to you? It's getting dangerous out here."

"Mom and Brodie are in the office. What do I tell them?"

"Charlie?" Mitch took over, "there's a men's room right around the corner to the right and across the hall next to it is a janitor's closet. Jump in the closet quick and the wall behind the utility cart is open. We'll wait for you. And move fast, sounds like some heavy artillery out there."

"Tell me about it." Another gunshot just as they reached the closet and the door opened by itself and someone yanked Charlie into darkness. "Don't forget Brodie."

Thirty-Seven

They sat on stacked boxes, under a dim lightbulb stuck in a white socket thing with a chain attached, enough box stacks to seat them all. Brodie had dropped the gun when he was yanked into the closet so they were now disarmed. At least he hadn't shot off his foot. Mitch and Kenny thought they should all wait it out until the shooting was over and everybody was dead and then they could just walk out of the place.

Charlie had a few problems with that. "One, the gun battle sounds like it's winding down to two combatants—the VanZants—both of whom must know of these lost spaces in the architecture, since they oversaw the most recent remodel job, and must have overseen or carried in themselves the furnishings upon which we lounge. Two, I don't know where Keegan is. Three, if I'm guessing correctly, there are at least four murdered federal investigators on the property and a few sheriff's deputies awaiting word on what to do when Washington sorts all this out. There's going to be a lot of bad blood between local and national agencies and we small folks are not going to count for much in the fracas.

"And nobody is going to want to admit that a pissed-off mother can wipe out such important investigations. It's either going to be totally hushed up or spun out of control and witnesses will have to be discredited or destroyed. And four, I have not found Maggie yet, dead or alive."

"Charlie, this is not Hollywood," Kenny said. "This is reality. There are lives on the line here—whether Maggie is dead or not."

"You bet there are and you're looking at them. You have any idea of the 'collateral damage' to the presently assembled there could be if somebody decides a fire would solve the problem? How is this space vented, do you know? Any loss of life here could be chalked up to the crazy mom up there getting even for the murder of her son. And we sit here inside the walls."

After a silence in which everyone stared at Charlie and then sideways-glanced at others to check out how crazy things were getting, Mitch said, "Charlie, you got to stop handling mystery writers."

This from the producer of *Jane of the Jungle* yet. Oh boy.

This tunnel-like space dead ended around a curve Charlie would bet came about when the circular auditorium was added and it was fitted with the lightbulb because it had already been wired as part of a room and was now used for storage. Kenny had found this one because it had an entrance to it off the men's room as well and the light had been left on, so he saw it through the crack at the back of a cupboard where toilet tissue and paper towels were stored. He'd stepped into the cupboard when he heard someone approaching.

It was Mitch. They had both been interrogated by the gentlemen in suits, their conversations recorded by someone and mixed with others in the past to entertain Charlie and company. The suits were called out of the room by someone behind Kenny and Mitch who were warned not to leave their seats. But the inquisitors never returned. The two had gotten into a "spat" and separated. Both being unarmed, they'd hidden in odd places and found other holes in the walls used for storage, some lit, some not. Both were looking for Charlie and her daughter.

"I saw you guys get captured. Who were those people?" Charlie asked.

"Sheriff's guys, apparently. They delivered us to the Feds and I haven't seen them since. I don't know what happened to them." Kenny's beard was growing out. On him it looked good, even with the dark patches around his eyes and the smudges.

"I do," Mitch said. "They were ordered to the parking lot, until priorities got untangled." He didn't look to have any more bruises than before. Charlie's life was sure hard on her friends.

"Kenny, why did you call to tell me to stay away from Jerry Parks?"

"He's a lunatic, that's why. He was moaning—all tied up in a closet and I let him loose. Tried to ram me, sock me. You'd think he'd been grateful but—"

"You let him loose? He tried to kill me," Brodie said. "He's probably going to find his gun and come after us again."

"Just because Charlie stuffed his cell phone in the used tampon receptacle in the ladies' room at the Islandia?"

"I vote we try to make a run for the parking lot. We're not that far from it here." Libby stood up to brush her tight little tush, not one male eye in the room ignoring the gesture, and then bent over to take a closer look at the writing on her box.

"What if he's got Keegan? And I have to find Maggie or what happened to her," Charlie insisted.

But Libby was too busy examining the contents of the box, pulling out smaller boxes to read labels, lifting the top box off to investigate the box beneath. "Like, you could put together a sweet little meth lab with all this. All you'd need is a chemical or two and a hot plate."

"You know how to make meth?" Charlie's voice gurgled like she'd never known it to do before.

"I don't know what the chemicals are or how long to cook it, but I could find out easy enough. Lots of other good ingredients here though."

"You could find out? Who are you running with now who'd know that?"

"Mom, don't start. We're in enough trouble without you losing it. You're driving me crazy."

"I'm driving *you* crazy?" Now Charlie was sputtering. Just like Edwina used to do. "Ohgod, when's your grandmother's plane due in?"

"I don't know, but she's a big girl. She could get a van or taxi from the airport. Jacob has a key to let her in." Libby shook her straggly hair in despair, ran her fingers through it and shook it again into perfect place to cup her face. Must have dried.

"I vote for Libby's idea," Mitch said. "And I think we better move before the shooting starts again."

"You got it," Kenny agreed.

"I'm in," Brodie added his blessing. "You're outnumbered, Charlie. You know it's best for Libby."

She nodded. It's horrible to have to make choices between those you love.

The first in line had just entered the broom closet when the light went out behind them. They were stumbling, reaching for each other as they moved around the janitors' cart and straggled out into the hall, making more noise than they wanted to as they knocked various items off onto the floor on the way.

Charlie blinked sticky contacts around, trying to focus on the dimmer shadow that was the front glass doors to outside and the parking lot somewhere at the end of the rainbow when she realized she'd lost touch with whoever was in front of her and reached back for whoever was behind. Something slid around her waist and yanked her out of the line, a hand clapped so tight over her mouth that it jerked her head back so she lost what little sight she'd had of her companions and she was lifted back into deeper shadow, unable to call out or even to swallow.

She barely felt the prick in her arm before a spreading weakness enveloped her.

Thirty-Eight

It was like sirens, humming a beautiful beckoning melody, lured Charlie from a sleep so deep it left her euphoric. Every cell of her body not only felt no pain but flowed, refreshed, to consciousness—almost like an orgasm and vaguely similar, but not as exhausting. Each intake of breath felt marvelous, renewing.

"Need help with depression? We all do sometimes. Why be miserable or just plain down when you don't have to?" a male voice, smooth as good scotch and as comforting, enticed over the sirens' background purring. "Studies show that Euphoria Four, just out of testing and soon to hit pharmacy shelves near you, makes all other mood medication pale in comparison." The sirens sighed in three-part harmony and in minor key, made you want to stretch like a cat. Charlie sighed too, too content and cozy to open her eyes.

"Tell your doctor about this amazing relief for the sadness-afflicted. Tell your doctor it might be right for you. Not suitable for children, pregnant or nursing women, adults with addictions or mental illness, anyone under treatment for cancer or diagnosed with attention deficit disorder, or people over eighty-five. Can cause loss of bladder control, heart palpitations, certain sexual side effects and dry mouth."

Then an unmistakable sound forced Charlie to open her eyes and her adrenalin to surge—Margaret Mildred Stutzman's giggle, unmistakable, an epiphany that brought on headache, dizziness, pounding heartbeat, a real urge to pee, and dry mouth.

"Maggie!" She sat up in a deep, dizzy darkness, a reeling

225

world she couldn't see, a cramping nausea. "Maggie, help me."

A rough hand pushed her back onto a soft surface that warped and buckled and tried to buck her off. There was nothing in her stomach but it tried to come up anyway.

"How do you like being on the other end of the power struggle this time and in a big way, big-deal Hollywood agent?" Jerry Parks said.

"Where's Maggie?"

"You'll be with her soon enough. First I just thought you'd like to know you murdered Dr. Grant Howard, Charlie. Know how? You backed up that no-talent Brodie Caulfield's pitch, that's how. I didn't believe it until you said it was true. I asked Howard and he said he didn't read the submissions but brought people like me and hotshots like you together. Well, you see where that got him. It got him dead. And you were nice enough to bring your friend Maggie to the Islandia and good old Dashiell was good enough to bring a bag of drugs with her name on them and then bring her back here. We'd decided to pin everything on Dashiell, but your friend Maggie offered herself up for sacrifice. You both have been a great help from the beginning."

"I heard Maggie. She's here."

"You smartass types like to dump on little people's dreams. Well, you don't have that right. This time, this little guy's gonna bring to an end all of your dreams." He pulled at Charlie's clothes. "All I wanted was time and money enough to write screenplays and be a father to my kid. But no, I wasn't good enough for big-deal Dr. Judy, creepy old hag. She had so much money, she couldn't have spent it all in a hundred years. But then she didn't get the chance, did she?"

"Caroline? Caroline, where are you? You need help, darling. Let me help you," Warren VanZant's soothing voice crooned like the sirens, hummed.

Charlie mustered the strength to knee Parks as he pulled at her underwear, but apparently didn't get him in the right socket.

"Your agent, Ridgeway, thought she had the goods on me, all the evidence that I had no rights to my daughter's money. Well, I got the goods on Dr. Judith Judd and her estate and double dealings and I'm going to write an exposé that will topple her empire and expose the pharmaceutical industry and the IRS and who knows what all? Got it all stashed somewhere safe. Going to make your Kenneth Cooper look like an amateur."

"Charlie." Mitch's voice. "We're here, do you have your cell? Let us know where you are."

"You don't have your cell, Charlie, I do. Just relax and enjoy the last chance you'll have to enjoy anything. You're soon going to join your friends but first I'm going to make you happier than you'll ever be again. What difference does it make if you're dead?"

An explosion. No, a gunshot. This one very close. Then silence. Then the lights. Charlie couldn't see Maggie anywhere. But she could see Jerry Parks. He was the one who was dead. She was half off the bed, he was on the floor next to it. She threw up spit and stomach juices on his face or what was left of it.

"Well, here we are full circle," Caroline VanZant's voice came, toneless, flat.

Charlie didn't know if the woman was on the PA or in the room. She did know the bereaved mother was dangerous. "Caroline, help me find Maggie and Keegan. We have to get out of here. The whole place is going to blow up and burn."

"Get off that bed and put on your clothes. You're disgusting."

Charlie rolled over to find herself in the Victorian room with the dippy chandelier. Caroline VanZant stood swaying in the warped doorway, her rifle leveled at Charlie. How could she level it when she was swaying? Charlie tried to grab a bed post and pull herself up. "No, really. It's a meth lab and they do that—blow up, I mean. We gotta hurry and find Maggie and Keegan."

The crazed part of Charlie's mind saw the whole room tilt

as she fell off the bed again, this time trying to crawl past Jerry Parks' ruined head to get to the stool in the bathroom, fighting the excruciating cramping in her body's uncentered center. The partially sane side hoped Caroline wouldn't shoot her and tried to figure out how many bullets were in that rifle and if there was a refill. The next thing she knew, she was on the floor of the shower, water beating over her and lavender shower gel suds everywhere.

Then skewered images of the tile and shower door and the long mirror in its frame with the trunnions and then the voice in the wardrobe and Jerry Parks' blood and tissue and yuck all over the floor. He didn't say anything but the wardrobe said, "Euphoria Four, on your druggist's shelves this month. Don't wait for a busy doctor to discover it. You be the first to tell the doctor about it and he or she will be the first to thank you." Caroline took her out into the hall. It tilted.

"Charlie, where are you? Answer me." Mitch on the PA.

"I'm here. Wherever here is."

"Caroline, please," Warren VanZant's voice next over the eerie-sounding sound system.

Charlie's hair dripped onto the lush terrycloth robe and the soft slip-ons were too big for her feet again. She smelled like lavender shower gel. She felt a little better.

"Don't listen to the voices." Caroline pulled Charlie along by the elbow. "I'm taking you to your Maggie. She's back where she started."

Maggie floated in the second eddy pool from the left, wrapped again in seaweed. But Caroline yanked Charlie on by and into the foliage behind it, through a door in the wall and into the space inside it. "I was going to use her to entice you out of hiding but now I don't have to. You must be very quiet. I have one bullet left. It is for the one who killed my son and tried to kill your Maggie and Luella too. Don't make me waste it on you or your friends, Charlie Greene. You wouldn't want that, would you?"

Charlie didn't have time to answer—her brain worked way

slow and the door that opened in front of her way fast. Here was the back door to the control room she'd known must exist. Mitch pleaded into a microphone for Charlie to answer him, Kenny and Sue Rippon tried to do CPR on Ruth Ann Singer, no longer very snappy, and Warren VanZant turned to face his wife. His skin turned too, turned as gray as his eyebrows and hair fringe.

Everyone froze but Kenny who rose slowly to his feet.

"Back on your knees, Mr. Cooper, or your agent is a dead woman. Everyone be very very very still. I want only the one man left who killed my son. The other is dead already."

"Caroline, listen to me, please. I can explain about Dashiell."

"Miss Ridgeway already has."

Charlie felt like an accordion deflating as she waffled to the floor to join Ruth Ann and Caroline VanZant used her last bullet.

"Maggie's in the eddy pool," Charlie insisted as Kenny tried to make her lie still on the floor of the auditorium while Caroline slouched exhausted in a front row seat and Mitch tried to contact the outside world on his cell. Sue Rippon cuddled Ruth Ann and rocked her in her arms.

"The medics say they've been ordered not to come in. They're waiting for word from higher up. Can we get the wounded to the gate?" Mitch said. "Looks like we should gather up the living and make a run for it."

Dr. Judy still entranced silently on the screen.

"Eddy pool," Charlie insisted and struggled out from under Kenny Cowper. "Must get Maggie too. Can't leave her. Whole place's gonna blow up in an earthquake."

"Christ, Cowper, can't you do anything right," Mitch said behind her and she left the clumsy slippers in the auditorium for Kenny to trip over and ran barefoot into the blood-spattered control room while Kenny informed Mitch where he could go and the sooner the better.

Charlie was in the dark space inside the walls before he

229

caught up with her and then he snagged the robe instead. She ran out of it. It was dark in here and he had a little trouble finding her and she had a lot of it finding the door out to the deck with the pools. He pleaded with her the whole time, swearing even. He insisted there was no door and they had no time to look for it if there was.

Charlie found it anyway and kicked it open, struggling against him and slipping out of his grasp because too much shower gel had left her slimy and because he was, when all was said and done, a gentleman by nature, and maybe because she was his agent. Agents aren't nearly as powerful as writers think, but the delusion is necessary for much-battered egos.

Hey, welcome back to some sanity, babe, her inner voice kicked in. I thought you were a goner there.

"Charlie, you are sick, trust me. I don't want to hurt you but I can't let you run around demented—everything will be okay."

Maggie was no longer stretched out in the second eddy pool on the left. She sort of sat and sort of leaned on its edge trying to unwrap stiff seaweed.

Thirty-Nine

Kenny couldn't believe Maggie was alive. He slid the terrycloth robe over Charlie's nakedness and they both helped Maggie out of the seaweed and still ended up with a naked woman. So Charlie put the robe around her best friend and Kenny took off his shirt to put it over Charlie. It came to her knees. "Isn't it weird how we worry about relative incidentals at times like these?"

Charlie was hugging Maggie and crying when Kenny's cell beckoned.

"Hilsten says to sneak out to the front gate fast. Medics in the parking lot say there's an imminent invasion and they've been ordered off the site. Charlie, you know the layout better than I do. He says don't go back to the auditorium. He and Sue have the remaining survivors almost to the gate. How do we get there from here fast?"

Maggie was still not herself so they had their hands full. Finally, Kenny picked her up and carried her.

"What about Keegan?" Charlie yelled over Maggie's protests and led the way outside and around the building to the service road. The drone of approaching helicopters was not far enough away when the girl named Roy came running toward them, grabbed Charlie, and raced her to the back of an already crowded ambulance. Then she yelled for everyone to duck and she and Kenny passed Maggie on to reaching arms of medics at the back. They were stuffed inside at a totally illegal number and burned rubber whizzing out of the lot and down over the ridge into obscurity before turning on lights but still without sirens.

231

"Was Libby's Jeep gone? What if she and Brodie waited for us in the parking lot?" Charlie was fast approaching hysteria and knew it.

"The Wrangler wasn't in the lot, Charlie," Mitch said from somewhere in the standing-room-only space.

"I can't get the door shut," a medic shouted. "Everyone stand as still as possible. I need a couple of volunteers to get off when we get to a safe place to stop. We won't have room to care for the sick."

"Let me off here," Kenny shouted. "Charlie, give me your keys, I'll get your truck. What hospital you guys headed for?"

"I'll go with him," Mitch shouted too and the medic at the door that wouldn't close nearly fell out when everyone jostled around to move out of Mitch's path as he made his way to the back.

"Me too," Charlie said.

"You have to go with us," Roy ordered. "You've been heavily drugged."

"Yeah," Mitch added as he and Kenny jumped out the back. "And you have to admit Maggie to the emergency room. She doesn't have any ID or insurance card."

"Somebody move it, I got a real sick lady—think I'm losing her," a male nurse yelled.

"Oh, and you think I do?" Charlie spread her arms to emphasize that all she wore was her contacts and Kenny's shirt. "Where do you suppose I'm keeping it? And the keys to the truck?" She squirmed out of Roy's grip and jumped, praying one of the guys would catch her.

"Move it!" The nurse screamed it this time.

The siren screamed too. Charlie scored a hit in poor Kenny's arms. Roy stared at them wide-eyed through a double window in the door as it closed and the ambulance took off downhill.

"Anybody got a flashlight?" Mitch asked without much hope.

Charlie had nothing but a purse in her truck with another

pair of shoes and a hidden key. Kenny and Mitch still had their cells. When they'd slipped out of sight of the main road to pick up Mitch's car first because it was closest, Charlie left a message for Libby on Mitch's cell. He'd had more time to check out the parking lot before their getaway and had remembered only a spa van and a couple of plain, white, unmarked, identical Chevy Blazers parked side-by-side, government issue without BORDER PATROL on the door.

Dawn threatened but not hard, there were still a lot of clouds and a rain smell to the air and little street lighting here. All the cul-de-sacs looked alike and everybody had a dog either inside the house or garage or out in fenced yards. Charlie kept squeaking her pain at stubbing bare toes. House cats prowled freely, hissing and moaning at them and each other. Porch lights came on.

Finally, Kenny picked her up again and ran after Mitch who'd spotted his car. By the time they reached it, helicopters flew low over the promontory's top. Searchlights swept across it and the Sea Spa at the Marina del Sol, searching for landing spots. Paratroopers dropped from others.

"Jeez, look at all the stuff they're wearing," Mitch whispered as the odd shapes with two legs floated down from above. The sound of heavy vehicles grinding up the main road they'd left a short time ago and still they stood entranced by the commotion in the sky. "Man, *Jane of the Jungle*'s starting to look hackneyed. You just can't outclass reality anymore."

Mitch's cell buzzed. Libby wanted to know what to do. She had Brodie and Keegan. Keegan had lost everyone and decided to wait out in the Wrangler when he heard more shooting. Libby and Brodie found him there. "You all go back to Les Artistes, honey, and get some sleep. I'll be there soon. I'm all right and so is Maggie."

The growing clacking and roaring waxed horrific. Houses lit up behind them, excited voices called to each other from yards, decks, porches. Even down where they were, the air filled with dust and the smell of jet fuels and smoke from

233

flares. Still they stood and watched, Charlie thinking about all her credentials somewhere in the Sea Spa and Maggie Stutzman's too, and Luella Ridgeway's along with who-knew-how-many murdered Feds.

"You know, if they're smart they'll have a roadblock set up somewhere down the road. They don't know everybody left up there is dead and the killer is on her way to a hospital. Seems likely some of the dead communicated our names to their headquarters before she blew them away." Mitch sighed, shivered. "All those dead Feds. Somebody's going to have to go down for this. Is poor Caroline VanZant going to be enough to satisfy egos? And won't that make for embarrassing headlines."

Kenny shook his head. "I still can't believe it. Sweet, soft spoken, little old lady—"

"Probably only in her fifties," Mitch said.

Charlie added, "Don't mess with mothers."

Behind them, some guy yelled, "We being invaded?"

"Washington's invading California," another answered.

"Yeah, they want to liberate our fruits and vegetables."

"Send for Governor Arnie. He'll take 'em out."

Charlie would have thought that with their homes so close to the invasion these people would have been less jocular. How could they know it wouldn't spill over into their neighborhoods? But then, they hadn't spent the weird night she had, didn't have their identifying documents up there awaiting discovery. "Let's get out of here if we can."

Mitch's car got them down to Charlie's truck without a roadblock. They figured it would be at the juncture of the turnoff to the marina. He left them there and took his car down. He had a pass into the marina and a legitimate right to be there. Charlie started the truck down after him and he called Kenny to say there was no roadblock, so she drove him down to his car which Mitch could get out of the Marina del Sol with his guest card and the three of them decided to try to get all their vehicles away.

They'd returned to the wye, Mitch in the lead, Charlie

sans license, underwear, or identification in the middle so they could try to help her out if need be, when the earth shook. Charlie's first thought was, wouldn't you know—*now* the earthquake of the century, like in a bad film. But the people on a lit balcony across the road did not appear affected and no cracks opened up around her, no buildings tumbled. A dark cloud billowed overhead, set back the dawn, and smelled like smoke.

"I knew it. There was a meth lab there and somebody blew it up."

Forty

Charlie, still with no identification but fully clothed, sat between her mother and Mitch Hilsten on rented folding chairs in the lovely garden of the Esterhazie mansion and watched as Libby Abigail Greene—stately and gorgeous—walked out of the wedding arbor on the arm of Douglas Esterhazie, heir to a fortune built by concrete, tall and better looking by the day and perfect for her but headed for Yale and success and some vacuous Buffy while Libby cheerfully headed for disaster. They would have been perfect for each other and Charlie would have been able to sleep nights. But noooo.

They could have had their wedding here and Libby could have been safe and cared for and—Edwina Greene nudged her, handed over a Kleenex before Charlie realized she'd been sniffling. Charlie's mother'd had an extreme makeover. She didn't look younger, but she did look better, sort of. For some reason, Charlie resented it anyway.

Edwina dabbed a tissue under her own eye and whispered, "I'd always hoped it would be you walking out from that arbor."

"Why would what's-her-name want me as bridesmaid?" Charlie was pretty sure it was Carol or Carolyn or something like that.

"I was thinking of you as the bride. You'd have been cared for, safe, and solvent. Edward could have discouraged your foolish, dangerous escapades. And I could sleep nights."

Charlie turned to look at her mother who, like Libby, was taller than she even though the hump had set in. Wow, I'm turning into my own mother. And I'm adopted.

Looking perfect for each other from behind too, Libby and Doug climbed the stairs to join Ed and the minister in the gazebo. The string ensemble segued into the opening strains of the wedding march. The minister turned his hands palm up, signaling the guests to rise. All heads swiveled to the arbor once more as the resplendent bride, confident and happy, appeared on her father's arm. He was elderly and shaky and what's-her-name had to move carefully to keep her gown out of his path, adjust her stride to accommodate his infirmities.

Tables sat under awnings on the lawns for the wedding dinner and, except for the bridal party, the seating was open. Charlie found a seat next to the minister in search of respite from her mother and Mitch and their reveries. Servers in maroon tuxedos brought trays filled with glasses of champagne for the wedding toast.

The minister was a portly gentleman and, his duties over, he removed his tux jacket and wiped his brow with a cloth handkerchief and when that didn't do the job, the linen napkin under his silverware. She congratulated him on a "service" that had been more good-natured than inspirational. He leaned backward and to one side to smile and nod at her, raised his goblet to hers, and emptied it. Charlie did too. Observant servers had them soon refilled.

During the teasing speeches to toast the couple by the groom's son and friends and the bride's father and friends, the reverend pulled out what he explained was a medibaggy. It had pockets for morning, noon, and night and separate zip-lock openings for each section.

"They're new. You can get small boxes of them free at your pharmacy. Very handy for the traveling medicated, which seems to be everyone these days." He proceeded to pour out one whole section into his palm, pop the handful of odd sized, shaped, and colored capsules into his mouth and wash them down with a shot of champagne.

Charlie couldn't bring herself to ask if he, by chance, suffered from dry mouth. After the week she'd had not much seemed strange today. The string ensemble continued to play, Ed and his bride did a little waltzing, Charlie emptied her champagne glass and it was refilled the minute she set it down. She was truly weary. She didn't feel like mixing. Just to sit still, fully dressed, with no need to run or hide or know terror for those she loved was such a blessing.

Doug, Libby, and Lori Schantz, had been buds all through high school and now they mimicked the bride and groom's formal dancing. The ensemble broke out in some modern thing that left the groom on the sidelines while the bride and the other kids danced in a foursome.

Betty Beesom had arrived on Jacob Forney's arm, a little wobbly but obviously enjoying it all. There was a breeze and enough chill in the air when the clouds came over the sun that the radiant heaters under the canvas canopies felt good.

Charlie had aches and bruises and bumps, but her innards had settled down after a double latte, nine hours of sleep, and two poached eggs on milk toast. None of which gave her a dry mouth. Even with her mother in the house.

Maggie and Luella were still in the hospital but recovering. Charlie, against all advice, had refused to be admitted. She figured she'd pretty well absorbed or eliminated the drugs and had no intention of having her stomach pumped.

The dinner was something of a blur, served on covered plates, no buffet style here in the midst of riches. Steak-caesar salad, lobster and crab chunks in a creamy butter sauce over rice— Charlie lost track. Suddenly the groom and Mitch were sitting on either side of her. "It was a beautiful wedding. I'm so happy for you. But I think I need another nine hours of sleep."

"I can't believe you made it here at all after what you've been through," Ed Esterhazie told her. "Thanks Charlie. It meant a lot to me."

Charlie let Mitch take her home early, both expecting to be met by somebody from the San Diego County Sheriff's Department and/or various local representatives of the federal government, at least a slew of news media types. No one met them but the cat.

She crawled into her sleep tee and a fuzzy robe. Mitch made hot tea and they settled in front of the TV to watch the news. Nothing about the invasion of the Sea Spa at the Marina del Sol or its condition now. Mitch got out his laptop to check the Internet, hers still hiding at the Esterhazies'. No news there either. She'd heard nothing about the condition of Detective Solomon, Deputy Saucier or Ruth Ann Singer, and assumed Caroline VanZant was in a cell somewhere. Kenny had gone back to his room at the Islandia to wait out events and continue his investigative research.

Charlie expected to be arrested for something any minute but was too sleepy to wait up. She woke when Edwina and Libby came home. The lamp was on and Mitch asleep in the chair with the ottoman and Tuxedo stretched out on her chest.

"Think Tux knows?" Libby asked her grandmother. "I've never seen him get that close to Mom without hissing."

"I wonder," Edwina said.

Forty-One

A week after the wedding there was still no news on the fate of the Sea Spa at the Marina del Sol or investigations into the streak of murders there, or the invasion by helicopters—as if nothing had happened. Mitch and Kenny were both down in San Diego now and reported no obituaries except for those of Grant Howard and Dr. Judith Judd. At least their deaths were listed as "still under investigation." A small notice of the burial of Dashiell Hammett and Raoul Segundo, both listed with cause of death as drowning and without mention of the possibility of foul play or being still under a coroner's investigation. Lone survivor for Dashiell was his mother and he was predeceased by his father, Welmer Hammett. For Raoul a daughter, Susan Rippon, predeceased by his parents and a brother, all with the surname of Jones.

The whole mess got weirder. And the weirdest of all was that when Kenny contacted the *Union-Tribune*, he was told that Jerry Parks had taken a job at another paper out of state when Kenny and Charlie and a few others knew for sure that the man was dead. And no mention of the dead Feds yet either. Charlie had seen at least four herself. It was like something hid the voices in the wardrobe as well as the pictures this time.

Plus the cat was acting funny—not that Tuxedo Greene had ever acted normally. She caught Doug and Lori, waiting for Libby to finish her makeup, watching the black feline with white chest and feet watch Charlie drag a bruised, sore, but grateful-to-be-alive-and-ambulatory bod about the living room.

Lori, a cute, short, bouncy brunette—the exact opposite

240

of Libby—and who would leave for Cornell in the fall, said, "I think he knows."

"I do too," Doug agreed.

"Knows what?" Charlie demanded. "What is going on?"

The two looked at her surprised, shrugged, shook their heads, said in unison of course, "About what?"

The really strange thing was that Tuxedo Greene hadn't hissed at her since she got back from San Diego County. He didn't rub on her legs and purr or anything but he didn't bite them either. "Must be the Diazepam."

"Oh, I took him off it, didn't I tell you? Kate said it made him insecure." Libby left with her friends for a buddy dinner at their old hangout, the Long Beach Diner. Kate, who cleaned their house, was the "cat whisperer" of Long Beach, as well as a no-nonsense person living among a nonsensical citizenry.

Charlie and her mother, who'd decided to stay until Libby's graduation rather than fly home and then back in a few days, would have delivery and doze in front of the TV. Charlie was getting stronger. Luella Ridgeway had been released from the hospital. Maggie was due home tomorrow and Charlie hoped to get to the office at least part of the day. She needed a little of the crazy normalcy there, the familiarity, the chaos, to convince herself life really could get back to normal as she knew it.

Charlie's first inkling of what was happening was when she went to work and opened an e-mail from Detective Gordon Solomon, recovering at home and wanting to know what Charlie knew about the reporter, Jerry Parks. He left a phone number and she called him.

"All I know is he decided he was the father of Dr. Judy's granddaughter and he found out Judd ordered her daughter to have nothing to do with him or her father, Warren VanZant, or forfeit a huge inheritance. The daughter obeyed. He told me he killed Judith Judd because of it."

"Charlie, do you know where he is?"

"Yeah, he's dead. Caroline shot him too. And I'm glad—he was seconds away from raping me. Didn't they find his body with all the others?"

"I don't know. I was half dead when I left and no one's allowed back at the moment."

"Well, when I got there, I counted four dead Feds at least, and then there was Warren VanZant. Caroline shot Jerry because he put her son in Luella's car with Luella and Maggie and sent it over the edge. Luella says she pushed Maggie out and went out after her, but Dashiell was in the front seat and he went over. She says Caroline rescued them and hid them but she was too drugged up to remember much else."

"You know how I got out of there?"

"You, Deputy Saucier, and Luella Ridgeway went out on the first ambulance. They wanted me to go out too but I had to look for Maggie and my daughter and—"

"Your daughter was up there?"

"Oh yeah, Mitch Hilsten and Kenneth Cooper and Brodie Caulfield and Keegan Monroe—I lose count. They all got there after you left. Gordy, someone planned to hush this all up somehow, huh? I haven't heard a word and no one's come to question me. Was there a lot of evidence destroyed by a major explosion on that promontory? The ambulances were told not to enter the Spa grounds. They waited in the parking lot. The *Union-Tribune* says Jerry Parks has left to work elsewhere but will give no more information."

"You know more than I do. So who killed Howard?"

"Jerry Parks. He was on a spree and very angry that the Institute would lead him on. Says he confronted Grant Howard about it and Howard admitted it. Blamed me for pointing out the exploitation of hopeful screenwriters and for being helpful by bringing Maggie to the Islandia and she'd already tried to confess to killing Dr. Judy, sooo—"

"Thanks. You've explained a lot. But you should have stayed away, like I told you to."

"If I had, you'd be dead. I can't help wonder how many dead there are up there. How their deaths will be explained away to families and colleagues. If the government investigation was so overpowered by personal problems at the Spa that it was an embarrassment as well as that these powerful people were so easily done away with by a grieving, angry, gray-haired mother with no prior criminal record. Of course one could be made up I suppose. How is Deputy Saucier?"

"Fine. Took the drugging and the recovery better than I did. How's Margaret Stutzman and who drove her back to the Spa from the Islandia?"

"She's recovering and according to Jerry Parks, Dashiell Hammett drove her back, driver's license or no. Says she was fed up with everything and went willingly. So, do I wait for a knock on the door and an arrest for whatever?"

"I suspect there are too many people who know what you do and that they've spread it around enough it would be difficult to hush up everything by now. The grieving, angry, gray-haired mother thing won't sit well. She may end up missing or something."

"She won't care, she was betrayed once too often. What worries me is that my identification and Maggie's and Luella's are still up there somewhere. The earth shook as we were driving away—we got out just before paratroopers started dropping and then had to get our cars. We left in the second ambulance."

"Paratroopers? Charlie, are you sure all the drugs had worn off yet?"

"Kenny and Mitch stood there and watched it with me and they weren't drugged and people in the neighborhoods came out in their yards to watch it too. No way they can cover this up. There were cameras rolling even. It has to be on the Internet by now even if it isn't in the papers."

"You can spin the Internet stuff as being faked, like by people who believe in alien invasions and everything. My guess is there's some kind of lid put on it locally from Washington while it's under investigation."

"How many people did the San Diego County Sheriff's Department lose, do you think?"

"I can't say and don't really know. I'm suddenly out of the loop because of my 'mental health after injuries sustained in the line of duty.' So is Lydia. We're just trying to figure out what's going on and what went on. If we speak up, our 'mental health' may be questioned."

Charlie wanted to tell him that the facts were very likely due to air anyway soon and he and Deputy Saucier needn't worry. But she couldn't be sure he wasn't recording this conversation for at least county officials if not federal as well.

Forty-Two

"The secret's Campbell's Cream of Celery Soup," Betty Beesom said of her famous hot dish at the compound's potluck to welcome Maggie Stutzman home from the hospital. As if that should be news—it was always the same dish and these gatherings nearly always in Charlie's kitchen breakfast nook—a high-backed wooden booth arrangement with a window that let in the sunlight and the awesome scent of the lemon tree.

Unless they met for brunch when it was Sara Lee Cinnamon Rolls, Betty always explained the secret of tuna noodle casserole was Campbell's. Only the crispy potato chip topping and chopped celery saved the watery canned tuna and mushy canned peas. Truth be known, Betty Beesom pretty much repeated everything these days. Charlie, Maggie, and Edwina exchanged looks—Charlie and Maggie smiled extra nice at Jacob Forney. He was a great baker and his onion-dill bread saved the day.

Charlie kicked Libby under the table when she made fun of his sparse beard and hair and mouthed, "We're going to need him," nodding in Betty's direction.

"What I don't understand," Jacob said seriously, with no apparent clue what all the nodding at the table was about, "is how this whole thing was kept a secret for so long and why?" He picked up the folded *Los Angeles Times* and pointed to the headline story which had originally appeared in the *New York Times*.

"Because my client, Kenneth Cooper, is a very savvy investigative reporter, was actually at the scene of most of

245

it and able to sell it to New York while no one was looking, and the local papers were kept in the dark or somehow convinced to play it down while the Feds tried to figure out what had happened and get the right spin on it or hope it would just go away, or something less embarrassing would come along to overshadow it. And unfortunately for them there was a lull in the carnage abroad, weather disasters, and terrorism, soooo—And as Gordy Solomon said, the CIA hated the FBI who hated the IRS and everybody hated the San Diego Sheriff's Department. Ee-eye-ee-eye-oh."

"I just find it hard to believe the VanZants and this Jerry Parks could have outwitted and overpowered the local and federal authorities that way. None of the three were professionals." Jacob Forney was an accountant and of an orderly mind set. Just exactly what this tiny settlement needed.

"Like Kenny said, the Feds wouldn't cooperate with each other and were too busy trying to track people by their cell phone signals to watch their backsides. Three different agencies not cooperating, competing with each other while everybody but the dead and unconscious were busy coordinating by cell. I expect that the local sheriff's department would have taken a lot of the heat if Kenny hadn't exposed how they'd been sidelined by a higher authority."

Kenny was the only person involved who would sit for a TV interview. Mitch had corroborated the story through a publicist and the video and stills from the Spa's neighbors below the crest. No government spokesmen would comment on the charges of a coverup except to make a blanket statement that the information in the article was being looked into and was no doubt blown out of proportion if there was any truth to it at all. One can compose pictures of anything these days, videos too can be "especially prepared." Such as faked footage of flying saucers and it was derisively suggested that Mr. Cooper might be better adapted to writing fiction.

"Why were people running around with boxes of paper and disks?" Libby wanted to know.

"Luella thinks the IRS was looking into colossal payments

by pharmaceutical companies to get endorsements on Dr. Judy's TV show without being in a commercial. Concealing taxable money from them."

"Why? Everybody does it," Jacob snorted. "Rich people, corporations, CEOs, officers of the New York Stock Exchange, mutual fund execs. That's the way business is done." Jacob had been demoralized and embittered by the venality of those in high places. He'd blown the whistle on his superiors in a well known accounting agency and of course lost his job. He now worked as a personal tax accountant for individuals and home businesses out of his house. Charlie, so benumbed by the book cooking in the entertainment industry, couldn't see what the fuss was all about. No, it wasn't right nor fair, but it certainly wasn't new.

In another conversation with Luella Ridgeway, Charlie learned that Ruth Ann Singer and Sue Rippon had finally revolted at the carnage and tried to stop Caroline but Ruth Ann had been shot. She did not survive the trip to the hospital. She'd worked her way up from sound engineer to Judith Judd's manager and was the one who'd done the mixing, at Caroline's command, of conversations on Dashiell's little recording devices long after he was dead with conversations recorded later. All this to flush Warren so his wife could shoot him too. Luella had the impression that the recorded voices could be activated from a console in the control room. Warren must die because he had helped Jerry send Dashiell over the cliff in Luella's car.

"All I remember of that was being in the grass with Luella's hand over my mouth watching a car roll down the hill and brake lights go on and off like someone was trying to stop it. But it was too late and it went over the cliff. Luella told me to lie real still. Next I knew, I was on a bed in a room and the room kept going around and around." Maggie was pale, colorless, droopy, tired, but alive. Charlie liked to think she saw occasional sparks of hope in her friend's eyes. Between what Parks had told Charlie—she wasn't sure she remembered it right—and what Luella had learned from Sue

Rippon and Dr. Judy's lawyer, it appeared that Jerry Parks killed Dr. Judy because her daughter had broken off their engagement. Judith Judd threatened to disinherit her altogether if she didn't find a more suitable father figure for Judy's granddaughter.

After meeting her daughter, Parks had met the doctor several times trying to find a story there and discovered her fabulous wealth. He wanted to do an exposé on the money to be made at what she did, but he didn't realize how much more of her wealth came from payments under the table offering exposure to pharmaceutical companies than from her PBS appearances. He'd planned to call it, "The TV Doc Documentary."

Still, his real yearning was to be a successful screenwriter and Judy's daughter had plenty of money from her mother so he wouldn't have to work anymore—could concentrate on making it writing screenplays until he became successful. Not to mention she would inherit a fortune from her mother someday.

And then Judith Judd declared him off limits and her daughter's father as well, so both men had it in for Dr. Judy. Warren had also had it in for the unlovable Dashiell and somehow the two men got together to blame Judd's murder on him. "But good old Maggie offered herself up so—"

"I really wasn't sure I hadn't done it. I just sort of wanted to hurt myself," Maggie said, eyes tearing up.

"He also killed Grant Howard to blame it on Maggie to further the questioning of her questionable morality and sanity and to vent his anger on the man who admitted he had no intention of reading any of the filmscript submissions, claimed he'd done his part by bringing the aspiring together with professionals in the business."

Had Raoul died because he suspected the two of killing the doctor or was it an accident? He had a heart attack in the water. His body was full of prescription drugs, not very carefully mixed. Dr. Judy and the Spa were practically smothered with them by drug companies trying to gain her approval.

Warren VanZant had met Jerry when the reporter was snooping around Judy and the spa for his story.

Luella suspected what was going on to build this fortune. It was perfectly legal but kept quiet because it might not sit right in a country where the silent majority was getting royally sick of getting royally soaked in the name of commerce.

The plan had been to put Dashiell's drugged body behind the wheel of Luella's car and send it over the cliff. They didn't want Luella talking to the Feds either so she could go along and Maggie too, to put an end to any investigation. Jerry, in his snooping around the place, had come across the stash of medications as well as all the places to hide in the narrowed halls in the walls and dead ends.

Charlie still didn't know if there had been a meth lab on the promontory or what might be left of the Sea Spa at the Marina del Sol, or what had caused the earth to quake and the explosion. It could have been something dropped from the helicopters or some of the paraphernalia the paratroopers had worn on the way down.

"It will be interesting to see how it all washes out in the press after Kenneth's exposé," Edwina said. "But the spin will continue—the whole truth may have to wait for the history books. Or it may just die away as things do in the news."

"I hope not, but you're right." Jacob stood to study the cat on top of the refrigerator. "What's the matter, fella? It's like he knows, huh?"

Tuxedo just stared wide-eyed at Charlie.

Forty-Three

Charlie sat in her office in Beverly Hills watching the sparrows build nests in the palms growing out of the sidewalk five stories below on Wilshire. They did this every spring, but this year there were a couple of mourning doves too, rubbing their necks together, picking at each other's feathers. Is that where the old-fashioned term "necking" came from?

Charlie took a deep breath and grabbed the desk top, a startling sense of loss seemed to suck out her soul, create an enormous vacuum in her chest, leave her dizzy and gasping.

"You gonna make it, Charlie?" Larry Mann, her gorgeous assistant, said softly from the doorway of his cubicle that protected her office from the hallway.

"Yeah, I just suddenly felt so empty and alone and worthless. God, I hope menopause isn't coming on this early."

"Well, no one's surprised at that but you. Look at it this way. You're going to have time to get some work done. Which by the way is stacking up around here. Lester P. wants to see some more of Brodie Caulfield's work. Uranus has rejected *Rites of Winter*."

"That was fast."

"Our new star client is going to need a manager pretty soon if this keeps up. But right now, you're it—you're needed. Cooper said something about a massage? Don't worry, I'm not going there. A massage before he goes into hiding to research the *Invasion at Home* book. Pitman's wants all subsidiary rights to the nursing home book. Corporate policy, they can't help it. Same ol', same ol' . . ."

"Screw that. I can sell it elsewhere." Charlie was on her feet looking for her shoes under her desk. "They know I never sign over all the goodies to the publisher. What's the word from Onyx on film rights?" Charlie was so incensed it took her a second to realize Larry had grabbed one shoe from her and was kneeling on the floor, slipping it onto her foot.

"Welcome back, Cinderella." He looked up with that sardonic smile that could melt a solar ice cap.

Charlie dragged a weary bod into the empty house, empty except for Tuxedo. Libby hadn't moved out yet but she would leave in a few days. There were signs of packing everywhere.

"You knew, didn't you, Tux?" She guessed she couldn't call him "that damn cat" now. "Everybody knew but me, huh?"

The damn cat watched her with eyes that were all iris while she slipped out of her shoes and opened a can of gross-smelling cat food, spooned a third of it into a clean bowl, and set it down beside the refrigerator. He just sat looking at it.

Libby and Edwina Greene had announced that Libby would move to Boulder and live with her grandmother for awhile, sort out what she wanted to do, get a little perspective on life.

"It will save you both some money and be a safe haven for her while she works things out."

"Safe haven? Boulder? That's not the Boulder I remember."

"And, Charlie, it will take one of the responsibilities off your back for a time. I'm afraid Maggie and Betty will be a continuing responsibility here. And your work has always been hectic."

"Edwina? You have a clue what you're taking on? You're not getting any younger."

"Raised you, didn't I? And you aren't either. Charlie, let me help out. You've got so much on your plate. And I see

251

two, no three gray hairs, my dear." Charlie's mother brushed at the hair above Charlie's forehead and sighed. "No surprise with the life you lead."

A tickle of hope at the back of her throat, Charlie considered no lying awake for the kid to come home, worrying about a car breakdown or worse. Coming home to a little peace after an exhausting day and a killer commute instead of arguments and more tension. And Libby wouldn't be alone and vulnerable in some apartment somewhere. Not just yet.

The house seemed so quiet already. A box of CDs sat on the kitchen table, another of toiletries on the counter by the sink. Then a memory sound of her daughter's hooting laughter, very faint. Kind of sad and creepy, like voices behind the door of a wardrobe. Tuxedo moved his gaze to the air beside her, one ear swiveling as if to pin down a sound. As if he'd heard the memory too.

Charlie sat on the floor next to the cat food. "I never dreamed it would come to this, did you? Maybe it will work out for all of us for awhile? I mean, that's all we've got is awhile, any of us, right?"

He didn't answer. He didn't blink.

"Oh come on, I'm a grown woman, dammit. A kick-ass Hollywood agent." But Charlie rolled over a sore body onto hands and knees, lowered her head, and butted foreheads with the creature. He blinked, put his cold nose on hers, and bent over his dish.

Charlie didn't understand what all that meant but paused, on her way to find tweezers and mirror in case any more gray hairs had appeared today, to say something she wouldn't have dreamed possible yesterday. "We'll both miss her. But at least we've got each other, huh?"